THE NAMELESS ONE
⊷ BOOK 1 OF THE CADE SAGA ⊶

www.randomhousechildrens.co.uk

THE
EDGE
IN
THE THIRD AGE OF FLIGHT

NEW HIVE

THE FARROW
RIDGES

DEE

HIVE

THE MIDWOOD
DECKS

GREAT GLADE

THE EASTERN
WOODS

THE TWILIGHT
WOODLANDS

THE
GORGES

THE EDGE CHRONICLES

THE NAMELESS ONE
⊷ BOOK 1 OF THE CADE SAGA ⊶

STEWART & RIDDELL

DOUBLEDAY

THE NAMELESS ONE
A DOUBLEDAY BOOK
Hardback 978 0 857 53234 3

Published in Great Britain by Doubleday,
an imprint of Random House Children's Publishers UK
A Random House Group Company

This edition published 2014

1 3 5 7 9 10 8 6 4 2

Set in Palatino

RANDOM HOUSE CHILDREN'S PUBLISHERS UK
61–63 Uxbridge Road, London W5 5SA

www.**randomhousechildrens**.co.uk
www.**totallyrandombooks**.co.uk
www.**randomhouse**.co.uk

Addresses for companies within The Random House Group Limited
can be found at: www.randomhouse.co.uk/offices.htm

THE RANDOM HOUSE GROUP Limited Reg. No. 954009

A CIP catalogue record for this book is available
from the British Library.

Printed and bound by CPI Group (UK) Ltd, Croydon, CR0 4YY

Paul: For Julie
Chris: For Jo

· INTRODUCTION ·

Far far away, jutting out into the emptiness beyond, like the figurehead of a mighty stone ship, is the Edge. A torrent of water pours endlessly over the lip of rock at its overhanging point; the Edgewater River.

The river's source lies far inland at a stone pool high above Riverrise, one of the three great cities of the Edge, deep in the heart of the Nightwoods. A mere trickle at first, the river grows broader and more powerful as it makes its way on into the mighty Deepwoods.

Dark and forbidding, the Deepwoods is a dangerous and inhospitable place. Once, its denizens believed that the Deepwoods went on for ever. Now, in this, the Third Age of Flight, none but the most primitive of tribes, cut off from civilization, believe this to be true. Yet there is no denying the vastness of the forest. It takes even the sleekest phrax-powered skyship several weeks to travel from one end to the other.

By the time the Edgewater reaches the great city of Hive, it has already become a mighty river, cascading down the falls between East and West Ridge. Anglers plunder its stocks of fish. Farmers dam and divert its waters to irrigate their fields. Waterwheels tap its power.

Past Great Glade it flows, the third and greatest city of the Edge; a bustling metropolis of stilthouse factories, parklands, teeming mercantile districts, lakeside mansions and magnificent schools and academies. Then, disappearing under the ground, the river passes beneath the Twilight Woods and into the Mire. It is only at the end of this bogland, with its sinking-sands and blow-holes, that the Edgewater forms once more. Here, close to the end of its long journey, the Edgewater is at its most magnificent. It sweeps past the ancient ruins of Undertown, beneath the mysterious floating city of Sanctaphrax and on over the jutting rock.

Just as the river flows through the Edge, so too does its history. It flows down the centuries, ever growing, ever changing, ever switching course. And nowhere is this more clearly to be seen than in Sanctaphrax.

The ancient city of lofty academics, built upon a vast floating rock that hovers above Undertown's ruins, is anchored to the ground by a great chain. More than half a millennium earlier, that chain was cut and Sanctaphrax floated away, along with half the scholars who had once bickered and quarrelled so vociferously over the finer points of the sky science they studied. No one thought it would ever be seen again.

But then it returned. And since then its deserted streets and buildings have become a magnet for those who wish to flee the stranglehold exerted by the authorities of the three great cities over their citizens.

Chief among these outcasts and dissidents are the so-called 'descenders' – nonconformist academics who climb down the mighty cliff face of the Edge to discover what lies below. For, just as primitive goblins believed that the Deepwoods were endless, so, in the past, it was believed that anything, or anyone, falling from the Edge would fall for ever. The descenders – with Nate Quarter perhaps the most famous descender of all – have proved otherwise. Unfortunately, however, these brave explorers are now in danger of their lives from those who, like the powerful Quove Lentis, High Professor of Flight, believe that such talk is heresy.

For that is the trouble. There are always those who try to obstruct advances; who prefer to preserve the ignorance of the past rather than embrace the enlighten-ment of the present. But time passes. Technology moves on. Advances are made. And no technological advance was ever more significant in the Edge than that which heralded the Third Age of Flight: the harnessing of the power of stormphrax.

Stormphrax. Solid lightning. The most wondrous substance ever to have existed . . .

Its origins lie far out in Open Sky beyond the Edge where violent lightning storms form. These storms are drawn to the Twilight Woods, where they release their pent-up energy in the form of colossal lightning bolts – lightning bolts that turn to solid crystal the moment they penetrate the forest's permanent golden glow. As the millennia passed, more and more of these solid lightning bolts plunged down into the dark earth, sinking deep, shattering into countless million crystals, until every trace was concealed beneath the ground.

And it is these crystals that the miners of the Eastern Woods dig out, in order for the scientists and engineers of the Third Age to harness their power – the explosive power that fuels the stilthouse factories of Great Glade and Hive, and lights up the permanent night of Riverrise. But that power also gave rise to arms. Phraxmuskets and cannon. Weapons that have left thousands of dead and injured in battlefields across the Edgelands.

Today, more than five hundred years after the power of stormphrax was first safely unleashed, the sky is crisscrossed with steam-trails left by the mighty cloud-barges and skytaverns that journey throughout the Edgelands, carrying goods, raw materials and travellers between the cities, journeying to Great Glade and Hive. To Riverrise. And also to other, more modest places throughout the Edge; places like New Hive and Four Lakes, the Gorges and the Northern Ridges, and dozens of small towns and backwater settlements, each one battling to grow and dreaming that one day they too might become great cities.

There are, however, individuals in the Edge who have become disillusioned with life in the Third Age of Flight.

Some hate the pace of change; some regret the loss of a more innocent way of life; many are scarred by a terrible war that broke out between Great Glade and Hive. Turning their backs on the great cities, these pioneers set out for the furthest outreaches of the Edge to carve for themselves a new and simpler life.

Pioneers like Cade Quarter, the callow son of a professor, who didn't even know that such a life might exist . . .

The Deepwoods, the Eastern Woods, the Mire and the Edgewater River. Undertown and Sanctaphrax. Great Glade, Riverrise and Hive. The Farrow Ridges. Names on a map.

Yet behind each name lie a thousand tales – tales that have been recorded in ancient scrolls, tales that have been passed down the generations by word of mouth – tales which even now are being told.

What follows is but one of those tales.

· CHAPTER ONE ·

Cade Quarter tightened the straps of his backpack and blew warmth into his cupped hands. The day had broken bright but cold, and here, high up at the top of the highest ironwood gantry in the Ledges, the icy wind that plucked at his tilderskin jacket cut like knives.

He'd been one of the first to arrive that morning. Two others were standing close by him on the narrow wooden platform that jutted out high above the treetops of the forest at the edge of the city of Great Glade. One was a tall mobgnome dressed in a quilted frockcoat that was grubby and frayed and crudely patched, with a scuffed leather over-bonnet and down-at-heel boots. The other was a young, sunken-eyed flathead goblin who didn't look as though he'd eaten in days.

Cade had tried to ignore them, but the narrowness of the gantry forced them to stand shoulder to shoulder with him. He didn't want to engage them in conversation,

to hear their life histories. He might like them. And after all, they were competition.

There was a flash of white in the sky and Cade looked up to see a flock of snowbirds passing overhead. Their muffled wingbeats sounded like gloved hands clapping.

'Wish *I* had wings,' came a muttered voice and, despite himself, Cade looked round to see the young goblin staring after the birds longingly. He caught Cade's gaze. 'Don't you?'

Cade shrugged and turned away, and was relieved when the mobgnome spoke up in his stead.

'A flathead with wings,' he chuckled. 'Freak like that, they'd cage you up and charge ten groats a viewing . . .'

'You know what I mean,' the flathead protested.

'Personally,' the mobgnome continued without missing a beat, 'I'd have my own phraxlighter and a pouch full of gold pieces – if wishes came true.' He scowled. 'Which they don't.'

The goblin turned away, looking crushed.

Just then, a klaxon sounded from the lower gantries, loud and rasping. Once. Then again. From below him, Cade heard the clatter of shod boot soles on the ironwood rungs of the gantry ladder and felt the wooden platform beneath his feet tremble. Others were about to arrive. Cade Quarter swallowed nervously and pulled on the straps at his shoulder.

He didn't want wings or wealth. If he had a wish, it was simply that his backpack wasn't quite so heavy. It could prove his downfall yet.

Literally.

· CHAPTER TWO ·

The mighty skytavern was tolley-roped securely to a vast docking-cradle, the largest of two dozen which were attached to the towering ironwood gantries of Great Glade. All around it, phraxbarges and phraxlighters were tethered to the hull, both fore and aft, at the upper decks and the lower, like gyle goblins tending to a grossmother.

Up at the skytavern's snub-nosed prow, a cluster of hovering phraxbarges were being unloaded. Long chains of goblins, from wiry underbiters to hulking great barrelchests, were passing foodstuffs one to the other from phraxbarge to hold with piston-like efficiency. There were casks of winesap and woodgrog, crates of knotcabbage, glimmer-onions and earth-apples, boxes of dried fruits, salted meats, pickled roots and spices – each one neatly labelled with its contents; haunches of tilder, barrels of lakemussels and long knotted strings of trussed-up woodcocks and speyturkeys . . .

Enough for the long voyage ahead, both for the opulent Great Salon where the rich and powerful dined, and the slop halls and hanging galleys of the lower decks – and with as much again to trade en route as the *Xanth Filatine* proceeded on its journey, stopping off at the isolated mooring posts and scrat-settlements that lay between the great cities of Riverrise and Hive.

The journey from Great Glade to Hive would take three weeks of hard steaming, with a following wind and an absence of storms, neither of which could be depended on. Even if the weather was favourable, there were still many stops to be made. For the sky-platforms built high in the trees, the market clearings in the depths of the forest, and the trader-settlements scratching a living, the passing of the skytavern was vital. Manufactured goods from the steam factories of the great cities were exchanged for the raw materials of the Deepwoods: pots for furs, phraxmuskets for buoyant wood, and a thousand other trades.

A phraxbarge tethered further down the hull was piled high with bundles of finely woven hammelhorn fleece blankets, which a company of stout, bare-armed grey goblins were pulling free with long-handled hooks, hoiking the goods onto their shoulders and transporting them down into the hold of the skytavern. Beside it, a group of lop-ears were unloading a second phraxbarge that was laden with crates of machine-turned pots and pans, which clanked together as they were set down. A third phraxbarge was weighed down with bolts of shot silk and embroidered taffeta, a fourth with caskets of phraxmuskets, while another swayed precariously as four stooped gyle goblins struggled with a large glass-topped case under the watchful eye of a tall fourthling in a black longcloak and battered conical hat.

'Careful, careful,' he was admonishing them, brandishing a gold-pommelled staff as he spoke. 'One slip and six months' work will have been in vain.'

'What are *they*?' demanded the holdmarshal, an officious-looking lop-ear in a short satin jacket and matching breeches, as the gyle goblins approached. He tapped the tally-board in his hand insistently with his leadstick. The goblins stopped and the holdmarshal peered down at the pale, jellylike objects set out in rows beneath the panel of glass.

'Prowlgrin eggs,' said the fourthling proudly. 'Fertilized and soon to hatch.'

'Livestock,' the holdmarshal muttered. He made a note and pointed to his left.

'Livestock?' the fourthling repeated. 'I was hoping to keep them in my cabin . . .'

The holdmarshal spoke through him. 'Livestock goes in the hold.' He glanced up. 'Bound for?'

'Hive,' the fourthling replied, and rubbed his thumb and index finger together. 'And worth a pretty penny too. They're pedigree greys from the finest stable in Great Glade. So I'd be grateful if—'

His voice was drowned out by the sound of barking and howling, and the two of them looked round to see a huge crate, dangling on ropes from the hook of a mighty crane as it swept past. The crate was subdivided inside, four by four, with each of the sixteen separate compartments temporary home to a prowlgrin. Orange, brown, black, mottled and striped, piebald and skewbald, the creatures' eyes were wide as they bellowed their fear and discomfort.

'Now, they're what I call prowlgrins,' the holdmarshal muttered as he made a note of their number on his tally-board. 'And bound for the phraxmines in the Eastern Woods, I'd wager.'

'Yet worth a fraction of these unhatched eggs,' the fourthling snorted, flapping a dismissive hand at the crate as a bevy of cloddertrogs steered it down onto the deck and began untying the ropes.

'Quite, quite,' said the holdmarshal, 'but if you want to keep livestock in your cabin, it means the rules have got to be stretched . . .' He held out a hand. 'And rule-stretching don't come cheap.'

The fourthling sighed and reached into his pocket. Drawing out a purse, he opened it and eyed the contents. 'Four gold pieces?' he ventured.

The holdmarshal smiled. 'Five.'

While the phraxbarges were being unloaded of their cargo and provisions at the prow of the skytavern, phraxlighters crowded the sky at the stern, waiting to drop off their passengers. Some of the vessels were elegant and narrow-bottomed, with dark, varnished wood cabins and brass ornamentation; some were sleek blondwood boats with striped awnings, while others were larger, with unfinished timbers and standing room only – the quality of the phraxlighters reflecting the status of their passengers and from which part of Great Glade they had come from.

A wealthy merchant and his wife stepped from a sharp-prowed vessel, followed by their luggage-bearing retinue of velvet-clad goblins, and were ushered to their stately apartments in the upper part of the stern. Mere strides away, half a dozen grey goblins – stilthouse workers by the look of their grubby homespun – were noisily bartering with the ticket-steward for an upgrade. An extended family of woodtrolls – with great-grandparents down to babes-in-arms – was being detained by a pair of flathead deck-guards. One of them had his hand on the butt of the phraxmusket at his belt.

'And I say they *are* weapons,' he was saying as he eyed the hatchets at the woodtrolls' belts.

'Tools of the trade,' said the head of the family, a

stocky, middle-aged troll with plaited side-whiskers. 'All male woodtrolls carry a hatchet. It's part of our woodlore.'

'I wouldn't know about that,' said the flathead, sounding bored. 'But if you want to travel on the *Xanth Filatine*, you surrender your weapons—'

'They're *not* weapons, I tell you. They're—'

'Oh, for the love of Earth and Sky,' came an imperious voice from behind them, and the woodtrolls turned to see two dark-robed academics glaring down at them.

The pair had endured this dead-end bickering in silence for long enough. The klaxon had already sounded twice. If it should sound a third time before they were on board then the gates would close and they would not be able to travel – and neither of them relished the idea of returning to the academy to face the wrath of Quove Lentis, High Professor of Flight, not now, not after what they'd done.

'Give him your axe,' the taller of the academics demanded. 'Or make way for those who truly do wish to travel.'

'This is a *phrax*vessel,' the shorter, stouter academic sneered, his nostrils flaring. 'It's not as though you're going to be asked to chop kindling.'

'*Valves approaching full steam!*' The engineer's voice rang out from high above as the phraxcradle creaked and hissed. '*Departure imminent!*'

With a grunt of irritation the woodtroll placed the hatchet into the outstretched hand of the flathead guard.

The other woodtrolls did the same. The two academics barged them aside.

'Two mid-range berths for Hive,' they chorused and reached inside their robes for the required fare.

As the steward finally allowed them aboard, a raucous screech echoed behind them, and the two academics turned to see a white raven emerge from a porthole and flap up into the sky. They eyed one another with a look of alarm.

'The High Professor's bird!'

'Then the High Professor knows we're on board,' came the reply. 'He has spies everywhere. We can't risk staying in our cabins now. We'll have to find somewhere else to hide out . . .'

Higher and higher the bird flew, its white wings flashing like blades of silver in the bright sun as it rose above the hustle and bustle of the Ledges, with its cranes and docking-cradles and phraxvessels of every shape and size. It flew, in a broad north-easterly arc, past New Lake and Old Forest, with the corn- and barleyfields of the Silver Pastures beyond rippling like water. Far ahead the stilthouses and steam-factories of East Glade stained the horizon with billowing clouds of white and yellow and grey. Then, wheeling round in the sky, and with the opulent town-houses and lakeside manors of Ambristown to its right, the white raven – Kraakan – headed directly over the Freeglades District. It swooped down low over the tower at Lake Landing, then as the lofty towers and turrets of the academies of the Cloud

Quarter loomed up far ahead, it soared back into the sky and gathered speed.

Kraakan had learned the hard way that the master's mood was dependent upon the speed with which it completed a task. With luck, the message it had delivered so swiftly to the lower decks would bring it not only praise but also a saucerful of rat-scraps.

The white raven was flying high above the outskirts of the Freeglades district when the distant sound of the phrax-klaxon echoed out across the sky.

One, two, three times.

· CHAPTER THREE ·

Cade Quarter trembled. It was time.

There were seven of them now standing at the top of the highest ironwood gantry in the Ledges. 'The Forlorn Hope', it was known as. The gantry's wooden boards sloped sharply down from where Cade and the others stood, ending abruptly in a sheer drop.

Originally used to roll timber down from logging ships into phraxbarges below, the sloping platform had fallen into disuse when a broader gantry had been constructed on the other side of the Ledges. Now it provided the best place for the desperate and penniless to attempt to board a departing skytavern without a ticket – a forlorn hope . . .

Cade glanced around him. Apart from the mobgnome and the young flathead, there were two young pink-eyed goblins, twins most like, the pair of them scrawny and sullen; a lop-ear goblin matron with dead eyes, a withered arm and a tattered basket strapped to her back, and, towering over the rest, a cloddertrog.

Unlike the others, the cloddertrog had no possessions with him to slow him down. He was powerfully built and looked fiercely determined, as if no one was going to get in his way. The scars on his face and arms suggested that he'd had his fair share of fights, and had survived them. As Cade watched, the cloddertrog braced himself, flexing his huge arms and bending his treetrunk legs at the knee.

He looked like he knew what he was doing, and Cade made a mental note to follow him as closely as he could.

As the third blast of the skytavern klaxon faded, Cade steadied himself. He smoothed down the front of his jacket and blew into his hands. He tried to slow the frantic beating of his heart.

He didn't want to be here at the top of this ironwood gantry. He didn't want to jump. In fact, he didn't want to leave Great Glade at all. But he had no choice. If he didn't get out of the city now, he was as good as dead . . .

At the far side of the gantries, the *Xanth Filatine* trembled and throbbed at the top of its docking-cradle. Steam poured from its mighty funnel, while a white-hot jet hissed from the propulsion duct beneath. And as the gathered crowds on the surrounding gantries waved and cheered, and the passengers waved back, the crew began unhitching the tolley ropes fore and aft.

Wait for it, Cade told himself.

The skytavern rose slowly from the cradle and inched forward in the sky. The crowds whooped and hollered.

Cade watched intently as the skytavern drifted up from the cradle and began to move slowly above the heads of the crowd, its massive hull with its flight-weights, cargo-hooks, hanging sky-floats and tether-rails casting them in shadow. Slowly, but gathering height and speed all the while, the *Xanth Filatine* moved past the lower scaffolding and platforms, over the swinging cargo-cranes, and approached the last and highest gantry: the Forlorn Hope.

'Wait for it . . . wait . . . for it . . .' Cade muttered, his eyes fixed on the cloddertrog.

Suddenly the lop-ear set off down the slope. Maybe with her withered arm, she felt she needed a head start. Whatever, the next moment, the others were off after her – the pink-eyed goblin twins shoving past the mobgnome, with the flathead close on their heels, while overhead the *Xanth Filatine* drew ever closer.

Cade hung back with the cloddertrog, who was eyeing the underside of the skytavern as it loomed. He was clearly choosing a spot to aim for; Cade followed his gaze. Below them, the others had reached the end of the ramp. But too soon. One after the other, they leaped and flailed and grasped hopelessly at the smooth snub-nosed prow of the vessel – and tumbled down through the air to their deaths.

And as the despairing screams of the mobgnome, flathead, lop-ear and pink-eyes rang out, the cloddertrog suddenly launched himself down the wooden slope at full pelt. Cade gulped and sprang after him, his boots

pounding on the juddering boards as he gathered speed.

Teeth clenched and arms outstretched, Cade launched himself off the end of the ramp, his eyes fixed on the line of tether-rails secured along the underside of the huge vessel. Below him, the treetops were a blur of green. The wind tugged at his backpack as he flew through the air.

Too heavy, he groaned, and cursed himself for loading himself down with all those weighty memories best left behind.

He thrust his arms forward, his hands curved, braced. His fingertips grazed the hard, nubbed planking but, unable to grasp a hold of the tether-rail he'd been aiming for, Cade fell – only to be caught by the wrist in a powerful grip.

He looked up. It was the cloddertrog, who had landed on a ledge below a porthole. His scarred face broke into a smile as he pulled Cade up to join him.

'Room for one more, I reckon,' he grunted.

Cade was about to thank him when the porthole abruptly flew open and a studded cudgel emerged. With a loud crack, the cudgel slammed into the side of the cloddertrog's head. He lost his grip, and with a cry more of surprise than pain plummeted down to the forest below. The cudgel withdrew and a moment later a bony hand with a large gold ring on one finger appeared at the open porthole. It grabbed Cade by the collar and dragged him bodily through the narrow porthole and into the skytavern.

The place smelled rank; a mixture of rancid fat and stale bodies. And it was dark. After the early-morning dazzle Cade was as good as blind. But he could hear well enough as a gruff voice spoke up.

'I like the small ones. They don't give no trouble . . . Let's see what the boss thinks.'

· CHAPTER FOUR ·

'What we got here, then?'
 Cade looked up to see two hefty flathead goblins standing over him. Their brow- and neckrings gleamed in the sputtering yellow of an oil lamp that hung down from an overhead beam. With a grunt, the nearer goblin extended a gold-ringed hand and pulled Cade to his feet with such force he felt as though his arm was being pulled out of its socket.

The flatheads Cade knew in Great Glade had adopted the ways of the city. They wore clothes of homespun or serge, with crushed funnel hats on their heads and boots on their feet. They grew up unadorned by neckrings or tattoos. But not these flatheads. These were old school, fresh from the darkest Deepwoods by the look of them. Tilderskin breeches, leather jerkins, fierce-eyed talismans around their necks. Barefoot. Tattooed and ringed. And heavily armed, with studded cudgels

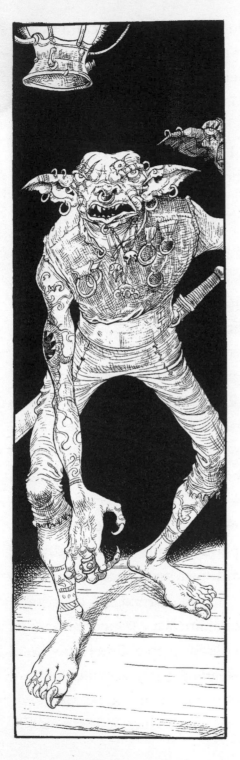

and jag-blade knives hanging at their belts. The ornate gold ring on the first goblin's finger looked out of place.

The second flat-head goblin peered at him from the shadows; swarthy and hard-faced. In addition to his other weapons, he had a crossbow slung over his shoulder.

'Mish-mash by the looks of him,' he said, his top lip curling. 'You a mish-mash, lad?' he demanded.

Cade stared back, confused.

'A fourthling,' said the second.

'Oh . . . y-yes . . .' Cade stammered. 'There's long-hair blood in my family. And slaughterer. And . . . and a bit of grey goblin, I believe, on my mother's side of the—'

The first flathead goblin cut him short. 'We didn't ask for your life history, mish-mash.' His big hands hovered near the weapons at his belt. 'You best come with us.'

Cade nodded again. He wasn't about to argue. His heart was still thumping from the frenzied dash down the slope of the Forlorn Hope. He could still hear the despairing cries of the other leapers, and see the look of horror on the face of the cloddertrog who had helped him . . .

His eyes were growing more accustomed to the smoke-laced gloom of the lower deck, and as he stumbled through the hull quarters, flanked on either side by the savage flathead goblins, Cade took in the strange, shadowy place he'd landed in. Down here in the bowels of the mighty ship, the skytavern was far larger than he'd imagined. Cavernous, in fact – though full to bursting with goblins, trogs and trolls from every part of the city.

Each group of travellers seemed to have its own patch of deck space, dimly lit by the foul-smelling greaselamps and tallow candles which hung from the beams. These makeshift camps were marked out by boxes of belongings or by tilderhides strung up to create makeshift partitions, or sometimes, Cade noticed, just by lines chalked onto the wooden floorboards.

A large family of tufted goblins were seated in a circle, earthenware bowls on their laps, as an old matron with a beaded topknot and filthy leather apron ladled out a thin barley gruel into each bowl from a steaming pot that was balanced upon a glowing brazier, suspended on a chain from the ceiling. One of the young'uns looked up, caught Cade's eye and grinned. He nudged the goblin seated beside him.

'A forlorn hoper,' he said in a guttural whine typical of the eastern districts of Great Glade. 'Don't look like he'll last long,' he added, and the pair of them laughed unpleasantly.

Cade felt the pointed tip of a loaded crossbow press into his side, and he stumbled on.

Behind one of the hanging tilderhides was a bunch of brutal-looking cloddertrogs. One of them was sharpening the curved blade of his longknife on a pale grey whetstone, the soft noise it made like the hiss of a hoverworm. Another was oiling the parts of a dismantled crossbow, while four more were attaching weights to the outer sides of a large square slingnet. A hipflask of something that smelled like rubbing alcohol was being passed from one to the other and quaffed. No one looked up as Cade and the flatheads passed.

All at once, a whooping line of goblin young'uns appeared from the shadows and cut directly in front of the three of them, causing them almost to trip. Cade thought the flatheads would be angry, but instead they chuckled and waited till the last of the young'uns had dashed past. Then, pushing Cade roughly, they set off again through the dark, shadow-filled world of the lower decks.

To his left, Cade passed an underbiter who was frying up something delicious-smelling in a skillet. To his right, two old woodtroll gaffers sat cross-legged on a woven blanket, deep in conversation and sharing a pipe. And a little way beyond them were a couple of shifty-looking fourthlings, hunkered down and examining the contents of a burlap sack. Cade noticed an embroidered silk kerchief, a handful of gold coins and a gem-encrusted bracelet before the fourthlings noticed him. Then they turned away, scowls on their twitchy faces.

The three of them seemed to be near the centre of the great vessel now, and the goblins led Cade through a series of mast-like central pillars, left then right, then right again. He realized that his heart was still thumping.

Abruptly the flatheads stopped beside a series of pillars that had been sectioned off by ironwood planks. The one with the crossbow turned to Cade and held out a calloused hand.

'Give me your pack,' he said.

'My . . . my pack?' Cade repeated. He'd forgotten he'd been wearing it, the heavy pack containing his worldly possessions which had almost cost him his life . . .

'You heard, my friend,' said the flathead. 'And take off your boots.'

Cade swallowed uneasily, but did as he was told. He'd never heard the word 'friend' used with such menace before.

While the flathead rummaged through his backpack, Cade kneeled down and untied his laces. He pulled the boots from his feet, then stood up. The wood was rough beneath his bare feet.

'No knives or nothing, then,' said the flathead. He returned the backpack, slamming it into Cade's chest.

'N-no,' he said. 'I didn't think that weapons were allowed on board a skytavern,' he said, aware, even as he spoke, just how many he'd already seen down here in the depths of the hull.

The flathead paused and surveyed the lowlife all around him as though for the first time: the thieves, the vagabonds, the assassins . . .

'They're not,' he said, and chuckled.

He turned away, raised a bunched fist and hammered on the wall of ironwood planks – which was when Cade noticed the small door set into it. It had no doorknob, no handle. From inside there came a single word that sounded muffled and oddly distant.

'Enter.'

The flathead goblin shouldered the door and held it open for Cade, who stepped forward. His backpack was slung over one shoulder, his boots dangled from his hand – his head and his heart were clamouring. The flathead goblin shoved Cade inside.

The walls had been whitewashed, and the ornate pewter sconces fixed to them held perfumed candles that gave off a soft light and the sweet fragrance of lemon-grass and woodjasmine. On the floor was a thicktuft woven rug of reds and oranges that was soft between his toes, and Cade understood why the flathead had insisted he should remove his boots. There were shelves lined with labelled boxes, and glass-fronted cabinets, and to one side a tall three-panel screen of bone-inlaid blackwood.

The sound of someone clearing his throat startled Cade. It had come from a floating sumpwood armchair chained to the centre of the floor, its curved back towards him. Slowly the armchair began to turn round.

A hand gripped the arm of the chair. It was slender, long-fingered, with pale, almost luminous skin and manicured nails, filed to points. A finger twitched and Cade felt the flatheads' hands grip his collar and arms before he was slammed face down onto the rug.

· CHAPTER FIVE ·

'A forlorn hoper,' growled the first flathead. 'Trying to hitch a free ride,' said the second goblin, and laughed.

'There's no such thing,' said a quiet voice, smooth as spidersilk. 'No one travels for free on the *Xanth Filatine*. To stay aboard you've got to pay the price.'

Cade couldn't move. The flathead goblins had both his arms twisted behind his back and his face was pressed down into the soft rug. It smelled of scented candle smoke and sumpwood resin.

'But I have no money,' he protested, his voice muffled and indistinct.

'Shall I show him, boss?' said one of the flatheads.

Cade winced as his right arm was pulled from behind his back and stretched out taut on the rug. The next moment he felt the flathead's foot pressing down on his hand, squashing it open. Out of the corner of his eye he

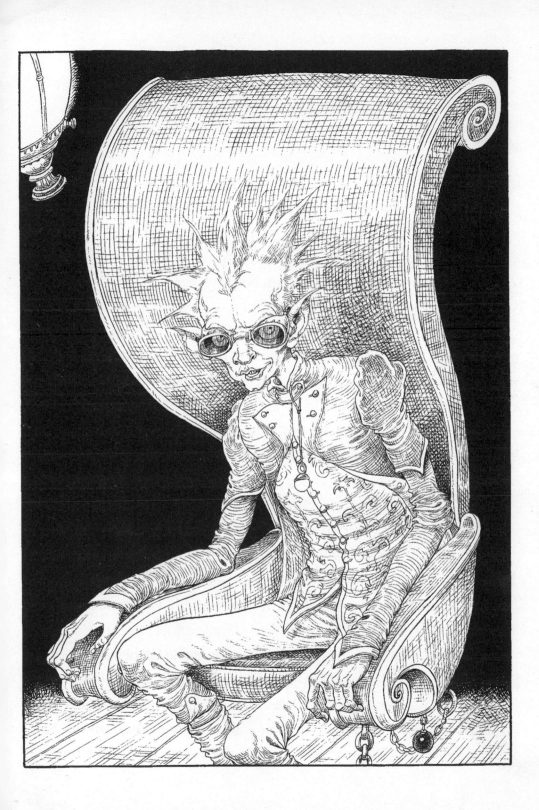

glimpsed a glint of metal and then, as the flathead knelt down, the jag-blade knife in his hand. The chain anchoring the floating sumpwood chair twitched. Cade tried to twist his head round to look up, but could not.

'Always so hasty, Teggtut,' said the voice. 'Let him up.'

Cade felt the goblins release their grip on his arms. He climbed slowly to his feet. A youth of roughly Cade's own age sat in the floating chair looking back at him.

He was unnaturally pale, with greased white hair fashioned into points and sticking up from his skull-like head. He was dressed in a faded smoke-grey topcoat and breeches, and wore a pair of bone-rimmed goggles with green-tinted glass that masked his eyes.

He was a fourthling. Like Cade. Half slaughterer perhaps, or grey goblin. And half . . . what?

'Drax Adereth,' the fourthling introduced himself as he climbed from the buoyant armchair, breaking into Cade's thoughts.

'Cade,' said Cade, trying to sound brave, unafraid. 'Cade Qu-Quarter.' There was a tremor in his voice.

Cade noticed that the fourthling, Drax Adereth, had a short silver blowpipe in his belt – a weapon, he knew, favoured by the nightwaifs of Riverrise.

Drax smiled. His teeth were small and even. 'Lucky for you, Cade Quarter, I'm a reasonable kind of fellow,' he said, nodding as he spoke. 'You got no money, I'm all right with that.' His brow furrowed. 'But to stay on board, there's still a price to pay.' His smile grew broader. 'That's just the way it is.'

'Price to pay,' Cade repeated.

'The skytavern's full of valuables,' Drax said, and the flatheads on either side of Cade growled in agreement. 'Just waiting for a quick-witted, light-fingered traveller to steal.'

'You want me to steal?' Cade said.

Drax's eyes turned to narrow slits behind the tinted goggles. 'You can go up to the upper decks, steal something of value and bring it back to me – or you can pay in another way.'

Even with the goggles, Drax Adereth's gaze felt uncomfortably penetrating. Cade looked away, and found himself staring at a glass bowl perched on top of one of the cabinets. There were things in it, piled high, like twists of knotted wood . . .

'You can have a week,' Drax said, smiling as he followed Cade's gaze.

'A week,' Cade said.

'A week to pay for your passage.' Drax turned back to Cade. 'And don't think you can just lie low,' he cautioned, his soft voice laden with menace. 'Because I know every inch of this ship. I'll find you. And you *will* pay . . .' A smile played at the corners of his narrow mouth. 'One way or the other.'

Cade stared at the glass bowl. Not wood, he thought. More like . . . fingers.

· CHAPTER SIX ·

'**A** week to pay for your passage.'
Cade's head spun as he left the dank, over-crowded depths of the lower hull, and climbed the narrow darkwood stairs. '*And you* will *pay, one way or the other.*'

Drax Adereth's voice, smooth and menacing, sounded over and over in Cade's mind. He tried to push away the memory of the amputated fingers as Drax Adereth had given him his warning; the brown, desiccated nubs packed into the glass bowl like so many pieces of dried wood. Each finger had belonged to someone. Someone down on their luck. Someone poor and needy and at the mercy of others.

Someone like him.

It hadn't always been this way, Cade thought bitterly. He was once the beloved son of celebrated Great Glade academics, Thadeus and Sensa Quarter. He had wanted for nothing.

True, his mother had died when he was only three years old, but his father had done everything in his power to ensure that his childhood was a happy and stable one. Cade had attended the Junior Academy along-side the other privileged children of academics. In the mornings he had chanted his cloud tables, learned wind currents and studied phrax crystals; in the afternoons he had played tensticks on the playing fields or raced sump-wood model skyships with his friends in the long gallery. Yes, life had been good. Until, that is, the fateful night when Thadeus had come to his bedchamber and woken him from a deep sleep.

'Pack your things, son,' he'd said. 'You've got to leave the Cloud Quarter tonight . . .'

The stairs leading up from the lower hull were steep and shallow, and Cade used the rope banisters secured to the panelled walls to help him up, but it was still hard going, and by the time he reached the top of the second flight of stairs he was short of breath. He paused and looked around him. Despite the climb, he knew he was still deep down in the great skytavern.

A long, thin, windowless galley extended both to his left and his right. Lining the inner wall were dozens of bunkbed frames, each one slung with hammocks, top and bottom. Packs and satchels, oilskin jackets and fustian overcoats hung on hooks between them; sacks and crates were stored underneath. Just like the Depths he'd left behind, the air here was hot and humid and rank with the smell of boiled knotcabbage, rancid tallowsmoke and countless unwashed bodies. And as Cade peered into the darkness, he made out dozens, maybe hundreds, of passengers.

Some were busying themselves with day-to-day tasks; stirring stewpots, patching and darning, grooming one another, keeping diaries. Some sat on blankets, alone and pensive, or with others, deep in hushed conversation. Most, though, lay on their hammocks, hands behind their heads, staring at the ceiling, or curled up asleep. All of them looked poor – but not as ragged and desperate as the denizens of the Depths. Judging by the bundles of tools and equipment he saw stowed beneath each hammock, Cade could tell that these were artisans and craftsmen – simple, hard-working folk who had managed to scrape together just enough to pay for these miserable little berths in the fetid bowels of the skytavern.

Cade didn't have the heart to steal from them. He'd have to venture further up to the higher decks . . .

He was about to continue up the next flight of stairs when he heard a low voice behind him. Cade turned to see a short, lean grey goblin watching him from the shadows. He was wearing filthy breeches which were too large for him and tied at the waist with twine, and a patched jacket which was too small and so threadbare it looked as though he'd been wearing it since he was a young'un. His features were sunken and gaunt, and together with the rags he wore, told Cade that this goblin came from the Depths.

'You're a forlorn hoper?' the goblin repeated, glancing round over his shoulders as he spoke.

'What?' said Cade, feigning ignorance.

The goblin shuffled closer, and Cade's nostrils flared involuntarily at the sour odour emanating from the goblin's clothes.

'I could tell, soon as I spotted you. Fresh-faced, well-clothed and with a pack on your back, but climbing up from the Depths,' he said, with a nod back down the steep staircase. 'Jumped the hull at Great Glade, I'll wager,' he added, 'and landed in Drax Adereth's kingdom . . .'

Cade swallowed, wondering whether to deny any knowledge of the fourthling gang boss. The goblin stroked his pointed chin and continued.

'Gave you a week, did he? Told you to steal enough valuables to pay for your passage?'

Cade nodded, the briefest jerk of his head.

'Thought as much,' said the goblin. He sighed. 'Only it ain't that simple, trust me.'

'But . . . but Drax said there were lots of wealthy travellers on board,' said Cade. 'In the upper decks . . .'

'Oh, there are. Don't get me wrong,' said the goblin with a rueful smile, 'but stealing up there among the rich folk is far more difficult than down here in the shadows. For one thing, it's bright and airy and we poor folk stand out. And then there's the skymarshals. Brutal lot, they are. Always on the lookout for lower-deckers without tickets.' He shook his head. 'They like nothing better than skyfiring a pickpocket.'

Cade swallowed. 'Skyfiring?'

The grey goblin rolled his eyes. 'You don't want to know, believe me,' he whispered. 'But it's worse than anything Drax Adereth can do to you.'

Cade trembled. 'So what should I do?' he asked.

The grey goblin merely shrugged. 'What's your name, lad?' he asked.

'Cade.'

'Cade,' the goblin repeated slowly, as though committing it to memory. 'I'm Brod,' he told him. 'I was a forlorn hoper like you. I jumped the hull in Hive eight voyages ago. Been trying to pay my passage ever since. But like I said, stealing from the upper decks is difficult, and I've never managed to get my hands on anything valuable enough to pay Drax off. And once Drax Adereth has his claws into you, he don't let go.' He shook his head miserably. 'I've tried to jump ship when the skytavern docked several times, but Drax's flatheads caught me each time. And I paid the price . . .'

The grey goblin held up his right hand. The index and middle fingers were missing.

'Drax Adereth did that?' said Cade.

Brod nodded. 'Now I stay down in the lower decks and try to keep out of his way for the most part. And look at me. I'm too broken down and ragged to stand a chance in the upper decks.' His eyes narrowed thoughtfully. 'But *you* might . . .'

He took Cade by the sleeve and Cade winced once more at the rank odour of the goblin.

'With a bit of luck and the right plan.'

· CHAPTER SEVEN ·

Cade followed Brod up the next flight of stairs. It opened up onto a deck that was broader but, since it housed twice as many hammocks, no less crowded. The airless space buzzed and hummed with activity and conversation.

'This is where the servants of the rich folk up top are quartered,' said Brod, pulling Cade back into the shadows by the hull wall. He scanned the crowded galley, his eyes narrowed in concentration. 'Wait here a moment,' he whispered before darting off between the hammocks.

Cade lost sight of the grey goblin, and after a few minutes was about to go after him when he felt a tap on the back. He spun round to see Brod smiling back at him, a scarlet topcoat in his hand.

'How did you do that?' Cade exclaimed.

'I've had lots of practice sneaking around down here,'

Brod laughed. 'But up there, it's a different matter,' he went on, his expression growing serious. 'No shadows to hide in. So you need to blend in.' He held up the scarlet topcoat. 'A footman's jacket, Cade. Put it on. A fresh-faced lad like yourself won't get noticed. Not like a shabby, grizzled old-timer like me.'

Cade nodded but said nothing. Even if the look of the old grey goblin didn't give him away, the smell certainly would.

'Now give me your backpack,' Brod was saying.

Cade hesitated. The pack contained all his worldly possessions, and though in truth they didn't add up to much in value, to him they were priceless.

'Footmen don't wear backpacks,' Brod insisted. 'I'll look after it for you while you go up top.'

Reluctantly Cade slipped the pack from his shoulders and handed it to the grey goblin. He put on the scarlet topcoat.

A smile broke out across Brod's face. 'You really look the part,' he said admiringly. 'Now, you need to take these stairs till you get to the fourth landing,' he instructed. 'To the left are the upper berth cabins, but they have guards posted outside every door. You want to go right, out onto the promenade deck. Try to look busy, as if you're on an errand, then hang around the deckstools and see what comes your way.' Brod gave Cade a wink, but then frowned, suddenly serious. 'And avoid the sky-marshals. Blue uniforms, black crushed funnel caps . . .'

He pushed Cade out of the doorway and up the stairs.

'Good luck,' he called after him. 'I'll be waiting down here for you.'

As Cade climbed the succession of staircases from landing to landing, the rough-hewn floorboards gave way to varnished corridors, and then carpeted ones. Portholes appeared on the outer walls. Similarly the lighting shifted by degrees from simple tallow candles, through lamps and lanterns, to ornate silver and crystal chandeliers set the length of the blondwood-panelled hallways, while the cabins that lined them became larger and more opulent with each successive staircase.

When he reached the fourth landing, Cade turned to the right as Brod had instructed, and stepped through an arch, its wooden frame decorated with carved vines and beady-eyed passionbirds, and out onto the open deck. Cade breathed in long and deep, drawing the warm pine-drenched air down into his lungs. After the rank atmosphere in the skytavern's depths, he thought it was the sweetest fragrance he had ever smelled.

Cade smoothed down his hair, then pulled at the cuffs of the topcoat as he tried to build up his confidence. *A message*, he told himself. *I have a message for . . . for the deck overseer . . . I'm looking for him . . . He's wanted back in the midships galley . . .*

His hands were shaking and his mouth felt dry. He was on his own now and felt oddly exposed. Even his backpack was gone, and with it everything he owned in the world.

Cade looked around. There were two outer decks

on the *Xanth Filatine*, one above the other, sweeping round the top levels of the stern and midships of the mighty vessel. For while the low-deck passengers had to content themselves with, at best, portholes, to see out, the travellers with berths on the upper levels were able to promenade on these open decks. Cade surveyed the travellers milling about him. Freeglades dignitaries and Ambristown stilthouse and mine owners by the look of them, their families in tow.

A tall, willowy couple, both dressed in ankle-length lemkinfur overcoats, were strolling towards him, arm in arm. The man carried a carved cane of tilderbone which *tip-tapped* on the dark varnished deckboards; his wife had a skittering fromp on a leash, its gem-encrusted collar sparkling in the midday sun. A corpulent figure wearing a frockcoat and breeches of dark huckaback, a silk shirt with lace at the collar and cuffs, and knee-length leather boots, was leaning over the deck-rail, looking out across the expanse of forest below with a bored expression on his face that suggested this was just one of many such journeys he had undertaken.

Young'uns ran up and down the open deck, just like those in the Depths below – except these wore expensive-looking clothes, had neatly cut hair and clean, polished faces . . .

Cade paused for a moment, and shined his boots as best he could on the backs of his legs, shifting from one foot to the other. He knew it probably made little difference, but it made him feel better.

Further along the promenade deck, Cade could see clusters of deckstools and upholstered sunbenches, where wealthy merchants and their wives, resplendent in bejewelled damask, taffeta trimmed with fur, and with dazzling jewellery at their necks, their ears, their fingers and toes, were seated. As he watched, they exchanged pleasantries with one another, clinked glasses of fine sapwine and nibbled on the canapés of pearlshrimp, smoked beltane and purple caviar being offered to them by servants in scarlet topcoats that matched the one he wore.

Cade was overwhelmed. It was all so exquisitely expensive, he thought; so luxurious, so opulent, so refined.

The skytavern, Cade now saw, glancing over the side, was cruising low in the sky. Its mighty hull was no more than half a dozen strides clear of the tallest treetops.

A little way off from the deckstools were spyglasses mounted on the deck-rails. As Cade watched, passengers rose from their stools and benches and took turns at the spyglasses to take in the spectacular views. And when they did so, they often left something behind, marking their place – an expensive beaded shawl, a pearl-handled purse, a quilted jacket with who knows what riches in its pockets.

Cade realized why Brod had suggested he visit this spot.

Taking a deep breath, he set off across the open deck, taking long, purposeful steps, and carefully weaving in and out of the promenading passengers. As he approached the first cluster of deckstools, he saw three underbiter matrons huddled together around the nearest spyglass, taking it in turn to look through the lens and point out the quarms and fromps and weezits they spotted in the forest below. One of them was ticking off the wildlife they had seen on a long card, illustrated with Deepwoods fauna.

'I do believe that's a rotsucker over there in that iron-wood pine,' one of them observed.

'Oh no, dear, far too small,' her companion corrected her. 'I think you'll find it's a daggerslash.'

On the stools behind them lay their shawls, parasols and purses, carelessly discarded. The purses had gold clasps and were studded with mirepearls. One lay open, its contents – silver powder-cases and little flasks of Riverrise tonics – spilling out on the velvet cushion of the deckstool.

Just one of these purses was all it would take, Cade thought, his fingers itching with excitement despite himself. He would be able to pay for his passage and Drax Adereth would be off his back.

Heart thumping, Cade approached the stools, only for a young tufted goblin in an embroidered waistcoat to beat him to it. As Cade watched open-mouthed, the goblin shot out a hand, grabbed the open purse and made off with it at full pelt back along the deck.

From behind Cade there came a gruff roar and, turning, he saw a large hammerhead goblin in the dark blue uniform of a skymarshal step out onto the deck and block the tufted goblin's escape.

'*Oof!*'

The tufted goblin ran into the hammerhead's barrel chest. He bounced off, and was sent sprawling on the dark varnished boards.

'Dirty little snatchpurse,' growled the skymarshal, picking up the now whimpering goblin by a tufted ear. 'I'd keep a closer eye on your valuables if I were you, madam,' he said, returning the purse to the horrified underbiter matron.

'Thank you, Marshal,' she simpered with a tusked smile.

'Lowdown filth!' exclaimed the second matron, turning from the spyglass.

'I trust he'll be adequately punished,' added the third, prodding the squealing tufted goblin with her parasol.

'Don't you worry about that, madam,' said the sky-marshal darkly. 'It's skyfiring for thievery on the *Xanth Filatine*.'

The hulking hammerhead barged past Cade without a second glance, dragging his prisoner with him. As they disappeared through the arch, Cade could hear the tufted goblin's high-pitched appeals for mercy growing increasingly urgent as they echoed up from the stair-well.

'I say, you, boy!' Cade turned to see the first underbiter matron staring at him through small, yellow-tinged eyes. 'Fetch me a glass of sparkling sapwine, and be quick about it!'

Cade nodded, then turned and hurried gratefully away.

· CHAPTER EIGHT ·

Cade headed back down the stairs. His nerve had gone, at least for the time being. Stealing was going to be a lot more difficult than he'd thought.

'You, there! Have you brought the phrax ice?'

Cade stopped on the bottom step. A tall fourthling in a conical hat had stuck his head out of one of the cabins along the corridor to Cade's right and was looking at him with an exasperated expression on his face.

'No?' the fourthling exclaimed. 'Well, for pity's sake, come in here and watch the eggs while I go and find out what's happened to it. I ordered two buckets of ice an hour ago . . . I mean, is that too much to ask?'

Cade looked about him. There was no one around, but even so, this was the upper decks and he didn't want to draw attention to himself.

'Er . . . yes, sir. Right away, sir,' he said, smoothing down the front of his scarlet footman's coat.

The fourthling gestured for him to enter the cabin.

Lying on the floor in the centre of the well-furnished compartment was a large wooden tray. A glass panel was propped against the wall next to it. Inside, the tray had been divided into forty compartments, each one lined with sweethay. There was a squirming jelly-like object lying in each one.

'They're prowlgrin eggs,' the fourthling told him. 'I've been trying to keep them cool, to delay the hatching. But this cabin's so warm it's set them off,' he explained.

Cade nodded, but was unable to tear his attention away from the sight of the quivering eggs.

'Just keep fanning them.' The fourthling placed a copperwood-leaf fan in Cade's hands and motioned an up-and-down movement with his arms. 'Like this. I'll be back as soon as I can.'

With that, the fourthling gathered his black longcloak about him and rushed out of the door.

Cade felt a draught on the nape of his neck. He looked round. The porthole behind him was open, and he began fanning the fresh air from the opening over the prowlgrin eggs.

The fourthling had mistaken him for a footman and Cade was now alone in his quarters. He scanned the cabin. There was a trunk by the floating sumpwood bed and a valise on the desk next to it. It would be so easy to rifle through them, pocket any valuables and make his escape . . .

But no. Cade couldn't bring himself to do it. The fourthling had trusted him, and deep down Cade knew that he was no thief.

He continued to fan the eggs rhythmically with the outstretched fronds of the fan. The eggs seemed to be cooling. The top few rows had stopped squirming now, and the others were slowing down.

Maybe, if he did a good job, the fourthling would reward him, Cade thought. It might not be much, but then anything would be better than nothing . . .

Suddenly an egg in the bottom row wobbled and stretched, and with a squelching, popping sound, split in two, a clear, gloopy liquid spilling out onto the bed of sweethay beneath it. Moments later, a tiny prowlgrin pup scrambled out, eyes closed, and mewling and kicking with its hind legs. Before Cade had a chance to react, the little creature propelled itself high in the air, over his head – and out of the open porthole.

'Oh no,' groaned Cade.

Watch the eggs, the fourthling had said . . .

Cade crossed to the porthole, reached up and gripped hold of the round window-frame. Then, bracing his legs, he heaved himself up and peered out. And there it was, perched on a tether-rail a dozen strides down the hull. The prowlgrin pup. It had its back to Cade, its wet grey fur gleaming in the afternoon sun.

'Come on,' said Cade, leaning out through the opening. 'Come here, boy.'

But the prowlgrin took no notice. Its body trembled as it readied itself to jump. Pushing the fan into the pocket of the crimson jacket, Cade thrust his arm out of the porthole and, grunting with effort, pulled him-

self through the narrow opening. It was a tight squeeze, with the frame of the porthole grazing his back and belly as his scarlet topcoat rode up. But he made it through and ended up outside, stooped over, one foot resting on the porthole, one hand clinging onto the frame – the other arm and leg dangling in mid-air as the *Xanth Filatine* flew on across the Deepwoods.

'Here, boy!' Cade shouted, pulling the fan from his pocket and waving it frantically.

The prowlgrin must have heard him. It turned and eyed him through large doleful eyes, thick with rheum, which it blinked away. Despite himself, Cade had to smile.

The air was drying

the little pup's fur, which had a translucent glossy sheen, smoke-grey in contrast to its bright yellow, jewel-like eyes. The creature was beautiful. A pedigree prowlgrin.

But how was he going to catch it?

Cade looked down at the copperwood-leaf fan in his hand . . .

Leaning out as far as he dared, Cade held out the fan horizontally, its leaves rustling in the steady wind. The prowlgrin's eyes fixed upon it.

'That's right, boy,' Cade urged. 'Go on. Jump onto the nice branch. You know you want to . . .'

Just then the prowlgrin's jaws parted, and with a soft, squeaky yelp it took a great leap towards the fan. Cade flinched involuntarily as the creature landed on the handle and held on tight.

Cade looked down. The prowlgrin looked up. Their eyes met, and Cade grinned. Then the prowlgrin pup blinked twice and nuzzled into Cade's hand, the soft fur, dry now, warm against his fingers. It began purring, loud and throaty and content.

'Good boy,' Cade cooed as he carefully climbed back into the cabin, holding the fan level. 'Good boy!'

The air was cold and, looking round, Cade saw that the fourthling had returned with two buckets of ice scraped from the metal hull of the skytavern's phraxchamber. The fourthling smiled as he saw the prowlgrin pup clinging to the fan in Cade's outstretched hand.

'You're a natural,' he said.

· CHAPTER NINE ·

'It's imprinted on you, Cade Quarter,' said Tillman Spoke.

'Imprinted?' Cade repeated.

'You were the first creature it saw once its eyes had opened. Now it thinks you're its mother. Or father.'

The prowlgrin pup purred softly and, still clinging onto the fan in Cade's hand, looked up at him lovingly. Cade grinned.

'And since we've made our introductions,' Tillman continued, 'might I suggest you also give our little friend here a name?'

'Can I?' said Cade. 'Are you sure?'

'Of course,' Tillman Spoke replied with a smile, folding his black longcloak and placing it beside the conical hat on the floating sumpwood desk. 'But make sure it ends with "ix". All pedigree prowlgrins have an "ix" at the end of their names.'

The pup purred, loud and rumbling in the back of its throat.

'Rumblix,' Cade said, and tickled the little creature under the chin, where there was a smudge of white fur in amongst the grey. 'I'm going to call you Rumblix.'

Spoke watched the pair of them, his green eyes twinkling. He reached up and raked his fingers through his thick salt-and-pepper hair, frowning thoughtfully.

'A footman on a mighty vessel like this . . .' he said. 'They must work you pretty hard.'

Cade felt himself blushing as he looked down at the scarlet topcoat he was wearing.

'Oh, I don't know,' he said, concentrating on the little prowlgrin pup. 'I'm new to all this . . . Joined the *Xanth Filatine* in Great Glade,' Cade added truthfully enough.

'Well, that makes two of us,' said Tillman Spoke, and laughed. 'I'm headed for Hive and a new life. Great Glade has too many memories for me now that I've retired from the Freeglade Lancers.'

Cade let out a low whistle. 'The Freeglade Lancers,' he repeated, his voice breathless with awe.

Dressed in their traditional green and white checker-board collars and white tunics emblazoned with a red banderbear, and carrying phraxmuskets and long iron-wood lances, the regiments of lancers on prowlgrinback had often marched ceremonially through the districts of Great Glade at the head of the militia.

The Freeglade Lancers were the elite – the toughest fighters and the most skilful riders – and they had a proud history. From the city's beginnings as a remote settlement in the heart of the vast and hostile Deep-woods, the lancers had patrolled its borders and kept its inhabitants safe. From the skirmishes and raids of the goblin wars a century earlier to the pitched battles of the war with Hive, when Cade was little more than a babe-in-arms, the Freeglade Lancers could be relied on to be at the centre of the fray, where the fighting was fiercest and their skill and courage was needed the most.

'You were a Freeglade Lancer,' Cade breathed.

'I was,' said Tillman Spoke, crossing the cabin to where the case of prowlgrin eggs lay on a cooling bed of phrax ice. Despite the warmth of the cabin, it had barely begun to melt, tiny droplets of water glistening on its surface. 'I fought in the war with Hive, took part in the prowlgrin charge that won the Battle of the Midwood Marshes.' His brow furrowed at the memory. 'Lost a lot of good lancers and fine prowlgrins in that fight.'

The fourthling fell silent as he stared down at the eggs nestling on the sweethay beneath the glass. Then he cleared his throat, and when he turned back to Cade there was a smile on Tillman Spoke's face.

'After the battle, they promoted me,' he said. 'I was made High Equerry of the prowlgrin stables. The well-being of the creatures was my responsibility, from the moment they hatched to the day they were retired, and every moment in between. I was in charge of their feeding, their grooming, their exercise. After all, as everyone knows, a lancer is only as good as his mount.'

Rumblix had stopped nuzzling Cade's neck and was snuffling about at his hip pocket.

Cade took hold of the pup and tickled him under his chin, behind his ears, at the top of his quivering nostrils. And Rumblix purred like a phraxengine – then wriggled out of Cade's grasp. Still purring, he began snuffling at Cade's pocket once more.

'What's the matter, boy?' said Cade. 'What are you looking for?'

Cade put his hand in his pocket – and a smile spread across his face as his fingers closed around a small paper-wrapped parcel inside. It was his breakfast, stowed there before he'd set off for the Forlorn Hope. He'd forgotten all about it. Rumblix began bouncing up and down, his mouth gaping and saliva dribbling down over his furry chin.

'Here we are,' said Cade.

He unwrapped the parcel and, taking a piece of salted tildermeat between his finger and thumb, held it out to the pup. Rumblix sniffed. His eyes widened. Then, with a slurp, he plucked the meat from Cade's hand and started chewing. A moment later, he was ready for another piece. 'He must have known it was there,' said Cade, looking up at the fourthling.

'He's a pure-bred grey,' said Tillman Spoke, nodding. 'Intelligent, obedient – and powerful jumpers.' He glanced back at the tray of eggs, with the phrax ice packed beneath it, keeping them cool. 'That's why this lot are so valuable.' He nodded. 'When I retired as High Equerry, they offered me a pension – but I opted for these instead. Forty pedigree grey eggs.' He grinned. 'It was an easy choice.'

'But what are you going to do with them all?' asked Cade.

'I'm going to start a new life,' said the fourthling, his face glowing with a mixture of pride and excitement, 'with some old friends of mine in Hive. They have stables and I have the eggs. We're going to raise and train high-jumpers.'

'High-jumpers . . . *Ouch!*' Cade exclaimed. 'Don't nip!' he told the pup, who backed off shame-facedly for a moment, before turning back and yelping for the next piece of tildermeat more eagerly than ever.

Cade couldn't help laughing.

'High-jumping,' Tillman Spoke explained. 'It's the most popular sport in Hive.'

'I've never heard of it,' said Cade.

'You wouldn't,' said Spoke. 'Not if you haven't been to Hive. But the goblins of Hive can't get enough of it. They have this course that runs down the great waterfall that divides the city. Fifty wooden ledges, fixed to the sides of the gorge at the back of the waterfall. They call them the "branches". Trained prowlgrins take it in turns to leap from branch to branch all the way from the top of the falls to the bottom, and the fastest one down wins. It's a nailbiting sport, all right. One slip, one misplaced foot, and you're a goner.' He nodded. 'But there's a handsome purse for the winner.'

Cade looked down at Rumblix. The little creature was so small it was hard to imagine him with a rider on his back.

'The thing is . . .' Spoke fell still.

Cade fed the pup the last of the dried meat and looked up.

'The thing is,' Spoke said again, 'I know you've just embarked on a career as a footman on this fine skytavern, so I hardly dare to ask, but . . .'

Cade's heart was thumping in his chest. Now that the food was all gone, Rumblix had curled himself up into a purring ball, his eyes closed. Cade looked down at him, stroking his fur, scarcely daring to believe his luck.

'But I'll just go ahead and ask anyway,' Spoke was saying. 'You see, like it or not, the pup has imprinted on you. And he's a valuable animal. If you just upped and left now, it could cause him irreparable damage – he could become untrainable. So what I'm asking is . . .'

Cade looked up to see the fourthling looking back at him, one eyebrow raised.

'Cade Quarter,' he said, 'I don't suppose you would be interested in turning in that scarlet topcoat and coming to work for me?'

· CHAPTER TEN ·

Cade watched as a hefty cloddertrog in a greasy white apron pulled on the rope, hand over massive hand, as he raised the bait log. Moments later, from the open hatch at the cloddertrog's feet, an ironwood spar at the end of the rope emerged. Cade swallowed as the cloddertrog swung the log onto the great stone slab in the centre of the open kitchen. He felt he would never get used to the sight.

The bait log was crawling with sky creatures – strange, translucent animals borne on the winds, who settled on the ironwood logs which were trailed from the sky-tavern each night and hauled up each morning. There were spherical mist-barnacles with soft blue shells and trailing tentacles, see-through wind-snakes coiled tightly around the wood, gelatinous hull-crawlers with eyes on stalks and vicious-looking claws, and gossamer-light cloud-spinners; tiny creatures the size of Cade's thumb, scarcely visible until covered in thick creamy batter.

Gnokgoblins in white conical hats gathered around the slab and began prising the sky creatures from the log. They chopped them up with cleavers and tossed them over their shoulders to others, who caught the chunks, coated them in batter and dropped them into bubbling vats of oil in a single, graceful movement.

Skyfare, it was called. The pieces sizzled and hissed, and Cade's mouth began to water.

He was sitting in one of the slop halls, the communal dining rooms that fed the ordinary passengers of the skytavern. It was a broad, low-ceilinged chamber with twenty buoyant sumpwood tables fixed to the floor by chains, clustered around a central kitchen. Here was the stone slab and the floor hatches through which the bait logs were lowered and raised, together with a circle of stoves on which pots, pans and fry-vats bubbled, and steam and smoke coiled up and rippled across the roof-beams in a greasy cloud.

On either side of Cade, his fellow diners jostled one another as they clutched the wooden platters they had purchased. A ripple of anticipation made the sumpwood table in front of Cade sway as the aroma of frying skyfare rose from the vats. As well as skyfare, there was an array of brightly coloured sauces to dip the battered pieces into, and cauldrons of snowbird and gullywing stew. And as much as you could eat for ten gladers.

No wonder the slop hall was so crowded, Cade thought.

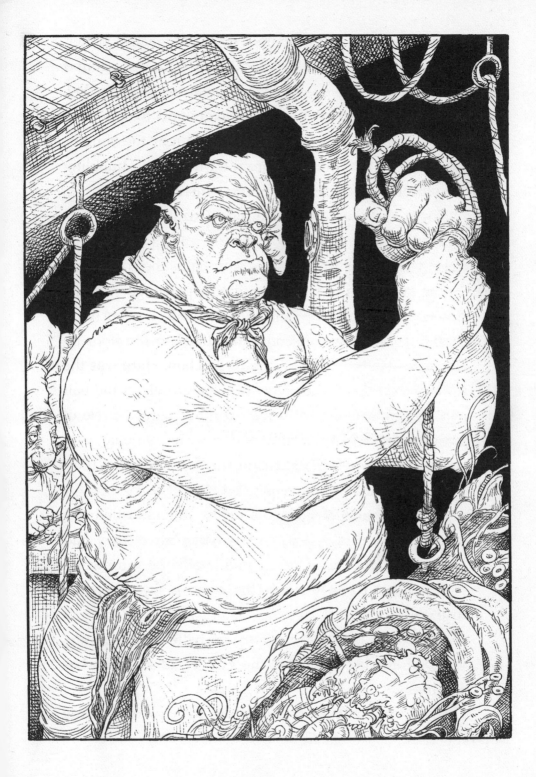

'Hold up yer platters!' the cloddertrog roared and, together with the gnokgoblin cooks, began to circulate around the sumpwood tables with the stew and skyfare.

Cade held his platter up above his head as the cooks passed, then returned it to the table in front of him. The platter was piled high. Already the excited clamour of the slop hall had descended into a low contented hum of slurps and chewing and muttered conversation. Cade took his spoon and knife from his topcoat and began to eat.

The stew was rich and creamy. The sauces were all different – some herby, some spicy, some sweet. And as for the skyfare, it was delicious. Not that some of it wasn't a bit unusual. Biting into the crunchy skin of a sky-worm, for instance, then sucking out the juicy pulp inside was something quite new to Cade, so different from the meals of tilder steaks and steam cabbage they had served at the Academy School in Great Glade.

Great Glade. Cade remembered his father's words the night his world had changed for ever, just a week earlier.

'Pack your things, son. You've got to leave the Cloud Quarter tonight . . .'

'But why?' Cade had protested, wiping the sleep from his eyes.

His father had looked white-faced and deadly serious. 'It's my brother, Nate,' his father had said. 'He has returned.'

Cade's uncle, Nate Quarter, was famous throughout the Edge, although Cade himself had never met him.

Nate Quarter had discovered the lost floating city of Sanctaphrax and founded a new city at the very tip of the Edge itself, where the mighty Edgewater River thundered down into the black abyss below. He was considered an enemy of flight by the academics of Great Glade and their leader, the powerful High Professor of Flight, Quove Lentis.

For Nate Quarter was a descender.

In the quest for knowledge he, and others like him, had lowered themselves on ropes down the cliff face of the Edge into the swirling depths where no skyvessel could follow. To Quove Lentis, this was heresy. Nate Quarter had disappeared into the darkness before Cade was even born, and his father – himself an academic in the School of Flight – had never spoken of his elder brother. Until, that is, that final night . . .

'The High Professor is using my brother's reappearance to purge the academy of any he suspects of supporting the descenders. And despite the fact that I've always made it clear that I don't agree with my brother's views, my name is at the top of Quove Lentis's list. Followed by yours, Cade.'

'But—' Cade had protested.

'No buts, son,' his father had said quietly. 'I have made arrangements. There's a cargo-handler down in the Ledges district who owes me a favour. He's agreed to put you up with his family until I can sort things out. It'll take a few days, but I'm sure this will all blow over once I've managed to convince the High Professor of

65

my loyalty. In the meantime, take these with you and promise me you'll look after them.'

His father had thrust a bundle of barkscrolls into his hands.

'I promise,' Cade had said.

His father had hugged him. 'Now, go . . . *go!*'

Now, here Cade was, sitting in the crowded slop hall of a mighty skytavern. He was no longer wearing the footman's scarlet topcoat. Folded up, it was serving as a cushion for Rumblix, who liked to nuzzle up contentedly into the soft material that smelled of his master. Instead, Cade was dressed in a smart black topcoat, courtesy of Tillman Spoke.

For the previous six days, Cade had set about making himself as useful as he could to his new employer. Each day he collected fresh ice from the mighty phraxchamber below the skytavern's steaming funnel and made sure the prowlgrin eggs were sufficiently cooled. He kept the cabin tidy, slept in a hammock in the corner, and looked after Rumblix, the little pup, who followed him around the cabin and fretted and pined whenever he left. Tillman Spoke busied himself with his accounts for hours on end, sitting at the sumpwood desk beside the open porthole, staring out at the passing clouds every so often, lost in thoughts of his new life in Hive.

Right now, though, Cade thought, the prowlgrin breeder would be taking his breakfast in the Grand Salon high above the slop hall. But nothing they served up there could be as delicious as this breakfast he was enjoying.

'Hold up yer platters!'

The cooks were coming round again, and Cade was about to hold up his platter for more when a hand reached out and grabbed his arm. It was large and powerful and had a large gold ring on one finger. Cade turned round, and found himself face to face with one of the flathead goblins from the Depths, his brow-rings gleaming in the low light. He smiled to reveal two rows of teeth, filed to points.

'We've been watching you, Cade Quarter,' he said. 'Drax gave you a week. One day to go.'

The goblin's grip tightened on Cade's arm, causing him to drop the platter, which fell clattering to the floor.

'That fourthling in the fancy cabin up top must have something worth stealing.' The goblin's smile faded and his eyes narrowed. 'A pedigree prowlgrin pup, for instance.'

Letting go of Cade's arm, the flathead barged his way out of the slop hall, pausing at the doorway to stare back.

'See you in the Depths tomorrow,' he said.

· CHAPTER ELEVEN ·

Cade was woken by the prowlgrin pup slurping at his face. He opened his eyes to see Rumblix perched above him, his paws gripping either side of the hammock and his head cocked to one side. The low sun was streaming in through the porthole. Two days had passed since Drax Adereth's deadline, and Cade hadn't left the cabin once. He hadn't dared.

'Hungry, boy?' he said as he sat up and wrapped his arms round the sleek, grey-furred creature. He tickled him under his chin. 'Always hungry, aren't you?'

Rumblix purred and pushed up on his powerful hind legs to nuzzle into Cade's chest.

'And growing bigger every day,' said Tillman Spoke from his seat at the floating sumpwood desk.

Cade swung his legs over the side of the hammock and climbed to his feet. 'What time is it?' he said, yawning.

'The dawn bell's just sounded,' said Tillman cheerfully

as he tidied the barkscrolls on the desk. 'I had an early breakfast in the Grand Salon.'

Cade's stomach gurgled. He would have liked some breakfast himself. Windsnappers in batter. Maybe some kerbiss-broth . . .

But that would have meant leaving the cabin, and Cade didn't want to risk it just yet. Unlike him, however, Rumblix was not prepared to wait. There was a bucket beneath the hammock. And it contained food. The smell of the pieces of skyfare that Cade had put in there was seeping enticingly through the gap between the top of the bucket and the heavy ironwood lid, driving the prowl-grin pup mad. Head down, Rumblix butted the bucket in an attempt to dislodge the lid, but to no avail, and he squealed with frustration.

'Here we are, then,' said Cade, pulling off the lid and laying it aside.

With a little yelp, Rumblix jumped forward and began to purr loudly. He was tall enough now to rest his front paws on the side of the bucket and plunge his head inside. Soon the throaty purring was replaced by slurping and swallowing as the prowlgrin pup gulped down the chunks of meat. Then, when every last piece was gone, he looked up, head cocked, and let out a small questioning chirrup. He was still hungry.

'Prowlgrin pups need a lot of looking after,' said Tillman, getting up from the desk and crossing the cabin. 'Feeding every few hours and regular grooming. Not to mention plenty of love and affection . . .'

He paused to pat the little pup on the head and tickle his nostrils. Rumblix purred appreciatively.

'But you're doing a fine job. I'm proud of you, Cade.'

Cade smiled delightedly, then bent down and reached under his hammock. There was a small casket standing next to the bucket. Cade dragged it out, opened the top and stared down at the contents for a moment, before selecting a long coarse file with a polished bone handle.

Tillman pulled up an armchair by the open porthole and settled down to watch.

'Here, boy,' Cade said, sitting himself down and patting the floor before him.

Rumblix trotted over obediently and slumped down between Cade's legs, his back towards him. Cade leaned over the top of the small creature, the file in his hand, and took the pup's front left paw. Then, one by one, he carefully filed each of the long curved claws to needle-sharp points. And when they were done, he started work on Rumblix's feet, filing off the ragged edges of his toenails and leaving them smooth and polished.

Cade returned the file to the chest and pulled out an earthenware pot. As he unstoppered the cork with his teeth, a sweet aromatic smell of sagemint, rock-fennel and blackwheat oil filled the cabin. Rumblix bounced up and down on his hind legs, trembling with excitement.

Tillman laughed.

'You like this bit, don't you, Rumblix, boy?' said Cade.

He dipped his fingers into the oily green ointment and started rubbing it into the prowlgrin pup's feet, while

Rumblix's purrs grew louder and louder.

Tillman nodded in appreciation. 'You're beginning to understand just how extraordinarily sensitive a prowlgrin's toes are,' he said. 'And how important it is to keep them supple and healthy with regular oiling.'

Cade nodded.

With their wide-apart eyes, Tillman had explained, prowlgrins could spot branches and perches to leap to, and their feet could sense whether a branch could take their weight, and for how long. In this way, a prowlgrin could gallop through the highest branches of the Deepwoods without ever missing a leap or falling to earth.

'When we get to

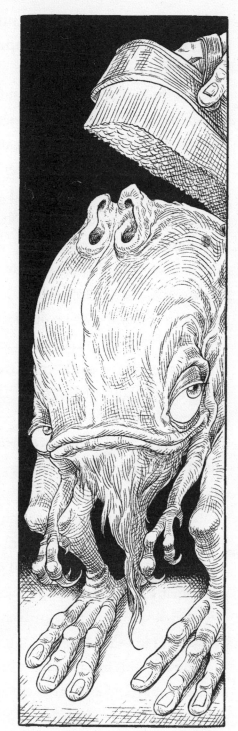

Hive, I'll take you riding through the forest. I tell you, Cade, sitting on a prowlgrin at full gallop is an experience you'll never forget.'

Cade looked up at the fourthling and, not for the first time, wondered whether he should come clean – tell him he wasn't a steward, but a forlorn hoper from the Lower Depths in debt to a gang boss . . .

'Trust a prowlgrin's leap and you'll never fall,' Tillman said with a gleam in his eyes.

Picking up a broad-toothed comb and a stiff-bristled dandy brush, Cade combed away the tangles from the prowlgrin's thick grey fur and brushed it till it was as sleek and gleaming as burnished pewter.

'You've done a fine job,' Tillman said, getting up from the armchair and going over to the tray of prowl-grin eggs. 'And watching you take care of this pup has convinced me that I can trust you to do a fine job as my head groom . . .'

'Tillman, there's something I should tell you—' Cade began.

'Trust,' Tillman said, examining the eggs. 'It is the most important thing there is – without trust, we have nothing.' He nudged the phrax ice beneath the tray of prowlgrin eggs with the tip of his boot. 'I think you ought to get more ice from the phraxchamber. This lot's melting away . . .' He looked up. 'What did you want to tell me?'

'Oh, it's not important,' said Cade, his face colour-ing. 'I've been meaning to get more ice, but I lost track of time.'

'Do you good to get out of the cabin, get some fresh air,' said Tillman, sitting back down at the sumpwood desk and opening one of the half-dozen ledgers stacked on its cluttered surface. 'After all, you've been shut up here for days.'

Cade swallowed. Tillman Spoke was right. The trouble was, Cade knew he couldn't hole up here indefinitely. He looked up at the fourthling.

'I'll get some just as soon as I've finished grooming Rumblix,' said Cade.

Tillman smiled. 'He looks fine to me,' he said.

'I haven't done his teeth yet,' said Cade. 'And his harness straps need loosening a bit . . .'

'First, go and get the ice, Cade,' said Tillman Spoke. 'The last thing we want is for any more of those eggs to hatch.'

Cade nodded and climbed to his feet. There was no point in arguing. Reluctantly he pulled on his cap and gloves, and placed the ice-pick in his belt. Then he closed the porthole. The last time he'd gone out and left it open, Rumblix had followed him, tracking him down to the slop hall and leaping delightedly onto his forearm when he'd found him. Cade had been impressed, but had hated to think of what might have happened to the young prowlgrin. He could have been stolen, or even fallen overboard. Needless to say, he hadn't mentioned Rumblix's little adventure to Tillman Spoke. Cade picked up the two empty buckets by the door and ventured out into the corridor.

He looked left, then right. The long copperwood-panelled corridor with its line of heavy darkwood cabin doors was deserted. Pulling his cap down low on his head, the peak concealing his face, Cade set off at a trot down the corridor and up the flights of stairs to the uppermost deck. As he neared the top, elegant couples and well-heeled merchants passed him, returning from their breakfasts in the Great Salon. Cade hurried by, keeping his head down. At the top of the stairs, he turned left and hurried along the covered gangway that led to midships.

Here, directly below the phraxchamber, phrax-engineers in long white topcoats, and their assistants in triple-waistcoats and shirtsleeves, clustered in groups around the pipes, gauges and levers that sprouted from the walls. They busied themselves with the myriad decisions and adjustments required to keep the great sky-tavern airborne, checking dials, scribbling on clipboards, releasing pressure valves that hissed and steamed; they paid no attention to the youth in the black topcoat and peaked cap among them.

Relieved, Cade reached the series of steep ladder-like steps that led up to the phraxchamber, and began to climb them. The flight platform above was usually deserted and he'd be able to gather the ice quickly and unobserved.

He could hear the phraxchamber above him, hissing and humming and creaking, together with the roar of the jet of air blasting out of the propulsion duct. A moment later, he emerged onto the flight platform, a broad ring of ironwood which encircled the base of the phraxchamber itself.

Cade stopped to catch his breath, hands on hips, and looked up. The giant metal-plated sphere of the phrax-chamber rose up before him, supported upon crisscross struts of scaffolding. At the top of the chamber was a tow-ering funnel from which huge clouds of ice-cold steam billowed in an unending torrent, while at the back of the chamber was the broad jutting pipe of the propulsion duct, out of which a jet of white-hot air roared, pushing the skytavern through the sky.

In the middle of the phraxchamber was a circular window of dense glass, through which an intermittent flash of light could be seen. Cade climbed the frost-covered steps and peered inside. Somewhere at the heart of the chamber was a shard of phrax crystal – solidified lightning, mined from beneath the Twilight Woods, and now keeping the mighty *Xanth Filatine* airborne and in flight with a never-ending series of controlled explosions.

Cade smiled sadly to himself. His father had worked for most of his life at the Institute of Phrax Studies – a part of the great School of Flight in the Cloud Quarter. He had explained to Cade how the power of lightning locked up in the phrax crystal could be released, caus-ing the huge chamber to become as buoyant as a flight rock, and intense heat and cold to be generated. The heat propelled the skytavern, while the cold flowed from the funnel as ice-cold steam and formed as ice on the outer casing of the phraxchamber.

As Cade stood in front of the ice-covered metal plates, he shivered. Gleaming pink and pale blue in the early morning light, the frozen rods and rippled curtains of ice resembled some curious miniature winter scene. It was beautiful, but bitterly cold. The ice sucked every trace of warmth from the air. Cade's eyes watered and the inner membrane of his nose stung and, as he set the buckets down and pulled the hammer from his belt, he was glad he was wearing the cap and gloves.

Tip-tip-tip. Tap-tap-tap . . .

The sound of the small pick hammering at the ice was not loud. But in Cade's anxious state, the noise seemed deafening. He worked quickly, making do with large chunks of ice rather than breaking them into smaller pieces, and when both buckets were full, he decided to take a different route back to the cabin.

With a bucket in each hand, Cade strode round the flight platform to the port side of the skytavern. He would return to the lower deck on the far side of the ship, then cut through. It was as he was rounding the front of the phraxchamber, and the roaring of the propulsion duct lessened, that Cade heard voices.

They were coming from a small maintenance cabin, half hidden among the scaffolding supporting the phraxchamber. Cade tiptoed down the stairs and past the door of the cabin, which stood ajar. Cautiously he craned his neck and peered inside.

Ice-rakes, phraxtorches, boltdrivers and hex-wrenches hung from hooks on the walls; a barrel of oil stood

beneath them. And crouched in the corner, round a glowing lufwood stove, were two figures in dark robes – robes
that Cade recognized at once. They were the same as the
ones his father used to wear; the robes of professors from
the School of Flight.

When one of the academics
looked up, Cade ducked
back and continued down
the steps. Whatever
these professors were
doing hiding out in
a tool shed, it was
none of his busi-
ness. He had bigger
things to worry
about – such as how
to keep all his fingers
until the skytavern
docked in Hive.

Reaching the corridor that
led to Tillman Spoke's cabin, Cade
allowed himself to relax. Things were going to be fine.
He'd just proved it. So long as he was vigilant and confident when he ventured out for ice, or food – or for any
other task that Tillman Spoke set – then no one would
even notice him. After all, the skytavern had hundreds
of passengers on board, and scores of crew; it would be
no problem to blend in. And Cade was congratulating
himself on keeping things in perspective when Drax

Adereth's two flathead heavies suddenly stepped out from the shadows at the far end of the corridor.

Cade froze.

Teggtut, the taller of the two flathead goblins, stepped forward. His eyes narrowed. Cade swallowed, then made a dash for the cabin door. He turned the handle – glancing back as he did so.

The flathead had stopped. He was glaring at him, then he raised a hand and ran a filthy-nailed finger slowly across the base of his throat. Cade swallowed again, and disappeared inside the cabin. He leaned back against the door for a moment, breathing unevenly, waiting for his thumping heart to quieten down.

Tillman Spoke was at his desk, slumped forward, his head resting on an open ledger as he quietly snored. The papers on the desk before him flapped and rustled as the wind came in through the open porthole above his head. Still trembling, Cade stole over to the tray of prowlgrin eggs and arranged the ice around and under it, and he was taking off his gloves when there was a soft knock on the door.

Cade jumped. Teggtut had decided to confront him after all.

He wished he was invisible. He wished the floor would swallow him up. He looked up at the porthole and wondered whether to try and make a run for it – but that would mean deserting Tillman Spoke and the promise of a new life, and that was the last thing he wanted to do . . .

With no other choice, Cade crossed the floor before

the flathead knocked again and woke Spoke up. Perhaps he could reason with him. Cade eased the door open a couple of inches.

'You!' he whispered, relieved to see Brod the grey goblin standing before him. He opened the door wider. 'Come in, come in.'

But the grey goblin shook his head. He looked ill at ease. His eyes were wide and darting and unable to meet Cade's gaze. Perhaps he'd spotted Drax Adereth's cronies in the corridor . . .

'Can't stop,' said Brod. 'Things to do. I . . . I just wanted to bring you this.' He brought Cade's backpack from behind his back and held it out. 'It took me a while to track you down . . .' His voice trailed away. 'But here it is. Better late than never, and all safe and sound.'

'Thank you, Brod,' said Cade, his face colouring. He'd assumed the grey goblin had stolen his possessions, worthless as they were to anyone but Cade. He took hold of the backpack, surprised and grateful that Brod had taken the trouble to return it to him, then reached into his pocket for some of the gladers that Tillman Spoke had given him for his meals. 'Let me thank you for your help,' he began.

But the grey goblin raised his hands and stepped backwards. 'No, no, I couldn't,' he said. 'Really. It was nothing . . .'

And with that, he turned on his heels and scuttled back along the corridor. Cade watched him for a moment, puzzled, then stepped back into the room and closed the door behind him. He crossed to his hammock and, stowing the backpack beneath it, fell into the gently swaying bed with a sigh of relief.

Only another week and a half and they would reach the safety of Hive. Above him, on his perch, Rumblix shifted on his oiled feet and let out an excited little whimper as he leaped from branch to branch in his sleep.

· CHAPTER TWELVE ·

*B*ang! Bang! Bang!
The pounding at the door shattered the warm, drowsy atmosphere in the cabin.

Bang! Bang! Bang! Bang!

Rumblix leaped from his perch at the end of Cade's hammock and scurried off into the shadows in the corner of the room. Cade clambered to his feet and was about to cross to the door, when Tillman Spoke stayed him with a sweep of his hand.

'Leave this to me,' he said, getting up from the sump-wood desk. He strode to the door and opened it. 'Well, if it isn't my old friend, the skymarshal,' he said smoothly.

Cade looked over Tillman Spoke's shoulder to see a severe-looking hammerhead goblin dressed in a blue uniform and black crushed funnel cap.

'Apologies for the intrusion, sir,' the skymarshal said.

'If it's about the prowlgrin eggs,' Tillman began,

'you should speak to the holdmarshal . . . I paid him five gold coins for the privilege of keeping them here with me. And I'm not paying a brass groat more.'

'It isn't that,' said the skymarshal, cutting him short. 'If you wouldn't mind, sir.' He pushed past Tillman Spoke and into the cabin. 'I'm afraid there's been a report . . .'

'A report?'

'Well, more like a tip-off, sir,' said the sky-marshal, his wide-set eyes scanning the cabin.

'I don't understand,' said Tillman Spoke, pulling himself up to his full height. 'If you're accusing me of something, then come out with it. I've got nothing to hide.'

'*You* might not have anything to hide, sir,' said the hammerhead

83

skymarshal, taking the phraxpistol from his belt. His eyes turned to Cade. 'But can your young friend here say the same?'

Cade flinched under the skymarshal's penetrating stare. 'I haven't done anything wrong,' he protested.

'There was a robbery up on the promenade deck, by the spyglasses,' the skymarshal said, ignoring Cade and talking directly to Tillman. 'A snatchpurse answering to the description of your assistant was seen fleeing the scene.'

'Cade?' said Tillman. 'Do you know anything about this?'

The sight of the rich goblin matrons at the spyglasses on the promenade deck flashed through Cade's mind and, despite himself, he felt his face begin to redden. 'No, nothing, Tillman, I swear . . .'

'Then you won't object if I search your belongings,' said the skymarshal, crossing swiftly to Cade's hammock and seizing the backpack which lay beneath it.

'They're just my personal things,' said Cade weakly as the hammerhead unfastened the straps at the top of the pack and rummaged about inside.

'And what have we here?' said the hammerhead, withdrawing his hand from the pack. His long-nailed fingers were clutching a small package, carelessly wrapped in brown paper.

'That? I . . .' Cade frowned. 'I've never seen it before in my life.'

He glanced up at Tillman Spoke, but the fourthling's

face was unreadable. The hammerhead tore the paper at one end of the package and shook it, and like a serpent emerging from sloughed skin, a long mire-pearl necklace slithered out into his open palm.

Cade gasped. 'It . . . it isn't mine,' he said.

'First honest word you've uttered,' said the skymarshal grimly. His eyes darted around the cabin, then fixed on the coathooks on the wall by the door.

'I didn't take it,' Cade protested, staring blankly at the stolen necklace.

'It's an old trick,' the skymarshal went on, putting the necklace in the pocket of his topcoat. He strode over and plucked the footman's jacket from the first coathook. He held it up to Tillman Spoke, his fingers and thumbs pinched at the shoulders. 'First they steal a uniform so they can get access to the upper decks without being noticed. Then, when they spot some rich goblin matron, they rob her. It's disgraceful,' he added, shaking his head. 'Thankfully, we skymarshals of the *Xanth Filatine* like to keep one step ahead . . .'

'Tillman . . . sir,' said Cade desperately. 'I had nothing to do with this. You've got to believe me . . .'

'I *did* believe you,' said Tillman Spoke coldly. 'I believed you were an honest footman looking for a new start.' He frowned. 'Are you – or have you ever been – a footman, Cade?'

Cade swallowed. 'N-no, sir, but—'

'Well, then,' said Tillman. 'It seems that the skymarshal here knows you a lot better than I do.' He shook his head sadly. 'You've disappointed me, lad,' he said. 'I can't pretend otherwise. I believed you. I *trusted* you. And it seems my trust was ill-judged.' He turned to the skymarshal. 'What do you intend to do with him?'

'You don't need to concern yourself with that, sir,' the skymarshal told him. 'He will be punished appropriately.'

'Please, please . . .' Cade persisted, but he knew his entreaties were falling on deaf ears.

Rumblix must have sensed that something was going on, because Cade could hear the pup whimpering and whining in the corner.

'Right,' said the hammerhead gruffly, seizing Cade by the arm. 'You come with me.' He scooped up Cade's backpack, then thrust the muzzle of the phraxmusket into Cade's side. 'And don't try anything stupid.'

Cade found himself being marched out of the cabin. He turned, craned his neck, looked back at Tillman Spoke. But the prowlgrin dealer had turned away and was gazing out of the open porthole.

'That'll teach me,' Cade heard him mutter.

Then the cabin door slammed shut.

With a grunt, the skymarshal twisted Cade's arm up behind his back and propelled him forward. Sharp jags of pain shot through Cade's shoulder and he bit his lip to stop himself crying out. At the staircase, the skymarshal shoved him a second time and Cade started to climb. Glancing back over his shoulder, he caught sight of a figure lurking in the shadows.

It was Brod the grey goblin. He was staring up at Cade, his eyes wide, brows drawn together and lower lip trembling; a look that was somewhere between guilt and pity. It was the same look the goblin had worn when he'd returned Cade's backpack to him earlier that day.

'Keep moving,' the skymarshal barked, and shoved Cade up the stairs.

At the top, the skymarshal pushed Cade roughly down one long covered gangway, then another. It was a part of the skytavern Cade had never ventured into and he soon lost his bearings. When they emerged into the light, he squinted against the brightness of the midday sun.

He found himself standing on a raised platform. To his left and right were jutting gantries, with large baskets hanging at the ends of ropes. One of them was being used. A family of opulent-looking fourthlings – mother, father and a pair of young'uns, the two of them squealing with delight – were being lowered down towards the treetops by a cloddertrog at the winch, so that they might get a better view of the forest-life below.

The skymarshal did not hesitate. Head high, jaw set and grip still tight on Cade's twisted arm, he continued along the platform. Glancing up painfully, Cade saw the great bulbous prow ahead of them and he wondered whether this was where they kept prisoners, in the hold below the prow, until they came to Hive, or even returned to Great Glade to be tried for their crimes.

Then the hammerhead came to an abrupt halt. He loosened his grip on Cade's arm, and rubbing his shoulder, Cade looked up. They were at the prow-rail, clouds scudding high overhead, and the mighty Deepwoods below, a carpet of green stretching off as far as the eye could see.

'I could chain you up in the fore-hold,' said the sky-marshal, as if reading Cade's thoughts. 'But your friends in the Depths would probably bribe one of the cargo-guards to let you go . . .'

'I haven't got any friends in the Depths,' protested Cade, only for the skymarshal to silence him with a hard blow to the head with the butt of his phraxmusket.

Stunned, Cade slumped to the deck. When he came to, he couldn't move his arms or legs. Craning his neck, Cade looked about him desperately. He was strapped by thick rope to a lufwood plank which was propped up against the rail of the prow. Cade's heart began to hammer in his chest.

Lufwood was a buoyant wood. He remembered how it had bounced about inside the woodburner at home, the flames bright purple through the glass. He remembered how once, sneaking off to the woodpile at the back of the house, he had set fire to one of the small logs. It had blazed across the sky like a shooting star.

Like a shooting star . . .

The smell of smoke penetrated Cade's thoughts. He turned. The skymarshal was standing beside the lufwood plank holding a blazing torch.

'No. Please. You can't . . .' Cade implored the hammer-head goblin.

'Oh, but I can,' smiled the skymarshal as he lowered the flaming torch to the base of the plank. There was a hiss and a crackle, and Cade smelled the familiar spicy smell of charred lufwood. He could feel the heat of the torch through the soles of his boots, and squirmed and wriggled and . . .

There was a muffled thud and a soft groan. The blazing torch clattered to the deck, extinguishing itself as it did so. Then the skymarshal slumped down heavily onto the boards, a thin, flute-tailed dart embedded in his neck.

Drax Adereth stepped out from behind a basket winch, returning his silver blowpipe to his belt as he did so. His eyes glinted behind the green glass of his bone-rimmed goggles. 'Haven't got any friends in the Depths?' he said. 'Shame on you, Cade Quarter.'

· CHAPTER THIRTEEN ·

'I'm interested, that's all,' Drax Adereth said softly, his mouth close to Cade's ear. 'Did you not believe me when I told you that you couldn't hide from me?'

They were back in Adereth's candlelit lair, deep down in the Depths of the skytavern.

Drax moved round and brought his face close to Cade's. Cade tried to avoid Drax's large pale eyes. Up close, his skin was white as candlewax, and Cade could see the maze of blue-grey veins that crisscrossed his temples. His breath was warm on Cade's face and smelled of fish and sour milk.

Behind Cade, the flathead goblin called Teggtut had one arm tightly round Cade's throat and the other out-stretched, pressing Cade's hand down hard on a small stone cutting-slab. Next to the slab was the glass bowl of severed fingers, brown and desiccated.

Drax held up the jag-blade knife and twisted it so that

its teeth glinted in the
candle light. The pupils
of his eyes widened as he
took in the quivering fear
in Cade's face.

'I wasn't going to let
that skymarshal rob me
of what's owed to me.'
Drax smiled as he held
the knife over Cade's
outstretched hand. 'One
finger or two?' he mused.
'Now let me see. I gave
you a week...seven days.
And then you hid from
me – for how long?'

'Two days, boss,'
growled Teggtut.

'I want to hear *him* say
it,' said Drax testily.

'T-two d-days,' stam-
mered Cade. Sweat was
trickling down his face,
stinging his eyes. But he
couldn't tear his gaze
away from the bowl of
severed fingers.

'Two days in hiding,'
said Drax.

Cade felt the blade touch the knuckle of his little finger. Then the knuckle of the finger next to it.

'Thought you were safe, didn't you. Locked away
up there in a cosy cabin with that rich fourthling
for protection. But you don't hide from Drax Adereth
that easily . . .' He held up the mire-pearl necklace and
dangled it before Cade's eyes. 'A little tip-off to the skymarshal to get you out of there. And then a little "tip-off"
for the marshal himself . . .' He giggled unpleasantly.

Cade flinched as he recalled Adereth casually tossing
the skymarshal's body from the prow.

'I've got this skytavern sewn up. Nothing happens
without my say-so. That skymarshal was in my pay and
had no business skyfiring you without my permission.'
He smiled. 'So here we are, Cade Quarter,' Drax continued,
all trace of humour gone. 'Back where we started.'

Cade felt the knife's pressure on his little finger. He wanted
to cry out, to scream for help, but here in the suffocating
Depths of the skytavern, what good would it do?

'You see, I'm not unreasonable,' Drax's voice intoned,
slow and measured, with a casual taunting inflection. 'If
someone works for me, pays their dues and doesn't try
to hide, I see them right. Just like I did for your friend,
Brod. He helped me out and now he's free to steal in
peace. But you, Cade Quarter, you think you're special.
You think you're better than everyone else down here.
You think the rules don't apply to you . . .'

'No, I don't. I . . .' Cade could feel the pressure of the
blade increasing slowly. Agonizingly slowly.

'Just like those two professors . . .'

'From the School of Flight?' Cade blurted out the words, then bit his tongue.

In front of him, Drax's face loomed close again, his large pale eyes narrowed. Cade felt the knife lift from his finger.

'That's right,' he said. 'How did you know?' Drax's voice was quizzical, interested. The slow taunting tone had gone.

'I . . . I saw them.'

'Did you now?' said Drax, smiling. He raised a hand. 'Let him go,' he said to the flathead goblin.

Teggtut relaxed his grip round Cade's neck then, glancing at Drax, released Cade's arm. Cade straightened up. Drax Adereth took a step backwards and looked him up and down.

'My master in Great Glade has an important message for the professors, which he has asked me to deliver. They work for him too, but they consider themselves so much better than me that soiling their fine robes coming down to the Depths is beneath them.'

Drax frowned. His voice was sincere; he sounded genuinely hurt.

Cade backed away, rubbing the knuckle of his little finger.

'Take me to them, Cade,' said Drax. 'I'll deliver my message and you'll be free to go.'

'You work for the High Professor of Flight?' said Cade.

Drax smiled. 'Everybody works for someone,' he said,

then added, 'Though if you do this little thing for me, I will consider your debt to me repaid.'

Quove Lentis!

Cade's heart lurched. The night he had fled his bed-chamber, Cade had paused only to gather up his most precious possessions, stuffing them into a backpack alongside the barkscrolls his father had entrusted to him. He had run through the deserted cloisters and court-yards of the Cloud Quarter and down the avenues of Ambristown to lose himself in the alleys and backstreets of the Ledges district. After an hour of searching he had found the small tumbledown house belonging to Lembit Flodd, a humble cargo-handler, and his young family. Lembit had been expecting him, and his wife had given him a warming mug of charlock tea before showing him to a hammock by the chimney place.

Cade would never forget the next day. Lembit had returned from the marketplace, his face ashen and the tufts on the end of his ears quivering.

'Quove Lentis's guards are searching the alleyways house by house. They'll be here within the hour,' he'd announced breathlessly. 'But that's not the worst of it . . .'

The tufted goblin's three tiny young'uns were clustered at his knee, looking up at their father's frightened face and whimpering.

'Your father, Cade. He's been found dead at the foot of the central tower of the School of Flight. They're say-ing he jumped. But none of us believe that. I'm so sorry, Cade . . .'

Cade's eyes had filled with tears, but he had dashed them away with clenched fists. 'And now they're searching for me. I can't stay here,' he'd said, grabbing his backpack and hurrying to the door. 'I won't put your lives in danger.'

It was then that he had looked up at the towering gantries rising up above the rooftops of the Ledges district and seen the ragged figures at the top of the highest one gazing expectantly at the sky.

'Who are they?' he'd asked.

Lembit Flodd had swallowed hard. 'Forlorn hopers,' he'd said . . .

Quove Lentis! The person who had been responsible for his father's death. Even here on board this skytavern sailing over the Deepwoods, Cade wasn't beyond the High Professor's reach. But Drax clearly didn't know who Cade was, and Cade didn't want to do anything to give himself away. If he just showed him where these professors were, Drax would let him go. It seemed a good deal.

Returning Drax's intense gaze, Cade nodded stiffly. And moments later, he was making his way back up through the skytavern, his backpack on his shoulders and Drax Adereth at his side.

'Don't look so worried, Cade,' said Drax as they climbed the steep ladders that led up to the flight platform. 'I left Teggtut and Mank down in the Depths, didn't I? *They're* the muscle.' He smiled. 'I just want to deliver my message.'

They emerged onto the platform as the orange sun was slipping down towards the treetops on the distant horizon. The skytavern had slowed right down and was flying low over the forest crown. The wind was balmy.

Cade paused by the maze of scaffolding that supported the great phraxchamber and pointed to the half-hidden door of the maintenance cabin. The purple glow of the lufwood stove was just visible beneath the door.

'They're in there,' he whispered.

Drax stepped forward and rapped lightly on the door. 'Second engineer needs the hex-wrenches,' he called out, then retreated as the handle turned and the door slowly opened.

The two academics that Cade had seen stepped out, both looking cold and miserable – and both holding phraxpistols.

'Lemtrius Korn and Hengruel Paxis,' said Drax, his arms crossed, hands buried inside his pale topcoat.

'Do we know you?' said the first academic, a short stout individual with a double chin and rimless glasses. His phraxpistol was cocked and pointed straight at Drax.

Behind him, his companion – younger, taller, thinner – blinked nervously.

Cade backed away uneasily towards the far railing of the flight platform. Below him, the tops of the tallest trees seemed almost to graze the hull of the low-flying skytavern. A thick stream of white steam rose from the funnel above.

'You don't know me,' conceded Drax Adereth, smiling thinly. 'But I know you. Cloud Quarter academics in charge of phraxship building, if I'm not mistaken. You paid for a fleet of twenty phraxvessels out of the treasury of the School of Flight. *Twenty* vessels.' He paused. 'Except that eight of them did not exist, did they? You must have made a tidy sum to line your own pockets.' He shook his head, his lips crimped with disappointment. 'My master doesn't appreciate cheats and swindlers . . .'

'How dare you!' thundered the older academic, his knuckles turning white as he squeezed the trigger of the phraxpistol.

Drax dropped to one knee, a small silver blowpipe raised to his lips.

Phut! Phut!

Cade clung to the rail at the back of the flight platform as Drax's deadly darts skewered first one, then the other academic through the throat. Both of them crumpled soundlessly to the floor.

Drax rose to his feet and turned to Cade.

Cade stared back at him, legs trembling, shocked by the gangleader's dead-eyed stare. He had just assassinated two professors, yet there was no sign of remorse or inner conflict in his face; no sign of any emotion at all.

'A . . . a message, you said,' Cade muttered anxiously. 'I would never have led you here if I'd known you were going to kill them . . .'

'That *was* the message,' said Drax, smiling.

Just then a high-pitched barking yelp sounded from the ladder below the flight platform and, in a flash of grey, Rumblix came bounding into view and launched himself at Cade. The prowlgrin pup landed in his arms and began licking his face excitedly. He must have escaped through the open porthole and tracked him here, Cade realized with a pang of pride.

'Clever boy,' he cooed, stroking Rumblix's fur.

'A pedigree grey,' noted Drax appreciatively, and Cade saw him draw another dart from an inside pocket of his faded topcoat and slot it into the blowpipe.

Cade glanced over his shoulder. The skytavern was low in the sky and slowing all the time, but the treetops still looked heart-stoppingly far below nonetheless. He looked back at Drax, who had a twisted smile on his face. The blowpipe was halfway to his lips.

'Teggtut told me about the pup,' Drax said. 'And now I see it, I think I want it. Trouble is, it seems to be attached to you, so I'm very much afraid, Cade Quarter, that as its new owner, I'm going to have to make it forget you . . .'

Cade spun round, ducking as he did so. Rumblix jumped down from his arms, then scampered to the edge of the flight platform and launched himself out into the air.

Phut!

A dart whistled through the air as Cade jumped after him, Tillman Spoke's words echoing in his head: '*Trust a prowlgrin's leap and you'll never fall.*'

· CHAPTER FOURTEEN ·

Judging his leap perfectly, Rumblix landed in a swaying treetop. Cade followed him down through the air, his arms and legs flailing wildly.

'*Oof!*' he gasped as he slammed into the branch just below the one Rumblix was balanced on.

The wood splintered under Cade's weight and he was falling again, branches bowing and snapping beneath him in a series of sickening cracks until he came to a jarring stop. His backpack had snagged on something and he hung there for a few moments, his eyes closed and legs dangling, praying that the leather straps of the backpack would not give.

Rumblix was squealing with alarm.

Cade opened his eyes. His gaze met Rumblix's wide-eyed stare. The prowlgrin had leaped down from his original perch, following the progression of broken branches that marked Cade's fall, and was now balancing expertly on a thin bough just to Cade's left.

'I'm all right, boy,' said Cade, though one glance up was enough to tell him that he was not.

His backpack was entangled in a large cluster of pine needles that fanned out from the end of a slender branch just above his head. As he looked around, the branch bent and quivered like a fishing pole under the strain of his weight – though it seemed to be holding. Cade hoped his backpack would do the same. Rumblix and he had landed at the top of an immense ironwood pine. He noted the huge fircones dangling from the branches above and below him, and the broad tree trunk they sprouted from, its craterous bark flecked with rivulets of glistening amber resin.

Above him, the mighty *Xanth Filatine* passed overhead and approached a lone platform that rose up above the forest canopy about three hundred strides away. The wooden scaffolding and ladders leading up to the platform reminded Cade of the docking gantries in Great Glade, though unlike them this platform, with its single cabin and lone water tank, was too small for a skyvessel as large as the *Xanth Filatine* to dock at.

In the forest to the west of the platform, the trees thinned out and gave way to an immense lake. And at the far side of the sun-flecked water, five magnificent falls cascaded down from the mouths of dark caverns that lined the top of towering ridges. Cade had never seen anything like it.

Slowly the skytavern swung round in the sky. The

white-hot jet of air from the propulsion duct abruptly cut, and the great vessel hovered in the air for a moment before dropping down lower still, amid loud hissing and clouds of steam. Then, as Cade watched, ropes were lowered from the decks up near the prow and a figure emerged from the cabin at the top of the platform.

Seizing the end of one of the ropes, the figure attached it to a bulging net, then reached up, grabbed hold of the rope again and tugged it hard. Moving on as the net was hoisted back into the air, he worked quickly, his movements agile, attaching boxes and crates to the other ropes. These were raised up to the skytavern in turn while, at the same time, fromthe stern, a long flexible pipe was lowered by half a dozen deckhands into the water tank. The sound of pumps creaking and water gurgling filled the air briefly as the skytavern's water supplies were replenished.

And then, as quickly as the loading had started, it was done. The ropes disappeared, the pipe recoiled and the *Xanth Filatine* rose majestically into the sky. The figure at the top of the platform stood for a moment, a dark silhouette against the sunset glow of the sky, before turning and disappearing back into the cabin.

The jet of air blasted from the propulsion duct of the *Xanth Filatine* once more as the skytavern soared up into the sky and away. Cade watched it go, relieved to be free of Adereth's clutches, but all too aware of his present predicament.

The light was fading fast. Soon it would be night, and

he was stuck at the top of this ironwood pine, unable to move for fear of . . .

There was a cracking, splintering sound, and through the straps of his backpack Cade felt the branch above him tremble.

'*HELP!*' he screamed.

· CHAPTER FIFTEEN ·

Above Cade, the slender branch gave out another ominous creak. He wanted to rub his aching shoulders, to relieve the pressure of the straps that were digging into him, but dared not. A wind was getting up, warm and blustery. It made his topcoat flap and brought tears to his eyes that he was too afraid of moving to wipe away. Beside him, perched on a branch that looked almost too thin to support his weight, Rumblix leaned forward and licked his hand.

'Thank you, boy,' said Cade. 'I'd pet you if I could, but . . .'

He looked down for the hundredth time, searching for some branch or other that, if the branch supporting him did break, he might land on. But it didn't look good. None of the broader branches were directly beneath him and, further down, everything melted into darkness.

The small phraxlighter rose from the platform and

started making its way towards the ironwood pine, steam billowing from its short funnel.

Cade's only chance was the approaching phraxlighter. Earth and Sky willing, it would reach him in time. Above him, the branch creaked again, and Cade fought back his panic by concentrating on the skyvessel.

It was closer now. Apart from being a fraction of the size of the mighty skytavern, the design was quite different – the most obvious difference the fact that, rather than being sited at the top of the vessel, the phraxchamber was mounted below the hull. But there were other features that set the small phrax-lighter apart.

Cold sweat trickled down Cade's face.

The prow was angled and came to a point. At the end of it was the carved head of an open-mouthed hoverworm.

Wind rustled through the branches, causing Cade to sway backwards and forwards. The branch gave another ominous creak . . .

The stern, which also came to a point but was unadorned, had two rudders fixed to its side. And just in front of it was a raised cabin which must house the flight-wheel, the rudder-levers – and the pilot.

Cade gritted his teeth, willing the phraxlighter on. Just a few strides more . . .

Creak.

He saw the figure at the controls peering out from the cabin.

Creak.

Leather hood. Yellow-tinted goggles. Scarf tightly wound and knotted. The pilot's face was masked, inscrutable . . .

Creak.

The phraxlighter came round in the sky and Cade breathed in the chilled steam as it passed by him. There was a whiff of toasted almonds about the smell. Through the window of the cabin, Cade could see the pilot's gloved hands dancing expertly over the hull-weight and rudder-levers as he brought the phraxlighter down lower in the sky. Then, smoothly and skilfully, taking care not to knock the fragile phraxchamber against the branches of the ironwood pine, he steered the small vessel directly beneath Cade and brought it to a hovering, chugging standstill.

Clouds of white steam billowed up around Cade, and a moment later he felt the toes of his boots graze the roof of the cabin. He let his knees buckle for a moment, then straightened. Reaching up, Cade pulled his backpack free from the branch, which sprang back with a whistle and a crack.

Yelping with alarm, Rumblix leaped from the tree and into Cade's arms. A warm surge of relief flooded through Cade's body as he cradled the pup and sank back down onto the roof of the cabin. The phraxlighter beneath him juddered as its propulsion duct roared, and the vessel rose from the ironwood pine and into the evening sky.

Cade gripped the side of the cabin roof, and as they gained speed, Rumblix burrowed inside his topcoat, his purrs mixing with the rumbling whirr of the vessel's phraxchamber. The phraxlighter rapidly crossed the three hundred strides between the ironwood pine and the platform, and began its descent to land. Cade looked down.

The platform was a spindly-looking construction, fashioned from lengths of ironwood pine that had been lashed together to form a high scaffolded tower. There was a flat platform at the top, with tying-posts and balustrades. Jutting out from the far corner were the tall cylindrical water tank and small timber cabin that Cade had spotted from the ironwood pine. Numerous crates and barrels were stacked around the sides of the cabin, together with winch-wheels, grappling irons and hooked cargo poles.

The phraxlighter flew over the cabin's flat roof and came down on the far side of the platform, where a curved iron docking-cradle jutted out from the timber scaffolding. With a soft *clunk* the phraxlighter came to rest in the cradle, and the phraxchamber's hum faded. Cade peered down from the cabin roof as the pilot emerged and tethered the phraxlighter securely to the mooring cleats. Then, straightening up, the pilot stepped off the vessel and onto the platform, pulling off his hood and goggles as he did so.

He was a fourthling, like Cade himself, tall and thickset, with skin the colour and texture of tanned leather; dark brown and with deep creases that crossed his brow and fanned out from the corners of his dark blue eyes. His black hair was oiled and swept back, and he wore a thick moustache, waxed at the ends in the fashion favoured by Great Glade sky mariners. As Cade looked down at him, the pilot reached up and scratched his chin, where thick stubble was growing, then broke into an easy smile. And when he spoke, his voice had a soft cultured quality more in keeping with an academic from the Cloud Quarter than a rough sky pilot from the Ledges.

'The name's Gart Ironside,' he said. 'Welcome to the Farrow Ridges.'

· CHAPTER SIXTEEN ·

'**B**loodoaks?' Cade breathed.

After the tension and terrors of the skytavern, it felt good to be sitting here at Gart Ironside's table on the flat roof of the cabin, next to a blazing brazier. Above, the darkening sky twinkled as constellations of stars flickered into existence.

'Bloodoaks.' Gart Ironside frowned. 'Flesh-eating trees of monstrous size, with mouths at the top of their gnarled trunks, ringed with razor-sharp teeth,' he explained with relish, reaching across the table and picking up the flagon of sweet sapwine. 'They wait for the tarry-vine – a lasso-like, parasitic creeper that grows in the branches above – to snare unfortunate victims in the surrounding forest and drag them back, kicking and screaming, to feed them.'

Cade looked at the flagon tilted and hovering above his goblet which, once again, seemed to be all but empty. The sapwine was delicious.

'Just a little,' said Cade, then watched contentedly as the pilot filled the goblet to the top. He took a sip and stared out across the moon-silvered treetops.

'Seen it with my own eyes,' Gart Ironside said, following Cade's gaze. 'And I'll never forget the sight as long as I live . . .' He paused for effect, and when he looked across at the pilot, Cade knew that he was waiting for a response.

For eight long years Gart Ironside had manned the lonely sky platform above the Farrow Ridges, just one of scores of watering stations on the convoluted route from Great Glade to Hive. And with barely a visitor to break the monotony. It was hardly surprising, Cade thought, that since rescuing him from the ironwood pine, Gart Ironside had hardly stopped talking for a moment.

Not that Cade had minded in the least. He'd listened with fascination as the pilot had described his former life in Great Glade; how he'd flown phraxvessels in its crowded skies, and built up a fleet of fast sleek skyships to transport phrax crystals from the mines in the Eastern Woods to the commodity markets of Great Glade. Gart had made a fortune, lived in an opulent mansion in New Lake, had the best seats at the thousandsticks matches, a stable of pedigree prowlgrins, and mixed with the richest merchants and most powerful academics in the city – only to lose it all in something he referred to simply as 'the great swindle'.

At this point, Gart had fallen silent and left Cade and Rumblix alone on the roof. Moments later, he was back, with a tray laden with food. And as night fell, they had enjoyed a supper of blackbread, sour-curds, roast sandfowl and salted tilder, pine nuts and forest fruits, all washed down with the best sapwine Cade had ever tasted.

Gart Ironside reached behind him for a couple of seasoned logs and tossed them into the brazier, which spat and hissed and blazed fiercely.

Cade sat forward, his elbows resting on the table. 'Would you tell me some more about the bloodoak you saw?' he asked, and saw Gart smile ruefully as the fire-light flickered on his weathered face.

'It was about three years ago,' he began. 'A leaper, like yourself . . . off the *Lucius Verginix* if memory serves. Anyway, he jumped ship one afternoon, just after the *Lucius* had taken on water, and ended up in the Western Woods. I saw him through my spyglass. A fourthling he was, in a ragged topcoat with a blanket-roll over one shoulder. I thought of setting out to see what had become of him. But, well, from experience, I know that most leapers jump for a reason – and they don't necessarily appreciate it when a platform pilot comes snooping around after them. So I left well alone.' He shuddered. 'Only wish I hadn't, given what happened . . .'

Despite the warmth from the brazier, Cade felt cold shivers tingling at the nape of his neck. He shifted round in the chair. Rumblix was snuffling about on the wooden floor, licking up the morsels of food that had been dropped.

'It was the following morning,' Gart continued grimly. 'Just after daybreak. I was down by the lake, pumping water to fill the platform's tank, when I heard this blood-curdling scream coming from the far side of the lake. It was the leaper. A loud, agonizing, gut-wrenching scream . . .'

Gart breathed in sharply, his gaze fixed on Cade's anxious face.

'I couldn't ignore it, so I jumped into my phraxlighter and set off as fast as I could. I was halfway across the mudflats when the cries abruptly fell still.' He paused. 'Five minutes after that, in a dank forest clearing that reeked of blood and decay, I discovered him. Or rather, what was left of him . . .'

Gart shook his head slowly from side to side. Then, pulling a kerchief from the pocket of his leather jerkin, he dabbed at his sweaty brow.

'He'd been swallowed up by a bloodoak. Head first,' he added. 'There was nothing I could do. All that remained in sight was his feet, with the tarry-vine that had lassoed him and lowered him down into the bloodoak's gaping mouth still wrapped around the tops of his boots.'

Cade realized his mouth was open.

Gart Ironside leaned forward, grasped his goblet and took a long deep swig of the sapwine, then wiped his moustache on the back of his hand. 'Still, it could have been worse,' he said.

'Worse?' exclaimed Cade. 'How could anything be worse than being eaten alive by a tree?'

'Hammerheads,' said Gart, a gleam in his eye. 'Wild hammerhead goblin tribes – the woods to the west of here are infested with them. Tall as a cloddertrog and twice as mean. Believe me, if they get their hands on a leaper, they'll make him scream for days.'

Cade took a gulp of sapwine.

'And then there's the lake,' the pilot went on, his voice hushed with dread. 'Lucky you didn't land in the lake.'

Gart held Cade's glance for a moment, his eyes wide. He was enjoying scaring his young guest. The pair of them sat forward closer to the blazing brazier. Cade warmed his hands in the flames, while the chills shot up and down his spine.

'Unfathomably deep, it is,' Gart told him, 'where the most fearsome of creatures dwell. Strange, half-formed things; fish-tailed, snagglemouthed, claws like rapiers.' He shook his head. 'And, of course, there are the caverns . . .'

Rumblix was whining by Cade's side, rubbing his flanks against his leg. Cade looked down, then patted his lap. The prowlgrin pup jumped up and nestled down as Cade stroked him pensively. The wine had gone to his head, which was beginning to swim.

'There's no knowing how deep they are nor what horrors they contain,' said Gart. 'But the tribes around here don't go near them. And they talk of the white trogs who live in their depths, and scare even them . . .'

Cade swallowed. What sort of place had he landed in? he wondered. A nightmare home to flesh-eating trees, torturing tribes, monstrous lake creatures and ghostly trogs . . .

He kept on stroking Rumblix's neck and flanks. The small creature had closed his eyes and was softly snoring. Cade felt his own eyelids grow heavy. He sank back into the wooden chair, which suddenly felt as soft as a heap of feathers.

Gart was still talking: '. . . and as for me, I stay up here on the platform, where I can see things coming, or stick to the phraxlighter. Eight years I've been in this desolate place and I'm proud to say I've yet to set foot on its soil.'

He snorted. 'Welcome to the Farrow Ridges . . .'

Cade nodded again, struggling to stay awake as Gart Ironside's words echoed in his head: '*Welcome to the Farrow Ridges . . .*'

Eyes shut and lulled by the rhythmic breathing of the prowlgrin pup in his lap, he allowed sleep to start lapping over him. And, as the moon rose higher in the sky, Cade heard the drowsy breeze whispering in the trees around him, their secretive murmurings punctuated by night creatures: quarms squealing, fromps coughing, a banderbear yodelling to its far-off mate.

'*. . . the Farrow Ridges . . . Farrow Ridges . . . Farrow Ridges . . .*'

· CHAPTER SEVENTEEN ·

Cade awoke to the bright sun shining in his eyes. There was a blanket over him that Gart Ironside must have thoughtfully placed there. It had kept the chill out during the night. But now Cade was too hot, and he threw the blanket aside and climbed to his feet, groaning as his head throbbed. Gart had also thought to put a tankard of water on the table, which Cade downed gratefully.

He wiped his mouth on his sleeve and looked around him, getting his bearings, sorting through the events of the previous ten days in his head. The almost skyfiring . . . The murder of the two professors . . . The leap from the *Xanth Filatine* and subsequent rescue by Gart Ironside, who had brought him here, to this spindly tower in the Farrow Ridges, a remote and insignificant backwater in the vastness of the mighty Deepwoods, so far from Cade's old home in Great Glade.

The wind had changed direction now, and the roar of

the five falls coursing down into the lake sounded more distant. A flock of long-legged white birds flapped low over the surface of the water, snapping at insects, then on across the mudflats on the far side of the lake, where they landed and began strutting about, jabbing their beaks into the mud in search of bugs and worms. Rumblix was perched on the back of the wooden chair, his eyes closed, gently snoring. Cade's backpack stood propped up against the chair leg.

Cade smiled to himself. This was everything that he owned in the world. Everything he cared about. A sleeping prowlgrin pup and a battered old backpack.

Cade laid the backpack on the table and untied the fastenings at the top.

Then, reaching in, he removed the contents, one by one. A pair of socks. A couple of shirts. A knife. His journal. A stubby leadwood pencil . . . Things closest to hand which he'd hurriedly stuffed into his backpack the night his father had told him to leave.

And then there were the three things he'd taken great care to pack.

Cade reached into the backpack and drew out a brass spyglass stamped with the initials *N.Q.* He turned it over in his hand. The spyglass had once belonged to Cade's uncle, Nate Quarter. His father had given it to him on his seventh birthday, but had never spoken about the famous descender himself until that fateful night.

Cade placed the spyglass on the table and reached once more into the backpack. He took out a small glass vial of perfume, and his eyes filled with tears.

It had belonged to his mother, Sensa, who, like his uncle, he had never known. She'd succumbed to the 'wasters' – a fever more prevalent in the poorer areas of Great Glade than the Cloud Quarter, and which turned a fit, healthy adult into a bag of bones in weeks – when Cade had been so very young. According to Cade's father, she had probably caught it while distributing alms to the down-and-outs of East Glade and Copperwood. For that was what she was like, he'd explained, always putting others before herself.

'A good person,' he'd always told Cade. 'Your mother was a good person.'

Cade unstoppered the vial and held it to his nose. He breathed deep the remnants of her sweet scent, his face taut with loss. It hadn't helped her, being a good person, he thought, sad – and not for the first time – that he'd had to grow up without a mother. Not that he would ever have confessed that to his father. Cade swallowed. His father had also been a good person.

And it hadn't helped him either.

Cade put the stopper back in the vial and placed it next to the spyglass on the table top. Slowly he reached into the backpack and removed the last, and bulkiest, item: the bundle of four scrolls, bound together with a ribbon bearing the name *Thadeus Quarter* in flowing script, that his father had pressed into his hand and made him promise to look after.

Cade slipped off the ribbon. He realized his hands were trembling. The memories of that night were still too fresh, too raw.

He unrolled the scrolls. The wind set them fluttering as he scanned the graphs and annotated diagrams, and neat clusters of numbers and symbols. He guessed they were equations of some sort, but they were far too complicated for him to decipher. All he knew for certain was that the scrolls must be important for his father to have entrusted them to him. Now his father was dead.

He would never see him again. And he missed him. He missed him so much.

Reaching up, he wiped away the tears that filmed his eyes, making the diagrams blur and dissolve. Slowly, thoughtfully, Cade rolled up the scrolls and re-tied them with the ribbon.

Before him, the Farrow Ridges spread out like a beautiful tapestry. To his left were tall jagged pinnacles of rock. The Needles, Gart had called them. Beyond them, like mighty steps, were the ridges themselves, with the gushing cascades of water – the Five Falls – tumbling from the five great caverns at their western end and splashing down into the deep dark-shadowed lake below. And, as Cade watched, as if to some signal, the flock of foraging white birds flapped their wings, rose up from the mudflats and wheeled round across the forest.

He returned his attention to the scrolls, turning them over thoughtfully in his hand. On the skytavern, when he'd met Tillman Spoke, the prowlgrin breeder, he'd dreamed of the possibility of a new life in Hive. He remembered the excitement and relief he'd felt when he imagined helping out in the stables, caring for the prowlgrins, watching them high-jumping down the Hive Falls . . .

But if Quove Lentis's spies could find him in Great Glade, what was to stop them searching him out in Hive? After all, the High Professor of Flight's spies were everywhere – even in the depths of the skytavern. Cade shivered as he pictured Drax Adereth's pale face staring back at him.

But here . . . Who would think to look for him in this 'desolate place', as Gart had called it, with its bloodoaks and hammerheads and trogs?

He looked up, just as the sun broke over the high forest behind him and spread out across the Farrow Lake. The slate-grey darkness turned to a dazzling display of burnished silver and gold. He noticed sallow-ash and weeping willoaks down at the water's edge that could provide timber to construct a small cabin, and tall reeds extending into the shallows that could thatch it . . .

A smile spread across Cade Quarter's face as the thought dawned. Perhaps, despite all its dangers, the Farrow Ridges might be the safest place to be.

· CHAPTER EIGHTEEN ·

Senses taut, Cade crept through the dark forest. The mighty ironwood pines rose up around him, their spreading branches far above cutting out the light. In the gloom of the forest floor, each cracked twig or rustling branch made Cade pause, and his heart thumped as he strained to hear where the sound had come from. Every movement he caught out of the corner of his eye made him flinch and grip the phraxmusket that Gart Ironside had given him all the tighter.

At his shoulders, Rumblix held onto the backpack with his powerful back legs and growled softly.

'It's all right, boy,' Cade reassured the pup. 'Not far now, and we should come out at the lake. Then we can follow the shoreline.'

Gart had offered to fly Cade to the north side of the lake in his phraxlighter, but Cade had politely refused. If he was to make the Farrow Ridges his home, Cade decided, then he'd have to get used to the surrounding forest, no matter how daunting that might be.

'Are you absolutely sure?' Gart Ironside had asked him. 'You're welcome to stay here. I've got room enough,' he went on. 'And I can always use a bit of help when the skyships come in . . .'

But Cade knew that this was not an option. He needed to lie low, to avoid the skyships – at least until Quove Lentis and his spies forgot about him. Down here on the ground he could find a quiet, out-of-the-way spot, build a dwelling place, teach himself to hunt, to fish. And lie low . . .

'Thank you, Gart,' he'd said, reading the disappointment in the pilot's eyes, 'but I need to be on my own right now . . .' He'd paused. 'And I'd appreciate it if you didn't tell anyone I was here.'

Gart had smiled and nodded knowingly.

'But at least let me give you some stuff to help you set up,' Gart had insisted. 'And if it makes you feel better, you can think of it as a loan,' he'd added when Cade had protested that he had no money. 'You can return them to me any time you like.'

As well as the phraxmusket, Gart had given Cade a net, a length of fishing line and a couple of hooks; some rope, nails and wire; a lantern, a small tarpaulin; fire-flints and a water pot. And tools. There was a hammer and a hack-saw, an axe and a spade, all of which were strapped onto the now bulging backpack on Cade's shoulders.

The lakeside hadn't looked too far from the top of the

platform. But with the weight on his back, and sights and sounds slowing him down, Cade's progress through the gloomy forest had been little more than a crawl. Then, just as he was beginning to lose heart and was considering retracing his steps back to the platform, the ground in front of him abruptly fell away.

Stepping carefully over gnarled tree roots, Cade emerged from the forest beside a vast body of water, its surface glittering like diamonds in the early-afternoon sun. He breathed in sharply and his face broke into a grin.

'We made it, lad,' he said to Rumblix as the prowlgrin pup jumped down beside him.

The sun splashed across Cade's face as he slipped the heavy backpack from his shoulders and walked down the sloping shore to the water's edge. There, he squatted down and dabbled his hands in the cold clear water, his gaze looking out across the still expanse of the lake. Next to him, Rumblix lapped at the water.

Now and then, a fish broke the surface, snatching at insects hovering above; birds flapped and tumbled overhead in the warm air. Their chittering and squawking cries echoed through the trees all around . . .

'The Farrow Lake,' Cade murmured, and he ruffled the prowlgrin's fur affectionately. 'Our new home.'

Rumblix looked round at him and purred.

Climbing to his feet, Cade peered up and down the shoreline. Towards the Five Falls to his left, the forest came down almost to the lake and he knew he would have to clear the trees before he could build anything

there. Far off to his right, however, he could see broad meadowlands stretching back from the water's edge to the treeline. It looked a more promising place and, hoiking the heavy pack back onto his shoulders, Cade headed north-west along the lake for a closer look.

In the bright sunshine of the lake edge, he walked at a brisk pace, Rumblix bounding along at his side. There were plump-looking waterbirds feeding on the soggy meadowlands in the distance.

They looked like they'd make good eating, Cade noted, if he could snare a few.

And then there were the footprints in the soft mud of the lakeshore all around – the footprints of the forest creatures that came down to the water to drink. Perhaps he could shoot a tilder. Or even a hammelhorn ... Properly smoked and stored, a fully-grown hammelhorn could feed him and Rumblix for months.

Cade's mouth watered at the prospect.

He scanned the lakeshore. There were tall pine trees and lichened outcrops of rock that Cade identified as possible look-out points, as well as dips and hollows where he might hide and lie in wait for quarry. And as he rounded a curved inlet and the meadowlands began, he came to a natural jetty of rock that jutted out into the lake and which, at its end, looked ideal for casting a fishing line from.

With every stride he took, Cade's optimism was growing ...

The other end of the rock jetty, Cade saw, was embedded in a low wind-shadowed ridge that rose up above the lake. He swung his backpack from his shoulders and dropped it to the ground. Then he stood back, hands on hips, eyes narrowed.

The ridge provided shelter and the rock jetty offered easy access to the lake. And, just as he'd seen from the flat roof of the lofty cabin, there was timber close by for him to construct a simple lean-to shelter, as well as thick meadowgrass and water-reeds growing in abundance to thatch a roof.

Cade turned and looked back across the lake. Gart Ironside's platform was now no more than a speck in the distance. No one would spot a small dwelling here. He smiled and patted Rumblix on his back and shoulders. It was the perfect spot for a cabin, Cade thought. Now all he had to do was build it.

But first things first . . .

Removing from his backpack the snare he'd fashioned back at Gart's place under the pilot's watchful eye, Cade carried it up to the edge of the forest. Then he set it at the base of a lufwood sapling, with the wire noose primed and taut and concealed in long grass, and the whole lot anchored to the tree with a length of rope.

'Sky willing,' he told Rumblix, 'we'll catch one of those plump birds for supper.'

He turned and, whistling tunelessly, gathered a couple of the straightest branches he could find and headed back down the slope to the lakeshore. There, in the shadow of the low ridge, he sharpened the branches into stakes and hammered them into the soft earth on either side of the rock jetty. Taking the tarpaulin Gart had given him, Cade tied the corners of one end to the stakes, then pegged the other end down at the top of the ridge, to form a tented lean-to.

It wasn't much, but it would provide some shelter in the days ahead as Cade set about the serious business of collecting timber and thatch, and building himself something more permanent.

Still whistling, Cade built a small brushwood fire, encircled with stones he'd collected from the lakeshore, and lit it with the sparks from his fire-flints. He set a small pot of water to heat on the flickering flames and placed handfuls of the wild nibblick he'd collected in the boiling water. And as the sun set below the trees, he lit the lantern that Gart Ironside had given him.

A breeze rose over the lake and a chill came into the air that made Cade shiver. Behind him, the forest sounds changed as the evening creatures started to stir, and strange howls and whooping calls echoed through the dark trees.

Suddenly, from close by, Cade heard heavy footfalls. A moment later there was the *twang* of his snare wire being tripped, followed by a soft and wheezing cry.

A waterfowl, perhaps? Cade thought. Maybe a tilder fawn?

He reached out and picked up the phraxmusket, then climbed to his feet. He spotted Rumblix halfway along the stretch of rock that jutted out into the lake.

'Here, boy!' he called.

The prowlgrin pup hesitated, then turned and came bounding over to Cade. Purring loudly, he nuzzled at Cade's knee.

'Time for supper, lad,' Cade told him, enjoying the normality of his own voice as he spoke to the young pup. He patted Rumblix's head. 'Let's see what we've caught.'

Cade set off across the meadow towards the treeline through the gathering darkness, Rumblix at his heels. A moment later he arrived at the spot where he'd set the snare. Cade prodded around the base of the tree with his boot. Rumblix looked up at him inquisitively, then let out a strange, shrill, high-pitched chattering. Cade was staring down at the ground in disbelief.

The snare had disappeared.

'I definitely heard it go off,' Cade muttered.

He looked around anxiously. Listened. But there was nothing there. He crouched down and inspected the base of the tree. The end of the rope was still tied around the trunk, but just beyond the knot, it had been severed. Cade fingered the frayed ends.

It was too ragged to have been cut with a knife. And there was no wetness, so nothing had bitten through the rope. Cade sat back on his haunches, his head spinning. The way the rope strands were stretched and feathered at the ends, it looked as though something had simply torn the rope in two; something unimaginably strong.

Cade swallowed. There was a hollow feeling in the pit of his stomach, and it wasn't caused by hunger. He reached out and hugged Rumblix tightly.

'Maybe,' he said, 'Gart Ironside is right to stay up there on that platform of his.'

· CHAPTER NINETEEN ·

The nibblick soup had tasted good, but Cade was still hungry. The night was cold, but with the glowing embers of the small fire and the body-heat of the prowlgrin pup curled up next to him, Cade was warm enough. His stomach gurgled, the sound mingling with the strange calls of the night creatures in the forests around him.

Up on Gart Ironside's platform they'd seemed reassuringly distant, but down here on the ground it was a different matter. The harsh coughing of tree fromps, the rasping sighs of weezits, the snuffles and grunts of creatures Cade couldn't identify, all seemed far too close for comfort. Several times, Cade thought he could hear scampering and tramping just beyond the flickering light cast by the dying fire, and had gripped the phraxmusket even more tightly. Once, Rumblix had stirred, opened an eye, his nostrils quivering, before going back to sleep.

And Cade had taken comfort from that. If there was any scent of danger, he could rely on the pup to alert him to it.

Just then, from the dark waters of the lake, there came a splash. A little way off, beyond the rock jetty, the lake churned and the water sparkled with a bright blue-green phosphorescence. It swirled and rippled in a dazzling underwater light display. Moments later, a monstrous creature broke the surface, a fish clutched in its snaggletoothed jaws. With powerful beats of its huge fins, the creature leaped high in the air, a luminescent shower of water pouring down behind it like the tail of a shooting star before it crashed back into the lake's boiling, glowing waters.

The sudden disturbance woke Rumblix who, frightened, leaped up into Cade's arms. Cade hugged the small creature, his gaze still fixed on the lake as the water became calm once more and the astonishing display of lights faded. He tickled the pup behind his ears.

'Easy, boy,' he said. 'Whatever that is, it can't get at us here.'

Rumblix nestled into the crook of his arm. Above the pair of them, the makeshift canopy fluttered as a wind got up and moonlit clouds billowed up into the night sky. Cade stared at the clouds as they scudded past.

That one, he thought, looks like a hammelhorn, horns and all. And that one could pass as a banderbear, dancing, one leg raised. And that . . .

'A prowlgrin,' he said drowsily, smiling as he stroked Rumblix at his side. 'It looks just like a prowlgrin, doesn't it, boy?'

The pup didn't stir. His breathing was coming slow and even. Reassured, Cade closed his eyes and moments later fell into a deep and dreamless sleep.

It was light when he woke. Dawn was breaking over the distant ridges behind him. He sat up, rubbed his eyes.

Before him, Cade saw plump birds waddling about on the shoreline, their webbed feet slapping the wet mud as they dibbed for shrimps and worms with their toothed beaks. He gazed out across the placid waters of the Farrow Lake and considered setting up a fishing line, then shuddered as he recalled the creature he'd seen the night before.

'Nibblick soup for breakfast,' he told himself, getting to his feet and scanning the meadowlands. 'With a few glade onions. Some lake-lettuce perhaps . . .'

He picked up the phraxmusket and whistled tunelessly as he eyed the plump birds on the lakeshore.

Cade stopped and frowned. The whistling was continuing, mimicking his own, and coming from the tree-line behind him.

'Hello?' he called.

'Hello?' a voice called back.

Rumblix had got to his feet, his eyes wide and his nostrils quivering. The whistling had started up again. The same badly executed melody that Cade had been whistling moments before.

'Hello?' he called again. 'Who's there?'

'Hello?' came the reply. 'Who's there?'

The voice was mocking him, repeating his own words back to him. A sweat broke out across Cade's brow. He skirted round the campfire and made his way across the meadow, phraxmusket raised and finger on the trigger.

He moved cautiously, with Rumblix at his heels, looking up at him from time to time for reassurance. Cade approached the treeline, not daring to venture into the forest in case of ambush.

Suddenly the whistling began again in the trees to his left. Cade peered into the shadows, but there was no one to be seen. The sound began to recede as the whistler moved away. Head down, phraxmusket raised, Cade crept along the edge of the forest. Rumblix followed close behind. The whistling continued, always keeping a dozen or so strides ahead of him.

As he went further, the meadowlands receded and the trees grew closer and closer to the lakeside. The Five Falls disappeared from view behind the trees even as their roaring grew louder, and Cade could no longer hear the whistling.

He paused, then cut down through the forest and emerged into a clearing at the edge of the lake. There was patchy grass beneath his feet, which gave way to sand closer to the water; two rounded boulders stood at the shoreline, half in and half out of the water.

Cade was just about to turn round and go back to his camp when one of the boulders moved . . .

Cade stumbled backwards with surprise, his mouth open as he stared. What he'd mistaken for a boulder was in fact the rounded back of a cloaked figure, which now rose and turned round. The figure reached up and lowered the hood that covered his head, and Cade found himself staring into the face of a grey goblin.

He had a broad round skull, a flattened nose, small ears pressed in close to the sides, a square jaw. His eyes, set deep in his craggy features, were crystal blue and twinkled with amusement as he held up his arm.

'*Tak-tak! Tak-tak!*'

A small striped creature came bounding out of the trees and jumped up onto the goblin's arm.

'*There* you are,' he said.

'*There* you are,' the creature repeated, the voice a perfect imitation of the grey goblin's.

Cade stared at the creature. It was some kind of lemkin by the look of it, but larger and with longer limbs than those kept as pets in Great Glade – as well as different-coloured fur: black and yellow rings, from the tip of its tail to the tops of its quivering ears, rather than the usual deep blue. Its pointed snout quivered and its jaws opened.

The grey goblin's eyes were fixed on the phraxmusket in Cade's hands as he flicked back his cloak to reveal a pair of phraxpistols in his belt. Cade lowered the musket. At his feet, Rumblix's nostrils flared as he sniffed at the hem of the grey goblin's cloak. The lemkin began whistling again.

'Tak-Tak here seems to have heard you whistling,' said the grey goblin, his eyes twinkling. '*Tak-tak*'s the noise he makes when he *isn't* mimicking someone else,' he added. He looked down at Rumblix. 'Fine creature you've got there,' the goblin observed. 'Pedigree grey, if I'm not mistaken.'

Cade nodded. 'We've made a camp by the meadowlands west of here,' he said. 'We didn't realize there was anyone else out here.'

'There ain't generally,' said the grey goblin, turning away and stooping over the other boulder.

Reaching out, he flipped it over and Cade saw that it too was not what it had first appeared to be. It was a small boat: a coracle made of leather stretched over a frame of bent willoak. The leather was shiny and smelled of the pine resin it had been painted with to make it waterproof. At the centre of the vessel was a wooden seat, grooved and worn from long use.

'Just Tak-Tak and me on the northern shore. And we generally keep ourselves to ourselves.' The goblin stood up and held out a hand. 'Thorne Lammergyre, fisher goblin.'

Cade shook the goblin's hand. 'Cade Quarter . . . trapper,' he said, hoping the title sound convincing.

The grey goblin raised his eyebrows. 'Trapper, eh?' he said quizzically, looking Cade's city clothes over. 'Had any luck?'

Cade shook his head and his stomach rumbled noisily. On Thorne Lammergyre's arm, Tak-Tak the lemkin mimicked the noise perfectly, and despite his embarrassment, Cade couldn't help laughing. The grey goblin laughed too, and then reached into his cloak and drew out two fat glistening lakefish.

'Here, take these,' he said, his blue eyes twinkling, 'to tide you over while you set up your traps.'

This grizzled grey goblin clearly had his doubts about Cade's ability to survive out here. Cade's face coloured.

'I . . . I fixed up a shelter,' he said defensively. 'Temporary, like. But I'm going to build something permanent,' he added. 'A cabin. With a jetty, and a store-room, and—'

'You know about building?' Thorne interrupted.

Cade shrugged. 'A little,' he said. 'Enough, I reckon,' he added uncertainly.

Thorne Lammergyre looked at him long and hard, but made no comment. 'I'll come visit,' he told Cade. 'See how you're getting on.' He frowned. 'If you'd like me to, that is.'

Cade knew he'd be a fool to turn down this offer – but he didn't want to appear needy. 'Drop by any time,' he said casually, and stuck out his hand.

'I shall,' said Thorne, shaking it firmly.

He turned back to his coracle and started pushing it into the water. Cade watched as the grey goblin jumped lightly into the little boat and pulled a broad copperwood paddle from beneath his big cloak. With quick, powerful strokes, he set off across the dark waters in the direction of the Five Falls. Cade shivered and tried not to think about what lurked beneath the surface.

Stowing the lakefish in his jacket, Cade waved to the fisher goblin. 'Goodbye. And thank you!' he called.

'Goodbye,' the lemkin's voice echoed back, mimicking Cade. 'And thank you!'

The water plashed softly on the sand at Cade's side as he made his way back along the edge of the lake. Fluffy white clouds drifted slowly across the sky.

Cade didn't realize that anything was wrong with his campsite at first. It was only when Rumblix dashed ahead, screeching at the top of his lungs, that Cade saw the chaos.

The awning he'd constructed had been torn down and tossed aside; the sharpened branches snapped in two. His fishing rod had been broken. Even the rocks he'd set to surround the small fire had been kicked or thrown away. His backpack had been upended and the contents strewn across the grass . . .

He spotted the spyglass, the brass gleaming in the sun. Next to it was the vial of perfume. Cade picked them up, thankful that neither had smashed.

But where were the scrolls?

He looked around him desperately. He felt sick and his scalp itched. He wanted to cry. It was barely two weeks since his father had entrusted him with those documents that had meant so much to him. And now he, Cade, had lost them.

But then he saw something out of the corner of his eye. Down by the stone jetty. Something white . . .

Turning on his heel, Cade ran headlong down to the lakeside. It was the scrolls. All four of them, still rolled up together.

The lake was lapping at one end and the parchment had gone a bit soggy. But that would dry. He had found them. That was the important thing.

Cade picked up the scrolls and turned round. Rumblix had leaped up onto the top of the ridge and was standing staring back across the meadowlands at the treeline, his nostrils quivering. Cade followed the pup's gaze and his eyes fell on the lufwood sapling where the day before he'd set the snare.

Cade trembled. Whatever he'd almost caught over there at the forest's edge must have returned. And judging by the state of his camp, it was angry.

· CHAPTER TWENTY ·

Cade propped himself up on his elbows and looked slowly around. Above him, the sky was clear and bright and tinged pinky-blue by the early-morning glow. Behind, the sun was coming up over the ridge, tipping the treetops with gold. To his left, the distant falls frothed white against the red rock behind as they tumbled down from the dark mouths of the caverns to the lake, their sound a distant, lulling roar. A light breeze was stirring the waters of the lake, and its surface was stippled and glistening.

A broad-backed purple beetle walked sedately past his outstretched boots, and Cade realized he was smiling. The Farrow Ridges were simply magnificent . . .

A series of low rumbling bellows from somewhere to his right caught his attention. He looked round. The noise was coming from the eastern shore of the lake. There, clustered at the water's edge, was a mighty herd of

hammelhorns, their huge, shaggy heads down, and long curling horns dipping as they drank.

As Cade watched, some broke off and began scraping the sweetkelp from the rocks and stones with their front hoofs, while others began to graze on clumps of succulent lake reeds. One of the largest hammelhorns turned its head and surveyed Cade impassively.

It was a bull, its long golden-brown hair gleaming in the dawn light and its massive horns glinting with menace.

Cade reached for his phraxmusket, raised it to his eye and took aim. In the distance, the bull stood staring back at him. Cade's finger tightened on the trigger. But then he relaxed his grip.

The hammelhorn was certainly a magnificent specimen, and with enough meat on its bones to feed Cade and Rumblix for several months. But that was the trouble. Without a smoke shed or meat cellar, he couldn't deal with an animal of such a size, and Cade couldn't bear to watch the carcass of such a noble beast rot by the lakeshore.

Besides, he thought, it could attract unwanted fearsome scavengers . . .

He lowered the phraxmusket, then climbed to his feet. Alerted by the movement, the hammelhorns turned to him as one, their dark eyes filled with mistrust. The bull lowered its head and pawed the ground, and Cade's heart pounded as, for a moment, he feared it was going to charge. The next moment it shook its shaggy head, turned away and trotted back into the forest, with the rest of the herd turning to follow it.

Rumblix opened his eyes, and his nostrils quivered as he sniffed the air. His gaze fell upon the last of the departing hammelhorns, and he looked up at Cade questioningly.

'Fish for breakfast,' Cade said. 'I know, I know, we had fish for supper,' he added, tickling the pup on the side of the head. 'But if we want to vary our diet, then I'd better get building.'

Cade boiled up some nibblick and glimmer-onion broth and, when it was bubbling, added the second of the plump lakefish that Thorne Lammergyre the fisher goblin had given him the day before.

Rumblix sniffed at the pot, then turned away and bounded out into the meadow behind the camp. The prowlgrin pup returned a while later with the carcass of a dead weezit clamped in his wide mouth. The smell of decaying meat was foul, but Rumblix seemed to find it intoxicating: prowlgrins love carrion, the older the better, and the prowlgrin pup was no exception.

'Ugh!' Cade groaned.

Ignoring him, Rumblix purred loudly, then began to crunch on the weezit's bones. Leaving him to it, Cade helped himself to the fish stew. It was delicious.

After breakfast, Cade unpacked his rucksack and laid out the items that Gart Ironside had given him. There was a pack of nails of various sizes, wrapped up in a length of greased leather; a set of hacksaw blades, and a whetstone for sharpening them. Attached to the outside of the backpack were tools, which Cade untied. He ran his thumb along the edge of the axe, examined the hacksaw, the short-handled spade, then picked up the hammer and bounced it up and down in his hand.

'Know your tools.' The words of his old woodwork teacher back at the Academy School in the Cloud Quarter echoed inside Cade's head.

Barkus Lumbergrove. He was an old woodtroll, as wide as he was tall, with a plaited beard and tufted knots in his grey hair. In the dusty old workshop, Cade and his schoolfriends had dozed at their floating sumpwood desks while Barkus Lumbergrove lectured them in that lilting voice of his, as soft and crackling as a lufwood stove.

'Choose your wood wisely, young scholars,' the woodtroll had intoned. 'Ironwood for strength. Copperwood for beauty. Sumpwood to float. And lullabee for the grain . . . A thousand different woods, each with a tale to tell, a gift to give . . .'

But Cade had nodded off, lost in dreams of thousand-sticks tournaments and phraxship races. Now, standing here in the Farrow Ridges, he wished he'd paid more attention to Barkus Lumbergrove and his lectures in woodlore.

Picking up the axe, Cade made his way across the meadowlands towards the treeline, with Rumblix gambolling along behind him, his tongue lolling. All he needed was enough timber to build a small cabin – two or three trees at the most, which he could split down and turn into rough-hewn timbers. Something light and easy to work. Sweet-maple, perhaps. Or gnarlwood. Then he could use the branches to make a latticework roof, topped with slabs of turf from the meadow . . .

Reaching the edge of the forest, Cade paused. Despite the bright sunshine, the woods were dark and forbidding, and Cade couldn't help thinking of the creature that had wrecked his campsite the previous day. He inspected the trees closest to him. One had a mottled orange trunk and broad, three-pronged leaves. Another was dark and gnarled, with twisted branches covered in small thorns. A third was tall and sturdy-looking, dark sap staining its bark a deep glistening brown. Cade didn't recognize any of them.

Looking around, he chose a couple of tall slender-trunked trees with feathery, purplish leaves and smooth bark. They looked like some kind of gladebirch, but Cade wasn't sure. They stood a couple of strides into the forest, but not too far into the forbidding gloom . . .

'Stand back, boy. But keep your eyes and nostrils open . . .' Cade said to Rumblix, then raised his axe and swung it at the first tree.

A sweet aromatic smell, like spices browning in a skillet, filled the air as the axe sliced a wedge-shaped divot out of the tree. With two more strokes, the tree fell with a pleasing creak and landed with a gentle thump on the forest floor. Delighted, Cade promptly felled the second tree in two strokes.

He took hold of the first trunk and was relieved to find that it was much lighter than it looked. He dragged it back to the lakeside, with Rumblix jumping on and off the trunk as though it was all a game.

Cade turned back and fetched the second tree, grateful that he hadn't had to stay in the forest for very long. Perhaps whatever had wrecked his camp had moved on. He hoped so, for he didn't like this feeling of unease he experienced whenever he approached the treeline.

He frowned. If he was to make this beautiful place his home, he knew he'd have to master his fear of the forest.

Once Cade had stripped the branches with the hacksaw, he split the trunks lengthways in two, and then in two again. He repeated this process several more times. It was tiring work, but the wood was soft and split easily – and as it did so, the pungent aromatic smell filled the air.

By the time the sun had reached its highest point over the glistening waters of the Farrow Lake, Cade had turned the two sweet-smelling trees into enough split logs for three walls. The fourth side, he decided, would be open on the lake side, and curtained with the tarpaulin. At least for now.

He spent the next few hours hammering the four upright corner logs into the soft soil in the shadow of the low ridge, and then attaching horizontal logs to them, using the nails. The timber was light, easy to handle, and the three walls of the little cabin rose with satisfying speed. Next, Cade took the branches and crisscrossed them to form a latticework roof, using the last of the nails to fix them in place. Then, picking up the spade, he strode back onto the meadowland.

The sun was lower by now, and turning from yellow to orange. Rumblix was asleep in a ball by the lakeside and snoring softly.

Using the spade to cut into the ground, Cade removed broad slices of turf, which he heaped into a pile. The soil anchoring the meadowgrass was rich and loamy and, as he dug, Cade began to consider the possibilities of planting a vegetable garden. Finally, when he had enough, Cade carried the turf back to the cabin and began laying it over the roof branches. Not only did the heavy sods cover the latticework beautifully, but their rich smell mingled with the aroma of the wood to create a pleasant heady fragrance. And with the last turf in place, and the tarpaulin rigged up to form a makeshift entrance, Cade was finally able to stand back and inspect his handiwork.

The cabin was modest, certainly, but sturdy and compact. He crouched down, pushed the tarpaulin aside and poked his head inside the dark interior. He breathed in the warm air, which smelled of meadowgrass and wood spice.

His little home was perfect. It was warm and dry and made him feel safe.

Backing out of the cabin, Cade climbed to his feet. The red sun was sliding down over the far western horizon and the forest was stirring into life as the night chorus began. Cade shivered as he considered what might be out there lurking in the distance. He looked back at his little cabin with its timber walls and turf roof.

He would sleep soundly tonight, he decided, and

tomorrow he'd dig a meat cellar, and then a smoke shed the day after. And then a veranda. Maybe a look-out tower . . .

Just then, something gripped his shoulder.

Cade spun round, the spade in his hand raised above his head.

'Thorne,' he gasped.

The grey goblin took a step backwards, his crystal-blue eyes fixed on Cade's waxen face. 'Whoa. Easy, lad!' the fisher goblin said, holding up his hand. 'Thought you might be able to use these.'

Cade looked at the three silver-grey lakefish hanging from his other hand, stretched out towards him. 'Th-thank you,' he said, trying to sound as though he hadn't just been scared half out of his wits. 'That's very thoughtful.'

Beside him, Rumblix stirred, then clambered to his feet. He yelped excitedly and bounded over to the grey goblin, his nostrils quivering.

Thorne patted the pup on the head, then handed Cade the fish.

The fisher goblin's coracle was strapped to his back and Cade couldn't help noticing how beautifully it had been constructed. The frame was made of thin strips of wood, which had been carefully curved and plaited together; the leather hull had been glued and stitched into position with absolute precision. Even the paddle that hung from Thorne's belt, with its ridged handle and fluted blade, displayed a skill and workmanship that would have made

Cade's old woodwork teacher proud.

'Been busy, I see,' said the grey goblin.

Cade turned and followed Thorne's gaze. Dark clouds scudded across the pink and orange sunset; the first stars began to twinkle in the east. In the fading light, Cade's little cabin suddenly looked makeshift and hastily thrown together.

'It's a start,' he said.

Thorne Lammergyre smiled, then slipped his beautifully crafted coracle from his shoulders and carried it to the lakeshore.

'Well, take care, Cade Quarter,' he called as he stepped into the coracle and set off across the lake. 'Looks like we're in for a storm tonight.'

Cade watched him

go, then turned back to his cabin, Rumblix growling around his knees.

''Fraid it's fish for supper again tonight,' he said with a sigh.

He laid the fish down on a flat rock, then started to set the fire. He arranged twigs and dry grass at the centre of the ring of rocks, and had just ignited it when the first large plump raindrops began to plash all around him.

· CHAPTER TWENTY-ONE ·

The rain grew heavier as black clouds rolled in on the rising wind. Rain and hail. Cade pulled his hat down firmly on his head, lowered the brim, turned up his collar.

A rich loamy scent filled the darkening air. The lake hissed and, from the far side of the meadowland, the forest rustled and rushed as the wind tore through the upper branches of the trees.

Cade eyed his little fire uneasily. It was struggling to keep going. He pinched the edges of his jacket between his fingers and thumbs, leaned forward, arms outstretched, and attempted to shield it from the increasing downpour. But it was hopeless. The fragile flames were snuffed out with a hiss and a wisp of steam, and the fire that Cade had hoped to grill the fish over was dead.

'Well, I'm not eating them raw,' Cade muttered to himself as he dropped the fish inside the pot. He secured the lid on top to keep out Rumblix – who just might – then surveyed the sky.

The dark banks of cloud were roiling and swirling, and in the distance, lightning glowed in their pleated folds. Far-off thunder grumbled, deep and forbidding.

'Looks like Thorne Lammergyre was right about that storm,' Cade told Rumblix. The pup was crouched down forlornly beside him, his grey fur black with wetness and his nostrils closed to the driving rain. 'Come on, boy,' said Cade. 'We can eat when this storm's passed.' He pulled the tarpaulin aside. 'Let's just get out of the rain for now.'

The prowlgrin pup bounded inside the cabin eagerly. Cade bowed his head and followed, pulling the tarpaulin down behind him. Rumblix shook himself, sending a spray of water droplets flying off into the air.

Cade grimaced as they hit his face, then smiled. He hadn't the heart to chide the little creature.

The cabin felt chill now; the fragrance of meadowgrass and wood had turned sour. And when Cade pulled off his hat he discovered that it was no longer dry either. Large drops were falling on his head – drops which, when he wiped at them with his hands, he found were thick with black mud.

He looked up at the roof, puzzled, only to see that the rain-sodden turf was slumping down between the crisscrossed beams and that water was dripping through, saturating the mud that had anchored the turf in place and melting it away little by little.

Outside, the storm was now directly overhead. Through the widening gaps in the roof, Cade saw blue-white flashes of lightning, which were followed almost immediately by deafening cracks and crashes of thunder. Cade hugged the trembling Rumblix to him with one arm and covered his head with the other. The wind had become monstrous. It was howling and bellowing like a wild beast; it clawed at the cabin, which flexed and creaked ominously.

All at once, behind him, the tarpaulin was ripped from its moorings and disappeared off along the lakeside, flapping like a wounded bird. Cade turned. Everything was in pitch darkness. The next moment, the sky exploded with lightning, and Cade saw the lake framed by the cabin entrance.

His stomach pitched. The waters had been stirred up by the howling gale into dark troughs and spume-flecked peaks. Driving rain billowed like sheets, turning the surface of the lake to a turbulent blur. The waves were crowned with dirty spindrift that was skimmed off and sent flying as the waves crested. They rolled towards him, crashing over the rock jetty and lapping at the entrance of the cabin.

Cade and Rumblix retreated into the far corner as the last of the disintegrating turf roof tiles were whipped away by the wind. The sky was bright with the dazzling lightning bolts that zigzagged down into the jagged treeline.

As Cade watched, open-mouthed, a blazing tree, the

flames dazzling white despite the torrential rain, rose up from the forest on the far shore, slowly, slowly, until its roots reached the treetops, when it was snatched away by the wind. It soared over the lake, rising higher with every passing second as the buoyant wood burned.

Moments later, it was joined by another one, and then another. And another. Until the whole lake was lit up by burning trees blazing trails across the indigo sky. It was beautiful . . .

Just then, a wave broke over the threshold of the cabin and swirled around Cade's feet. The ground turned to quicksand and the timber walls swayed as the shallow foundations of the cabin dissolved. In his arms, Rumblix let out a desolate howl.

'I know, boy. I know,' Cade said, reaching down and grabbing his backpack. 'We'd best get out of here before the whole lot collapses.'

But Rumblix didn't need to be told. He leaped out of Cade's grasp and dashed from the cabin, bounding across the meadowlands as fast as his legs would carry him. Cade set off after him, his head down and body stooped.

All at once the air seemed to explode around him. Blinded and deafened, Cade dived forward and landed flat on his front. When he looked up, he saw that the cabin must have been hit by lightning because it had burst into flames. One by one, the split logs shot up into the air like blazing rockets as what was left of his cabin disappeared into the storm-ravaged night.

Cade groaned and buried his head in his arms. He hadn't done a single thing right. He could see that now. He'd built his cabin too near the lake. He'd roofed it with turf. And as for the wood he'd used, it might have been light and easy to work, but by the way it had burned, it was obviously the worst type of timber he could have chosen.

He remembered how proud he'd been of his little cabin when he'd shown it to Thorne Lammergyre earlier. The fisher goblin hadn't said anything about the cabin, but had warned him about the approaching storm. Now Cade knew why.

Trembling, cold and wet, with the rain and hail beating down on him, Cade felt a complete failure. All his hopes and dreams of a new life in the Farrow Ridges had been destroyed. Soaked, flooded and set ablaze in a single night.

Cade climbed slowly to his feet and trudged over to the prowlgrin pup. Out here in the meadowlands they were exposed to the full force of the wind and rain, as well as the deadly lightning. Cade knew they needed to find shelter in the forest, despite the terror it held for him. He took a few stumbling steps towards the dark treeline, only for a flash of lightning to confirm his worst fears.

There, lit up with awful clarity, was a monstrous creature.

It was powerfully built, but bent over, with long arms that dangled down so low its knuckles grazed the ground. Its legs were thick and bowed. And set upon broad,

muscle-knotted shoulders was a head that was large and lumpen and hideously misshapen. Heavy jutting brows topped tiny deep-set eyes; a lopsided jaw was studded with fangs, while the skull – devoid of any hair – was a mass of bone mounds, at the centre of which was a thick ridge that extended down the back of the head and spine.

'No, no . . .' Cade murmured, his voice tight in his throat.

He tried to turn, to run, but he could not. His feet felt rooted to the spot.

The lightning faded and the meadowlands and the forest beyond were plunged into impenetrable blackness. The wind screamed. The thunder roared. The waves of the lake pounded on the shore. Yet above the cacophony of the storm, Cade could hear something else. He was sure he could. The sound of footfalls, loud and lumbering, as the terrible creature came crashing down across the meadowlands towards him.

He couldn't breathe. He couldn't scream. He felt his legs buckle beneath him . . .

· CHAPTER TWENTY-TWO ·

'Who are you?' Cade's voice was barely more than a whisper, and there was a heaviness in his chest that tightened as he took a breath.

'Don't try to talk,' said the girl.

She was beautiful, with gleaming jet-black hair, olive skin and the greenest eyes Cade had ever seen. They shone like shards of jade as she looked down at him.

'Thorne was so worried,' she told him.

Cade realized he was lying in a bed with a soft mattress and a quilt pulled up over his chest. The girl was standing over him, so close he could smell her warmth and a fragrance like woodjasmine and new-mown hay as she pressed a compress to his forehead. It felt deliciously cool.

'I'm Celestia Helmstoft,' she said. 'Thorne asked me to look after you. You've been ill with lake-fever.'

'But—' Cade began.

Celestia put her finger to his lips, and Cade felt shivers jangling up and down his body at the softness of her touch. Her green eyes sparkled.

'I said, don't try to talk,' she chided him gently, then straightened up, leaving the cold compress on Cade's brow. 'Lie still and rest,' she said, and before Cade had a chance to speak, she had turned and left his side.

A moment later, he heard her footsteps on the stairs.

Cade reached up and removed the compress from his forehead. It was made of folded white damask soaked in a fragrant salve with a sweet, musky smell that he could not identify.

As he propped himself up on his elbows, his head felt light and the room swayed gently. At first, he thought it must be the effects of the fever, until he realized that the bed was floating. Made of buoyant sumpwood and anchored in place by two chains, one at each end, the bed was hovering at the centre of a cone-shaped room, which rose up to a shadowy point high above his head. Honey-coloured timber had been used for the beams, which had been spliced and dovetailed together with pinpoint precision. The walls were made of plaited strips of willow, and varnished with a deep copper glaze.

Cade lay back on the pillow with a sigh. The workmanship was superb, and reminded him of the fisher goblin's meticulously constructed coracle. This hive hut must be Thorne Lammergyre's house, Cade realized, and he felt a pang of embarrassment when he thought of the miserable little shelter he had shown Thorne so proudly just before the storm struck.

The memory of the storm came back to him in all its horror. How it had raged. How the Farrow Lake had turned into a turbulent maelstrom that had thrashed and pounded and flooded his cabin. The crash of thunder. The dazzle of lightning. The burning trees, soaring over the lake.

And the creature: monstrous, misshapen, illuminated at the edge of the forest in the blue-white light, staring back at him . . .

Had he really seen it? Or had, even then, this fever the girl had mentioned, taken hold of his senses?

Cade's gaze strayed. There was a table to his left, and a three-legged stool, and beyond that, standing in shadow, a large ironwood chest. His jacket and breeches lay neatly folded on the top, with his boots on the floor beside it. At the far side of the room was the circular staircase the girl, Celestia, had disappeared down. The polished blackwood banister gleamed in the sunlight that streamed in through a large triangular window. Cade peered out.

The view was of the Farrow Lake, an unbroken vista over its still, silvery surface and the Western Woods beyond, so calm and peaceful now, beautiful in the morning light.

The stairs creaked and Cade heard the sound of footsteps. A moment later Celestia's black hair and radiant face appeared, and Cade was struck by her beauty all over again.

'It's been two days,' she said briskly. 'You need to eat.' She was holding a wooden tray in her hands; a steaming bowl, a spoon and a drinking cup were set upon it.

Cade's throat felt raw and, despite the quilt, he was cold and shivery, and very light-headed. The last thing he felt, though, was hungry.

Celestia set the tray down on the table, then pulled up the stool and sat down. She reached out and placed the back of her hand against Cade's brow, and he was startled by how cool it felt.

'You're burning up,' she told him. 'I made you some broth. But first . . .' She picked up the cup. 'Drink this.'

'Do I have to?' said Cade weakly.

'It'll make you feel better,' she told him simply.

Reluctantly Cade took the cup, put it to his lips and drained the contents in one painful gulp. It tasted bitter, fiery, with a sour, mouldy aftertaste.

He lay back. Almost at once, the heaviness in his chest began to shift, and the strength returned to his body in a warm, fluid rush. He sat up. His head was clear; his throat had eased . . .

'What *was* that?' he said, amazed.

The green-eyed girl smiled. 'Charlock root, lakebane, camphor-berry.' She reeled off the herbs matter-of-factly. 'And . . .' She paused. 'Just the tiniest touch of hover-worm venom.'

'Venom!' Cade exclaimed, dropping the cup and clutching his throat.

'To speed the effect,' said Celestia calmly – though by the look in her eyes, she was plainly enjoying Cade's alarm. 'It worked, didn't it?'

Cade was forced to nod.

'Now, eat,' Celestia said sternly, passing Cade the wooden bowl and spoon. 'Lakefish broth,' she said as Cade tried a spoonful. 'And before you ask,' she added, 'no, there's no hoverworm venom in it.'

Celestia got up and walked over to the stairs and, for the first time, Cade noticed the clothes she wore. A tooled leather jacket with rings, loops and pouches sewn onto the arms, from which various vials, small bundles and packets were hanging. Tight-fitting leggings, reinforced at the knees, and heavy boots,

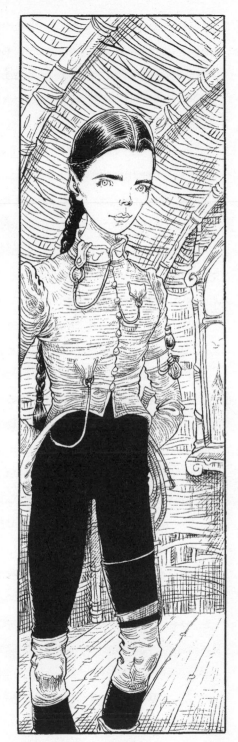

cross-tied and buckled at the ankle. A knife was holstered to one leg and a whip was coiled at her belt.

Celestia Helmstoft was Cade's age, but she was clearly no novice out here in the Deepwoods. Cade felt suddenly young and foolish.

'Finish the broth, then get dressed,' Celestia called to him as she descended the stairs. 'Thorne'll be back from the lake soon and he'll be pleased to see you up.'

'Thank you,' Cade called after her.

He ate the broth quickly, his appetite now fully restored. Then, leaping out of bed, he hastily dressed, his fingers fumbling over jacket buttons and boot buckles, painfully aware of how flimsy and inappropriate his city clothes now seemed.

Once dressed, Cade slowly descended the stairs, marvelling at the skill involved in the making of the spiral staircase with its triangular treads, its carved spindles and coil of banister. At the bottom, he stepped into a room that was similar to the bedchamber, but larger. It was fashioned from the same conjunction of beams and plaited willow, and there were five windows set high in the walls.

There was a large stove at one side of the room, with a spiral chimney that snaked its way up to the beamed ceiling and outside. Suspended on ropes from the beams was a rack, from which pots, pans and skillets, ladles and knives hung on hooks. Three buoyant chairs at the centre of the room swayed gently on the end of chains attached to the copperwood floorboards. A row of hooks by the arched door were laden with tools and weapons – axes, hammers, saws; fishing rods and nets; bows and arrows, lances, harpoons, and what looked like an old phrax-musket, adapted with a spyglass at one end and a long, thin muzzle at the other.

And there, returning a snare to its hook, was Thorne Lammergyre.

'Cade Quarter,' he said, striding across the room to the bottom of the stairs and gripping Cade by the shoulders. 'I've been worried about you. How do you feel, lad?'

'Good as new,' Cade said. 'Celestia gave me some medicine . . .'

'Celestia is highly skill-ed in the healing arts,' said Thorne approvingly. 'Among many other things. Her father, Blatch

Helmstoft, has taught her well, and what she hasn't learned from him, she has picked up from the goblin tribes of the Western Woods. She's a good friend to have out here, Cade,' he added, showing him to a chair.

'You're a good friend too,' said Cade, sitting in one of the floating chairs.

'Not as good as I should have been,' said Thorne, shaking his head. He sat down next to Cade. 'I knew that storm would sorely test that little cabin of yours, and yet you seemed so pleased with it I didn't have the heart to point out its failings. I should have insisted you come back here with me.'

'It wasn't your fault—' Cade began, his face colouring with shame and embarrassment – but the grey goblin held up his hand to silence him.

'Folks have to look out for each other here in the Deepwoods,' said Thorne, 'else we're no better than the savage trogs infesting the water caverns. I tell you, it fair broke my heart when I found you lying there in the lake meadow, your cabin gone and a fever burning you up . . .'

Cade reached out and patted the grey goblin on the arm. 'But you *did* look out for me,' he said gratefully. 'You brought me back here. You sent for Celestia . . .'

Just then Rumblix came bounding in through the open door, yelping and squealing with delight. Half a dozen strides from Cade, he launched himself into the air on his powerful hind legs. Cade opened his arms wide, and the pup slammed against his chest, all but knocking the pair of them out of the chair and onto the ground.

'Rumblix! Rumblix!' Cade laughed as the pup's tongue slurped at his face. 'I missed you too, boy!' he told him.

From the doorway, he heard Celestia laugh. 'That's a fine pup you've got there. But in need of attention. I've fed and watered him, greased his feet, groomed his coat,' she said. 'And I've left you some kit for him. Make sure you use it.'

Cade nodded. 'Thank you, Celestia,' he said. 'Thank you for everything.'

Sleek and healthy-looking, Rumblix wriggled and squirmed in his lap.

'My father and I live in a tree cabin to the west of the lake,' said Celestia, fastening the ties of her cape at her throat. 'You must come and visit us.'

'I'd like that,' said Cade as he managed to disentangle himself from Rumblix's grasping paws and place him down on the floor.

Celestia swept back her hair; her green eyes sparkled. 'Good luck, Cade Quarter,' she said. Then, with a little wave, she stepped out of the doorway and was gone.

Thorne turned to Cade, his face serious. 'There's something I want to show you,' he said and pulled a roll of parchment from the inside of his jacket. 'I was working on it while you were recovering.'

He led Cade across the room to a table, unrolled the parchment and fixed it in place with four flat pebbles, one placed at each corner. Cade looked at the leadstick sketch drawn onto it; the bisected lines, the calculations, the block-print annotations.

'What is it?' he asked.

'This,' said Thorne, his blue eyes twinkling, 'is your new cabin.'

· CHAPTER TWENTY-THREE ·

Had it really been less than three weeks since he and Thorne had begun work on his new cabin? Cade wondered as he pulled the scroll from his inside pocket and unrolled it.

The parchment was looking somewhat the worse for wear, frayed at the edges and with dried mud smeared in places. The actual drawings that Thorne had made were, however, still clear. A one-room cabin set against the side of the ridge and raised on stilts, and with a set of stairs leading down to the rock jetty from a jutting veranda. Behind the cabin, there was a storeroom carved into the cliff. The design was simple enough, but when Cade had first seen it, he had to admit he'd been daunted – though he had tried hard not to show it.

The first stage had taken a week. An ironwood tree had been chopped down and turned into planks and posts. Then the stilts were put in place – stout ironwood stakes sunk deep into holes in the ground and anchored with rocks, then strengthened with diagonal crossbeams. Afterwards, the pair of them had constructed a platform of ironwood planks on top. The result was sturdy, and high enough to escape even the worst flooding from the lake.

Next it was time to dig out the space for the storeroom by tunnelling into the ridge. But on the first morning of that second week, when Thorne Lammergyre came down for breakfast in the hive hut, Cade had noticed that the grey goblin looked hollow-eyed and unusually gaunt. Cade had been sleeping in a hammock slung from the ceiling beams beside the lufwood stove, and had got up especially early to lay out the hand-picks and spades they would need.

'Are you all right?' he'd asked.

Thorne had stared past him, out of the window and across the lake, which was wreathed in coils of early morning mist.

'Thorne?' Cade had touched his arm. 'Thorne, what is it?'

The goblin had flinched, then re-focused his gaze. 'I'm . . . Sorry, lad. I was miles away. Back at the Midwood Marshes.'

Cade had frowned. 'The Midwood Marshes?'

'It's a long story,' Thorne had sighed. 'There was a battle there—'

'A famous battle,' Cade had broken in. 'I've heard of it. Between the armies of Great Glade and Hive . . . That was a long time ago.'

'Aye, well, sometimes I relive those times. And my part in them . . .' Thorne had hesitated, his eyes glazing over as memories played inside his head. 'War's a terrible thing, Cade,' the grey goblin had said quietly, before slumping down at the table. 'I'm afraid I'm not going to be much use to you for a day or so,' he'd added weakly.

And so Cade had set off alone along the lakeshore to the site of his new cabin, and had begun to dig. He'd made good progress. The air had filled with a cloud of earthy dust, and the platform had soon become laden with a fast-growing heap of pale yellow sandstone.

By the time the sun had reached its zenith on that first day of digging, Cade had been able to stand inside the shallow hole he'd hacked out of the cliff. The muscles in his arms and shoulders throbbed with exertion, and he'd been hot, with sweat running down his face and back. But shaded from the sun in the ever-deepening hole, the temperature had been far lower than outside – perfect for the storeroom which Cade could already see in his mind's eye, stocked to the ceiling with cured meat, smoked fish and provisions of all kinds, foraged from the surrounding woods . . .

Cade had shuddered as the image of the misshapen creature he'd seen on the night of the storm invaded his thoughts. *Had* it simply been a fever-induced figment of his imagination? Cade had hoped so, yet ever since that night he had avoided going into the forest alone. And when chopping down the ironwood trees for the cabin had meant venturing into the dappled shadows beyond the treeline, he was grateful to have Thorne at his side.

Fortunately Thorne had recovered the following day and between them, the storeroom had been excavated in a week, with Cade loosening the rock, and Thorne shovelling it outside then loading it onto a barrow which he pushed to the end of the jetty and tipped into the lake. Four steps were cut into the rock which led down into the main room. The ceiling was levelled out, and wooden props were set along the side walls to strengthen the structure.

By the beginning of the third week, with the storeroom finally completed, it had been time to start work on the cabin itself. Whereas the stilts, the veranda and the stairs that led down to the jetty had been made of ironwood, Thorne's plans had indicated that two different timbers should be used for the little dwelling. It would mean heading back into the forest.

Thorne had found Cade poring over the plans in the hall of the hive hut.

'Looks like it was your turn to be afflicted by memories last night, judging by those dark circles beneath your eyes,' the grey goblin had observed.

'We have to go logging again?' Cade had asked miserably.

'That's right,' Thorne had said. 'We need lufwood – a light and buoyant timber – for the walls. And leadwood for the roof shingles. It's good and heavy. It'll anchor everything down. And best of all, it's lightning-proof.' Thorne had smiled. 'Cheer up, Cade,' he'd added. 'I've asked Celestia to lend us a hand.'

Sure enough, when Cade and Thorne had arrived back at the site of his new cabin, Celestia was waiting for them, sitting in the saddle of her prowlgrin, Calix. Cade remembered how her hair had been tied back with a cord of red silk, and her green eyes had looked straight into his, making him blush and turn away.

The three of them had walked up the meadowlands and into the forest, with Calix and Rumblix trotting along behind them, and Cade had found himself glancing around anxiously. Every shadow had seemed suspicious; every rustling leaf and cracking twig had set his senses jangling.

Calm down, he'd told himself. It's all right. There's nothing there.

Thorne had soon spotted what he was searching for: a lufwood tree some twenty strides or so tall, its rough bark dark and pitted and pale leaves dense overhead. The goblin had handed Cade one of the two axes he carried in his backpack and the pair of them had set to work cutting down the tree. As Cade got into a smooth rhythm, driving the hard edge of the axe into the wood, his fears had gradually subsided.

The lufwood tree had proved much easier to cut down than the ironwood, and minutes later Thorne had stood back and bellowed, 'Timber down!'

The tree had fallen with a whisper and a thump.

When they'd stripped the branches and sawn the massive trunk in two, Thorne and Celestia had tied one of the logs to ropes, which they attached to Calix's saddle.

'Come on, boy,' Celestia had said, taking the prowl-grin by his bridle.

Calix had grunted and pulled forward and, with Cade at the back, pushing, the log slowly shifted forward. Leaving Thorne to find a leadwood tree, the two of them had hauled the lufwood log out of the forest and down the meadowlands and unloaded it next to the platform. Then they had returned for the second log. It was when they were halfway back down the meadowlands that Cade had heard Celestia laugh.

'What is it?' he'd asked.

'Oh, nothing,' she'd said. 'It's just . . . When I first saw you lying on that bed, all pale and shaking and burning up with the fever, I thought, uh-oh, a city boy. He's not going to last long out here in the Deepwoods. Yet here you are, with your very own cabin half built.'

'Thanks to Thorne,' Cade had said. 'And you,' he'd added bashfully.

'Oh, we've helped a little,' Celestia had said lightly. She'd fixed Cade with her piercing green eyes. 'But you've done most of the work. Not bad for a city boy.'

At the sound of Celestia's praise, Cade had felt as buoyant as blazing lufwood – and almost as hot. He'd lowered his gaze, his face burning.

'Thank you,' he'd murmured.

They had returned to Thorne in the forest to discover that the grey goblin had chopped down a leadwood tree, sawn off the lower branches and already split them into dozens of thin, rectangular pieces.

'Your shingles,' he'd said, looking up. 'Ten more branches should do it.'

They'd spent the rest of that day making the shingles, and that evening, with the forest darkening around them, they had loaded them onto Calix, who carried them back to the lakeside. Then Celestia had left them, galloping on Calix through the treetops to the hanging cabin she shared with her father, and which Cade longed to see.

'I'm sorry I can't stay and help,' she'd told Cade as she left, 'but I promised my father I'd be home by nightfall.'

'You . . . you'll come back to see the cabin when it's finished, won't you?' Cade had called after her.

'When do you think that'll be?' Celestia had asked.

'Three days, I'd say,' Thorne broke in.

'See you in three days, then,' Celestia's voice had floated back to them. 'City boy.'

The following day, Thorne and Cade had erected the walls of the cabin, which they strengthened with ceiling beams as the sun set and the light began to fail. On the next day, while Cade – under Thorne's instructions – had knocked up a banister around the veranda, the grey goblin had put a window into each side of the cabin and a door at the front.

Now it was the final day of construction, and as Cade stood looking at Thorne's tattered, mud-smeared plans, all that remained to be done was fixing the shingles to the roof. With a lot of hard work, and the help of his friends, it had taken less than three weeks to build a perfect home beside the beautiful waters of the Farrow Lake.

The previous evening, Thorne Lammergyre had shown him how to fix the leadwood shingles in place. First he drilled two holes at the top of the piece of wood with a bradawl, one on each side, then he nailed it to the crossbeam, taking care to align it with the neighbouring shingles. He had made it look easy. But it was not easy – as Cade found out as he set to work that morning.

Thorne was out on the lake checking his nets, and Celestia had said she would visit later. Cade wanted to have the roof finished before either of them returned.

The timber was hard and shiny. Sawing it had proved difficult, but Cade soon found that it was close to impossible to bore the holes without either the point of the awl skidding off to one side or, worse, splitting the shingle in two. And even with the holes in place, more often than not when it came to fixing the tiles to the roof, Cade managed to bring the hammer down hard on his fingers and thumb. His left hand was a mass of bruises and swellings.

'Not that way, you greenhorn,' said Cade, imitating the grey goblin's gruff voice as he struggled with the shingles. 'I swear, if you were any wetter behind the ears, you'd drown.'

He could mimic Thorne's voice almost as well as that pet lemkin of his. And as Cade and Thorne had worked together, they had fallen into an easy, gently mocking banter.

'All right, all right – old-timer,' Cade replied to himself

in his own voice. 'When I've finished bashing my thumbs, I'll fashion you a walking stick . . .'

Cade carried on both sides of the conversation as he secured the shingles to the sloping roof row by row, continuing up from the bottom to the top. He was on the very last one, carefully *tap-tap-tapping* the nail into the beam beneath and crooning, 'Nearly there, old-timer. Nearly there . . .' when he heard Rumblix yelping and squealing with excitement below. He looked down to see the prowlgrin pup dashing up the meadowlands towards the edge of the forest where, a moment later, Celestia Helmstoft appeared, sitting astride her own prowlgrin, Calix.

Cade's heartbeat quickened. Her long black hair

was up and, as she approached, the low sun glinted on the silver clasps. She raised a hand when she saw Cade staring at her, and smiled.

'Greetings, city boy!' she called out. 'Am I mistaken, or were you talking to yourself up there?'

'Of course not, Celestia,' Cade called back, and laughed. 'You probably heard Thorne's lemkin.'

The girl tugged lightly at Calix's reins and the prowlgrin started into a gallop. Rumblix kept up, bouncing around at his side. Cade finished knocking the nail into place, then climbed down the ladder.

Celestia pulled up beside him. Cade realized that instead of the tooled leather jacket she usually wore, she had on a sleeveless homespun tunic and mid-calf breeches.

'The cabin's looking wonderful,' she was saying. 'Is it finished?'

Cade beamed proudly. 'Just this minute,' he said.

'Excellent,' said Celestia. She swung her leg over Calix's back and jumped down lightly to the ground. 'Then I've come at just the right moment.' She patted the leather satchel at her side. 'I've brought a bottle of my father's finest sapwine. I thought we could all celebrate . . .' She frowned and looked around. 'Where's Thorne?'

'He's checking his nets,' said Cade, and looked across the lake at the sun, which was hovering above the horizon, large and blood-red. 'He should be back soon.' He laughed. 'It'll be fish for supper again, no doubt. I think I'm turning into a fish!'

Celestia's face suddenly became deadly serious. She reached out and ran her finger across one side of Cade's neck, then the other.

'I think you're right,' she said darkly.

'What . . . what do you mean?' Cade asked.

'Gills,' she said, and threw back her head in laughter. 'You're growing gills. Let's go and check them out,' she said, and with that she sprinted down the jetty, and then kicked off her boots and launched herself into the lake. 'Come on!' she shouted.

For a moment, Cade hesitated. But only for a moment.

Kicking off his own boots, he sprinted down the jutting rock and dived into the cool, dark water. He grabbed Celestia's legs and pulled her down. And Celestia – who was at least as good a swimmer as he was – shoved his head down under the water. Writhing and splashing, the pair of them ducked and dived and dunked one another over and over. They swallowed water when they were pushed down, and spluttered and gasped for breath when they resurfaced.

Celestia's skin was blushed red with the setting sun. Cade couldn't keep his eyes off her. He had never felt so happy before. And when Celestia joined in his laughter, he almost dared to believe that she felt the same way.

· CHAPTER TWENTY-FOUR ·

'I've got to hand it to you, lad,' said Thorne, licking the grease from his fingers, one by one. 'You certainly know how to roast lakefowl.'

'You like it, then?' said Cade a little bashfully.

'Like it?' said Thorne. He took a piece of blackbread and mopped up the juices on his wooden plate, then looked up. 'Finest cooking I've tasted since back in Hive, when . . .' The grey goblin hesitated and his expression darkened.

'When?' Cade prompted him.

But Thorne was frowning now and looking down at his empty plate. 'It doesn't matter,' he said quietly.

'Let me get you some more,' said Cade, breaking the awkward silence that followed.

He pushed his chair back and, taking Thorne's plate, crossed the small cabin to the stone hearth where two more plump birds sizzled on a spit above a crackling log fire.

That morning, he'd shot three of the waterfowl that grazed the meadowlands with the phraxmusket Gart Ironside had lent him. The creatures were slow and awkward, and Cade had felt a twinge of guilt each time one of the musket-balls found its target. But he'd consoled himself that each of the ungainly birds had met its end quickly and painlessly – and would make good eating.

Back at his new cabin, he had sat on the veranda overlooking the lake and plucked and gutted the birds as Rumblix looked on, his wide mouth open and tongue lolling. Cade tossed the giblets to the prowlgrin pup, who gobbled them down greedily before leaping onto the veranda rail and begging for more, his whiplash tail a blur of movement.

'That's all for now, boy,' said Cade. 'Got to save some for our guest.'

Entering the cabin, Cade crossed to the stone wall and ducked through the small doorway that led down into the storeroom. He took down a string of glimmer-onions from a hook in the low ceiling, then selected other vegetables from several sacks on the floor.

Cade had been busy in the last week. Besides the forage sacks full of polderbeets and strings of glimmer-onions from the meadowlands, there was a bucket of salted lakefish, a box of drying field mushrooms, and bundles of sweet lake-kale hanging over by the far wall. The storeroom wasn't full exactly, but it was a good start. And soon, Cade told himself as he climbed the rock-cut

steps back up to the cabin, as he grew more confident, he'd start foraging in the surrounding forest.

Cade sat down at the beautifully crafted copperwood table that Thorne Lammergyre had made him and set to work on the polderbeets and glimmer-onions, peeling and chopping and dicing. Then, after searing the pieces in sizzling oil, he tossed the whole lot into a stewpot of water, which he set to boil over the hearth. He added sticks and split logs to the fire, then blew long and hard into the embers until the whole lot burst into flames.

The aromatic smells of cooking soon filled the cabin as Cade cleared the table and then set two places for supper. He put chairs out on either side of the table: two high-backed lufwood seats that he and Thorne had made together only a week earlier, but already looking as if they had always been there – much like the cabin itself.

Cade looked around his new home – at the hammock in the corner, beside a log night-stand; the veranda, with its floating sumpwood bench and magnificent view of the distant Five Falls, and the ironwood mantelpiece above the blazing hearth. At one end of the mantelpiece was the brass spyglass, his uncle's initials – N.Q. – glinting in the firelight. At the other end stood the vial of perfume that had belonged to his mother, Sensa. In the middle, pinned to the log wall above the mantelpiece, were the four parchment scrolls that Thadeus, his father, had entrusted him with.

Cade swallowed as the memory of his father's face came back to him. The careworn lines that furrowed his brow when he was lost in concentration; the greying hair at his temples, grown whiter with the worries of his position in the academy. And yet, despite it all, his father had always made him feel safe, protected from the plots and intrigues that were rife in the Cloud Quarter. His eyes filled with tears . . .

Cade stood back as the flickering firelight illuminated his precious objects. They were all he had from his old life, and here, in his new life, it was these that made his little cabin in the wilds of the vast Deepwoods feel like home.

Thorne had arrived at dusk, a casket of freshly made sapwine under his arm and a couple of newly turned goblets in his pocket. And as the lakefowl roasted over the fire, they had toasted their friendship.

The wine was strong and sweet, and one gobletful had been enough to make Cade feel distinctly light-headed. But as he served up roast lakefowl and beet-stew, Cade noticed that Thorne was drinking freely and deeply. And as he did so, the grey goblin began to talk.

He told Cade about his childhood in Hive, living in one of the bustling districts below the central falls, where his father had owned a modest tallow-candle store. At twelve years old, Thorne had won a scholarship to the famous academy on the Sumpwood Bridge. And as he spoke of his days studying the extraordinary properties of phrax crystals, Thorne's eyes had lit up with pleasure. But at sixteen, his career as an academic was ended when his father died and Thorne had to return to run the candle store.

'Those were dark days,' Thorne said, refilling his goblet, then draining it in one draught. 'The High Council of Hive was corrupted by greed and the lust for power. They trebled the militia, turned the city into a vast military camp, and they barrelled any who raised their voices in protest . . .'

'Barrelled?' said Cade, placing a second helping of roast lakefowl in front of Thorne.

The grey goblin didn't seem to notice it. His eyes were heavy-lidded, and his voice low.

'They were put in barrels and dropped over the falls – smashed to pieces on the rocks below. For weeks, the waters beneath the Sumpwood Bridge flowed red . . .'

Thorne helped himself to more sapwine. Outside, the sun had set and, through the open door, the sky above the lake was a riot of oranges, purples and reds. Cade lit a lantern and placed it on the table between them. There was a look of pain in the goblin's face. He was pale, and his hands had begun to shake. He looked up, his eyes sunken and dark and fixed on Cade.

'I had the nightmare again last night,' he said breathily. 'About the Battle of the Midwood Marshes . . .'

He took a slurp of wine, shook his head. Rumblix, who was curled up at Cade's feet, fast asleep, whimpered softly as though he sensed the goblin's distress. Outside, the sunset colours slowly faded.

'It always starts the same way,' Thorne began.

Cade swallowed.

'The war with Great Glade has begun, and I've been

pressganged into the First Low Town Regiment of the Hive Militia, along with my friends, Grablock and Grasp, and Chafe Sireswill . . . We're dressed in uniform. Burnished copperwood helmets. Dark grey breeches. White waistcoats. And heavy overcoats with embroidered patches on the sleeves.'

He paused. Closed his eyes. Cade saw his hands tighten round the bowl of the sapwine goblet in an effort to stop them from shaking.

'We're marching through the Deepwoods. Dappled sunlight on the forest floor. Laughing, joking, trying to keep our spirits up. Then the sky darkens.

'It starts to rain. Hot, torrential rain that hisses and steams and turns the ground to a quagmire. There's crashing thunder

and blinding lightning. Except it isn't; it's phraxfire. Explosions of phraxcannon. The dazzle of exploding shells. White-hot leadwood bullets are cutting through the air like buzzing woodwasps . . .

'We fall to the wet ground. The order comes to load, to take aim, to fire . . .

'All at once a shell explodes just to my right. The air – it's filled with mud and blood and body parts. And it stinks. Burning hair. Flesh. Grablock and Grasp. Gone. Ripped to shreds.' He swallowed. 'Then . . . then I hear a voice. Weak. Whispering. I roll over to see . . . to see . . .'

Thorne paused to take a gulp of sapwine, then a deep breath – and then another gulp. Cade watched the goblin's face twitch with pain.

'It's . . . It's Chafe Sireswill. Known him since we were both young'uns, I had. And he's lying in the mud . . . Or rather, what's left of him.' Thorne closed his eyes. 'One arm is missing . . . There's a gaping hole in his stomach . . . The left side of his face is smashed in. Jaw crushed. Cheek smashed. One eyeball torn from its shattered socket . . .

' "Thorne . . . Thorne . . ." he's whispering . . .'

Thorne opened his eyes again and fixed Cade with a wild-eyed stare. Cade trembled.

'I crawl towards him. All around me, the ground is littered with the dead and the dying. I seize Chafe's hand, whispering promises and reassurances I know are untrue. He *won't* be all right. He *won't* pull through . . .'

Thorne paused and drained his goblet once more,

before filling it from the casket. It was almost empty, and Thorne had to tip the small barrel upside down to drain the last of the fiery sapwine from it.

'I . . . I see a flicker of recognition pass across Chafe's face. He knows who I am. And then . . . then . . .' Thorne lowered his head and rubbed his eyes with a finger and thumb, slowly, kneading them, as though trying to squeeze the memories away. 'Then it's over. He's gone. Earth and Sky take his spirit,' he added reverently.

'Then I hear a squelching thud. I look up to see a Freeglade Lancer on prowlgrinback standing before me. His lance is raised. I want to tell him that I am no enemy of Great Glade; that I have been pressganged into fighting for the Hive Militia. That I hate the Grand Council's warmongering as much as any Great Glader. But I know there is no point. His face is twisted with hatred for his enemy . . .

'For me.'

Thorne put down his goblet and held his head in his hands. Cade waited for what seemed like an eternity until finally the grey goblin lowered his hands again. He stared back at Cade.

'It's him or me, you see,' he said. 'Him or me. I raise my phraxmusket and I fire . . .'

Cade held his breath.

'It clicks. Uselessly. I fire again. Same thing. There must be mud in the firing chamber. I see the look of triumph in the rider's eyes as he raises his lance . . .'

The grey goblin's eyes welled up.

'I grip the phraxmusket by the muzzle and swing it. Desperate. The stock hits the side of the lancer's head hard. There's a splintering crack. Blood. He tumbles from his prowlgrin and falls to the ground and I'm on him, knife drawn, and I'm stabbing and stabbing and stabbing . . .'

He looked up at Cade. The tears had spilled over and were streaming down his face.

'And then I wake up.'

Thorne Lammergyre fell still. Apart from the sound of the lake lapping softly at the jetty, the air was silent.

'That dream has plagued me for years. I returned to Hive after the war. The High Council were overthrown and a new, fairer one elected . . . But the dream wouldn't go away.'

He wiped his face on his sleeve, sniffed.

'You see, there were just too many memories in Hive. And then there was the fear. Fear that greed and power could corrupt the city again; that the dark days could return. I couldn't live like that.' He shook his head. 'Which is the reason I came here to the Farrow Ridges, as far away from the great cities and their politics as I could get,' he said. 'To set up a new life. A good and simple life. I have tried to cut myself off from the past.' He shuddered. 'But sometimes, even after all these years, it comes back to me . . .'

By now the moon had set, and though the sky was ablaze with twinkling pinpoints of light, the inside of the cabin was cloaked in shadow. Cade leaned forward and turned up the lantern, raising the wick until the yellow light flickered on the fisher goblin's face. He looked calmer now.

'Is it me, or is there a chill in the air?' Thorne asked, shivering. Getting to his feet a little unsteadily, he crossed to the hearth and warmed himself by the fire. 'What have we here?' he asked, looking down at the mantelpiece.

Cade followed his gaze. 'Oh, the spyglass belonged to my uncle. Nate Quarter,' he explained. 'And the perfume—'

'No, not them,' said Thorne. '*These*.' He squinted at the scrolls that Cade had pinned to the wall. He turned. 'Where do they come from?'

'My father did them,' Cade told him. 'He was a phrax-scientist in the Cloud Quarter . . .'

'Was?' said Thorne.

'He . . . he died,' said Cade sadly. The reality of his loss was still painfully raw. 'He left me the scrolls,' he added. 'They are part of *my* past. I put them there to remind me of him.'

Thorne turned back to them. He pored over the annotated diagrams and spidery calculations, his fingers tracing over first one, then the next, then the next scroll. When he turned back to Cade, his eyes were wide with excitement.

'It's not the past you have here, lad,' Thorne told him. 'It is the future!'

· CHAPTER TWENTY-FIVE ·

Cade opened his eyes. Yellow sunlight was streaming in through the cabin windows. He lay back in his hammock, his hands behind his head, and stared up at the ceiling beams above his head.

Thorne Lammergyre had studied Cade's father's diagrams late into the night, making page after page of notes in the small tilderleather-bound book that he kept in his waistcoat pocket. The diagrams were about phrax crystals, but when Cade pressed him for details, all Thorne would say was that it would be easier if he demonstrated what the diagrams meant, rather than trying to explain them in words. And that this would 'take a little while'.

'Maybe a week or so,' he'd added.

Unable to keep his eyes open, Cade had left the grey goblin to his note-taking, and stumbled off to his hammock. Now, in the morning light, Cade saw that

Thorne had pinned the drawings back on the wall above the mantelpiece, and must have let himself out.

Cade sat up and was just stifling a yawn when Rumblix woke up from his perch at the end of the hammock and leaped onto his chest. The pup began to lick Cade's face furiously.

'Whoa, boy! Easy!' Cade laughed, pushing the enthusiastic prowlgrin pup away. 'If I wanted a wash I'd jump in the lake!'

And as Cade tousled the pup's fur, Rumblix licked at him all the more eagerly, his tail flicking back and forth. Cade climbed to his feet and Rumblix jumped down after him, wide-eyed and yelping.

'Hungry?'

Cade crossed over to the stewpot which, now the fire was out, was resting at an angle above the hearth. Inside it were the congealed remains of the beet-stew and the second helping of lakefowl that Thorne hadn't eaten the night before. Cade carried the pot out onto the veranda and emptied it into Rumblix's feeding trough. The pup barged him out of the way and devoured the leftovers greedily.

'Hey, city boy!' came a voice.

Cade looked up from the trough to see Celestia mounted on her prowlgrin, Calix, standing on the cabin roof. Beside them was a second prowlgrin, black with flecks of orange in its beard; bridled and saddled – but riderless. Celestia's green eyes sparkled mischievously as she gazed down at Cade.

'Burrlix, here, is for you,' she said. 'Quick, put some clothes on and we'll go for a ride.'

Cade pulled the top of his nightshirt closed and shivered as he gazed at the two prowlgrins perched on the lufwood shingles above him. Both creatures were snorting, puffs of white steamy breath billowing from their flaring nostrils into the chill early-morning air.

The black prowlgrin looked big, his powerful hind legs quivering and his blue eyes swivelling round to gaze at Cade. As Cade stared back, the prowlgrin drew back his lips to reveal two rows of sharp white teeth, then pawed at the roof shingles with his long, sensitive toes.

'Don't keep Burrlix waiting,' Celestia urged him. 'He's looking forward to his morning gallop.'

Cade swallowed. 'But I've never ridden a prowlgrin before,' he confessed.

'There's nothing to it,' Celestia laughed. 'All you have to do is hold on. Burrlix will do the rest.'

Cade looked at the creature uncertainly; at the bridle secured round his great head, the narrow saddle with its stirrups, the reins . . .

'Besides,' Celestia continued brightly, 'it'll be good for that little pup of yours. It's high time he was introduced to the forest. He'll learn branch-leaping from the others – just like pups do in the wild. Now, come *on*!'

Cade had planned to clear a plot in the meadowlands that day; pull up the coarse meadowgrass, remove the rocks and stones, till the soil ready for the planting of a vegetable garden. Hard, back-breaking work . . .

'I did have plans,' he said. 'But I suppose they can wait.'

He ducked back into the cabin, and a few minutes later returned in jacket and breeches, a canteen of water slung over one shoulder and a rolled blanket over the other, together with his phraxmusket. He'd noted the phraxpistols holstered at Celestia's side, and the bedroll strapped to her saddle. And Thorne was always telling him to be prepared at all times . . .

Celestia looked him over with approval. 'You're learning,' she said, and Cade was pleased she hadn't added the teasing words, 'city boy'.

She twitched the reins in her hand and Calix jumped down onto the veranda, followed by Cade's mount, Burrlix. Rumblix ran in circles around the adult prowlgrins' legs, chittering excitedly.

'Put your left foot in the stirrup,' said Celestia, taking Burrlix's halter and holding him steady. 'That's it. Hold onto the reins, then swing your right leg over the saddle.'

Cade did as he was told, trying to ignore the way his legs were shaking.

'Relax,' said Celestia gently. 'Trust your prowlgrin.' She smiled. 'When you were ill, you talked about how you used to watch the Freeglade Lancers riding through the streets of Great Glade, wishing that you could be one of them. Remember?'

'I do,' Cade admitted.

'Well, imagine you're a lancer,' said Celestia. 'Grip with your legs. Flick the reins . . .' she instructed, demonstrating the actions as she spoke. 'And hold on tight.'

With a sudden lurch that threw Cade back in the saddle, Burrlix trotted across the veranda and jumped down onto the lakeshore. Cade held on with his hands and legs as tightly as he could. Celestia, on Calix, cantered past him, with Rumblix scampering behind.

They crossed the meadowlands behind the cabin at full tilt. And with the wind in his face and the lakeside a blur of blue and green, Cade revelled in the sense of speed as the two great prowlgrins pounded over the soft, reed-spiked ground and leaped up over any rocks and bushes in their way.

A moment later, Cade's heart leaped into his mouth as he realized that they were approaching the treeline. A giant lullabee tree, its trunk as broad and lumpy as a stone wall, rose up in front of him. Instinctively he tugged at the reins, yanking them backwards to slow the galloping prowlgrin down. But if anything Burrlix seemed to gather speed. The side of the tree got closer and . . .

'Whoa!' Cade cried out as Burrlix braced his powerful back legs and kicked off, and Cade found himself soaring up vertically into the air.

Gripping on tightly with his hands and legs, Cade looked up as the trunk of the lullabee tree smudged past in a blur. Suddenly Burrlix thrust out his front legs, clawed paws outstretched, and they landed on a branch, with Calix and Celestia on one side of them, and Rumblix

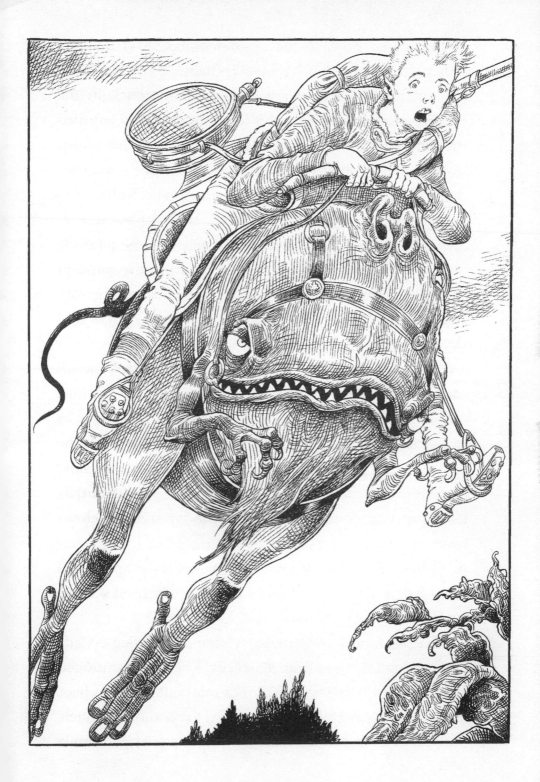

on the other – but only for a moment. Before Cade had a chance even to catch his breath, Burrlix had flexed his legs and jumped again – this time soaring high through the forest to the jutting branch of a huge lufwood, twenty strides away. And from there, without hesitation, he leaped again, onto the bark-stripped branch of a mighty ironwood pine.

Higher and higher they climbed through the shadowy forest, tree after giant tree, until all at once they burst through the canopy, and Cade was momentarily blinded by dazzling sunlight. When his eyes adjusted, Cade saw that all around, like a mighty green carpet, the Deepwoods extended as far as the eye could see. Without a moment's hesitation, the prowlgrins bounded across the treetops on feet sensitive to the sway and give of the highest branches.

The sensation of hurtling across the top of the forest on prowlgrinback was like nothing Cade had ever experienced. Nothing could have prepared him for it – not the leap from the Forlorn Hope, nor the swell of the sky-tavern, nor the speed of Gart Ironside's phraxlighter. All of them paled in comparison to this sensation. This was wild and wonderful. It was like riding the wind – and Cade hoped it would never end.

Then suddenly, up ahead, Calix and Celestia disappeared from view. Then Rumblix . . .

And seconds later, when Burrlix reached the same spot in the dense green forest canopy, he too leaped through the gap in the branches and down into the leaf-scented shadows below. They were descending now, coming down through the branches of the trees as sure-footed as on their ascent, and even faster. A copperwood blurred past, followed by an ironwood, a lufwood, a sutterpine, a redoak, and what could have been a couple of white-willows – Cade wasn't sure. Then all at once they came to a halt, just above the forest floor on the edge of a large clearing.

Celestia, Calix and Rumblix were waiting for them, perched on one of the stout lower branches of a spreading bucknut tree. Celestia pointed to the massive trunk of an ironwood pine on the far side of the clearing.

'Welcome to my little tree-cabin,' she said.

· CHAPTER TWENTY-SIX ·

Cade peered into the green gloom, puzzled for a moment. And then, looking up into the branches of the massive ironwood pine, he saw it: a vast construction that resembled a skyship, some thirty strides in length and three storeys high, each storey separated from the next by finely carved pillars.

The rounded roof had a platform at its centre, and had been clad with red, yellow and black wooden tiles set in intricate diamond-shaped patterns; a tower to the left was crowned with a high chimney, white smoke coiling out from the top. There were jutting domed structures at each end of the building, complete with balconies, balustrades and steps that linked one storey to the next. The uppermost floor had a row of eight arched windows, all but one closed to the outside world by shutters; the middle floor was set back a couple of strides and enclosed by a veranda, while the lowest floor was open to the elements.

The building was truly magnificent. It wouldn't have looked out of place among the palaces and academies of the Cloud Quarter, or the opulent mansions of New Lake – apart from one thing. Unlike the buildings in Great Glade, which were anchored to the earth, either on stilts or stone foundations, Celestia's home was suspended high above the ground on metal chains that were bolted to a broad, sturdy ironwood branch. A cluster of giant ironwood cones had been attached to the bottom of the building by ropes, weighting it down and preventing it from swinging when the wind got up.

Cade let out a long low whistle. '"Little tree-cabin", you said,' he murmured. 'I've never seen anything so grand.'

Celestia laughed. 'It took my father and Thorne ten years to build,' she said, then nodded thoughtfully. 'And at the end of it, my father had taught Thorne everything he knew. My father was a skyship builder in Great Glade. A master craftsman,' she added. 'You see, that's how it works out here in the Deepwoods. We help each other and pass on whatever skills and talents we have freely. Not like in the big cities where everyone is only out for themselves.'

Cade turned to Celestia. 'I'm not sure I have any skills or talents,' he said ruefully.

Celestia smiled. 'Don't worry, city boy,' she told him. 'I'll teach you. Now, come and meet my father,' she said, twitching Calix's reins. He leaped off the bucknut branch and down to the ground.

Cade, Burrlix and Rumblix landed on the forest floor beside her, and the three prowlgrins trotted across the clearing to the immense ironwood tree towering above them. The lowest branches were too high even for a powerful prowlgrin to reach. But wooden pegs had been hammered into the bark of the trunk in a rising spiral, and it was these the prowlgrins used to climb the tree, leaping from one peg to the next.

Arriving at the branch that the tree-cabin was slung from, Celestia set off along it until the red, yellow and black tiled roof was directly beneath her. Then she twitched the reins again, and Calix jumped down onto one of the cabin's jutting balconies. Cade followed, and was relieved when Burrlix landed squarely and steadily on the wooden boards.

'Jump off, then,' said Celestia, who had already dismounted.

Cade did so, and Celestia tethered the three prowlgrins to cross-posts, gave them water and some dried offal. Then the two of them headed down the short staircase to the storey below and through an arched door.

The smell of the chamber struck Cade first. It was a heady mixture of spice, woodsap and pungent spirits. The windows were shuttered, and as he followed Celestia through the darkened chamber, Cade glimpsed shelves, cupboards and cabinets crowded with bottles, vials and pots of all shapes and sizes. From hooks overhead hung bundles of dried roots and feathery clusters of medicinal plants.

'This was my mother's chamber,' said Celestia. 'She taught me the art of healing. It's mine now,' she added. She stepped through the doorway at the far end of the room. 'Come on, Cade,' she called back to him, and Cade had to tear himself away from the mesmerizing display.

He entered a long, narrow study lined with shelves of barkscrolls and bound parchments. Ahead of him, a figure was perched on the seat of a floating sumpwood desk. The light from an open window streamed down on a range of barbed arrowheads he was inspecting one by one with long-nailed fingers. He was thin and spidery. He wore wire-framed glasses with small round lenses. His head was large and bald on top, but with a ruff of thick white hair that stuck out over his ears. He had the bushiest eyebrows Cade had ever seen.

'You've found more arrowheads,' said Celestia.

'Yes, yes, yes,' said her father, without looking up. 'Except I'm beginning to think they might be harpoons.' His nimble fingers darted over one of the objects. 'See the grooves here? See these barbs?'

'And they're from the caverns?' Celestia said.

'Farthest in I've been so far,' he said, and laughed, the sound high-pitched and flutey, 'though I still haven't come across a single white trog.' He hesitated. 'Which isn't, of course, to say they're not there. The caverns are enormous, Celestia. Miles and miles of tunnels. I can't begin to imagine how deep they go.'

'It's my father's latest obsession,' Celestia told Cade with a smile. 'Exploring the caverns behind the Five Falls.'

Her father spun round, almost tipping himself off the buoyant desk seat. 'Company,' he chirped. His beady black eyes fell on Cade. 'I had no idea.'

'This is Cade,' said Celestia. 'Cade Quarter.' She smiled reassuringly at Cade. 'And this is my father, Blatch Helmstoft.'

'My pleasure,' Blatch squeaked, and thrust out a hand to Cade, who went to shake it, only for Blatch's hand to dart back untouched to the objects on the table. 'Quarter. Quarter. Quarter,' he said thoughtfully. 'You're not related to the notorious descender by any chance?'

'He's my uncle, sir,' Cade told him.

'When I say notorious, don't get me wrong,' said Blatch Helmstoft quickly. 'I have a lot of time for descending. And descenders. Their quest for knowledge is an inspiration to us all . . . Mind you, not that those fools back in the Cloud Quarter agreed. Made it all but impossible for them. *And* their sympathizers. That's why I decided to leave Great Glade.' He paused. 'I built several skyships for descending expeditions and the School of Flight objected. Made my life impossible. So I came out here with my dear wife and little baby Celestia to pursue other interests . . .'

Cade smiled politely.

'I spent the first ten years cataloguing the tree species of the Western Woods. Rather useful, I might say, since I was building my little cabin at the time. Of course, I'm a skyship builder so I did rather go over the top. Once I'd started I just couldn't resist adding a cabin here and a balcony there – what with all this beautiful timber at my disposal. Did you know that there are seven previously unknown sub-species of sumpwood in this very room.'

'No, sir,' Cade replied, looking around uncertainly.

'For the last five years, I've been studying water-spiders around the shores of the Farrow Lake. I found one particularly fascinating specimen drowned at the bottom of the falls. It could only have come from the caverns. I'd been meaning to explore them for years, but had been so busy with other things I'd simply never got round to it. But now I'm making up for lost time. I've been investigating the caverns for . . . let me think . . .

three weeks now!' He gave a thin tinkling laugh. 'You really must come with me, Celestia dear, and bring your young friend.'

'It will have to be another time, Father,' said Celestia. 'Cade and I have other plans – I'm taking him into the Western Woods to gather shriekroot.'

'You are?' said Cade, surprised.

'Well, do take care, Celestia, dear,' said her father absentmindedly.

'I shall, Father,' Celestia told him. 'Come on, Cade.'

She headed back down the narrow study, and Cade followed. When he looked back, the small figure was hunched over the arrowheads – or harpoonheads – once more, as though he'd already forgotten Cade and his daughter had ever been there.

Back on the rooftop balcony, Celestia unhitched the prowlgrins and jumped up onto Calix's back. Cade climbed onto Burrlix, with Rumblix scurrying excitedly round the prowlgrin's feet.

'What is shriekroot, Celestia?' he asked. 'And where exactly do we gather it?'

'Follow me and you'll find out,' said Celestia, her green eyes sparkling, 'city boy.'

· CHAPTER TWENTY-SEVEN ·

The Western Woods were darker and even more brooding than the forest that fringed the meadowlands. The trees were taller and seemed to grow closer together, plaited to one another with swathes of dark-leafed and tendrilled creepers. Shards of sunlight twinkled in the forest canopy, though little penetrated the shadowy depths below.

In the saddle, Cade gripped the reins and pressed his legs tightly to Burrlix's flanks as his prowlgrin leaped through the forest. There were creatures all around them. Cade could hear them. Fromps emitting their strange coughing call. Screeching quarms and filbits. Insects with iridescent blue or green or orange wings flashed past. A black and orange lammerkeen came swinging through the forest, its huge golden eyes scanning the branches for fruit. Seeing the prowlgrins and riders, it unfurled its long, curling snout and hooted at them mournfully before disappearing down into the forest depths. In the distance, a swarm of woodwasps droned round a massive, papery nest as big as Cade's cabin, and Celestia changed course to give it a wide berth.

They had been riding for an hour or more, and Cade was getting used to the swaying rhythm of his leaping prowlgrin. A tired Rumblix clung to the pommel of his saddle, eyes half closed. They left the nest behind them and were approaching a dense cluster of maroon-leafed lufwoods that rose up from the surrounding canopy like the walls of a stockade, when Calix and Burrlix both let out snorts of alarm.

As they landed in the branches of the tallest lufwood, Celestia brought Calix to a halt and, holding tightly to the saddle, Cade felt Burrlix pause also. In front of him, Rumblix was now wide awake and whining softly, his grey fur standing on end.

'They can sense it,' said Celestia, dismounting. 'The bloodoak. Its glade must be just below us.'

Cade's jaw dropped. Bloodoak. He remembered Gart Ironside speaking of the razor-toothed, flesh-eating tree in hushed tones that night on the sky platform – and of the parasitic tarry-vine that took root in its branches, slithering through the forest in search of prey to fasten onto, then drag back to feed to its host.

'So why are we stopping?' said Cade, with an uneasy feeling.

'Because this is where shriekroot grows,' Celestia said. 'It is one of the strange but beautiful things about the

Deepwoods that, even in a place of horror and death, you also find a plant of such powerful healing.' She frowned thoughtfully. 'If I'd had shriekroot back then, my mother would almost certainly still be alive . . .'

She paused for a moment, busying herself checking her backpack and equipment. Cade climbed slowly down from Burrlix's saddle.

'Celestia?' he said gently, and touched her arm.

She looked up at him. Her eyes were filled with pain. 'She was exploring the Farrow Ridges with my father,' she told him quietly. 'Climbing a cliff face – when a great slab of rock came away in her arms. She fell and landed badly. Very badly. Shattered the bone in her right leg. Father rescued her and carried her home, but . . .' Celestia shook her head. 'Infection set in. She developed a terrible raging fever and there was nothing I could do to cool it.'

Cade watched as Celestia tried her best to pull herself together. She swallowed. She took a deep breath.

'When nothing in her medicine chamber worked,' she went on at last, 'I scoured her scrolls and journals – which is where I discovered her notes on shriekroot, and how to find it. So I left my father tending to her and set off into the Western Woods.'

Celestia's voice had become so low that Cade had to strain to hear.

'But I was so young. I didn't know what I was doing . . .' She sighed. 'It took me for ever. And when I got back, she . . . my mother . . . she was dead.' She smiled weakly, blinking away a tear. 'But I'm older and wiser now,' she said. 'And I know what I'm doing. Come, and I'll show you.'

She adjusted the straps of her backpack and checked her phraxpistols. Then she turned and began to climb down the tree. Cade patted Rumblix, and the other two prowlgrins, who were visibly trembling, their whiplash tails down flat against their rumps, then he reluctantly followed Celestia.

In the gloom at the foot of the lufwood tree, he found her waiting for him. As he stepped down onto the ground, Celestia put a finger to her lips, then beckoned, and the two of them crossed the forest floor. It was soft and bouncy, like a mattress, thick with leaf-fall and needle-drop. She gestured towards the ground, then got down on her knees. Cade did the same, peering into the gloomy clearing that had opened up just ahead of them.

Cade became aware that the forest here was utterly silent and the air was still, and chill, and laced with a sour-sweet, almost metallic odour – an odour that seemed to grow more pungent with every second that passed.

At the centre of the clearing was a solitary tree, broad-trunked and with four splayed branches at the top, which divided and sub-divided into a dark-leafed crown that cast the clearing beneath it into gloom. The tree's pale bark was a mass of bumps and nodules that, in the poor light, gleamed with a red, sticky wetness, and made it look like nothing so much as diseased skin covered with blisters and weeping sores.

Cade shivered as he stared at the bloodoak. It looked, and smelled, even more horrific than he had imagined it to be from Gart Ironside's description. Cade scanned the branches of the bloodoak for the tarry-vine that he knew must be rooted there – but couldn't make out anything in the shadows. In contrast, at the base of the tree, he could clearly see a white mound of jutting ribcages, angular hip bones and skulls with empty, staring eye sockets.

Just then, from the top of the broad trunk, there was a deep belching noise, followed by an eruption of bleached white bones which flew up into the air, then cascaded down, clattering around the base of the tree on the top of the others. The pungent stench grew more intense and Cade covered his nose and mouth with his hand. He looked round at Celestia, to see that she was pointing. He followed the line of her outstretched finger and his gaze fell on a plant that sprouted from the midst of the bone mound at the base of the bloodoak.

It was tall and bushy, with a thick central stem and a mass of spiked leaves which were shiny and crimson and stark against the whiteness of the bleached bones.

It was the shriekroot.

Celestia unshouldered her longbow, then slipped her rucksack from her back and opened it.

Cade sat back on his heels and watched her in silence.

First she pulled a length of rope from the rucksack and uncoiled it, then carefully tied a noose at one end. Next, she pulled an arrow from her quiver and attached it to that end with a piece of twine. She worked methodically, her fingers quick and dextrous. When the noose was securely attached, she picked up the bow, climbed to her feet and placed the arrow in position. She raised the bow and pulled back the drawstring.

Cade saw the tight muscles in her arms knotting up both above and below her crooked elbow; saw her close one eye . . .

With a low twang, the arrow leaped from the bow and flew through the air across the clearing, taking the rope with it. It grazed the top of the spade-shaped leaves and plunged down into the bone-strewn mound on the other side. As it did so, the looped noose dropped over the plant, snagging on a couple of the lower leaves as it fell.

Celestia jiggled the end of the rope, sending ripples running down its length. The noose wavered for a moment at the spiked ends of the leaves, then fell to the earth. She tugged gently. The noose closed around the plant's stem. Then, with a swift movement, she jerked the rope hard towards her. Around the stem, the bones began to shift.

All at once, in a shower of dark red earth and white bone, the shriekroot burst from the ground. It was a mass of tubers, all of them plump and taut. For a moment, the root remained suspended in the air just above the bone mound, a thin, fibrous tendril anchoring it to the ground. Then, with a *crack*, the tendril snapped. The root leaped free, and at the same time, the air filled with a blood-curdling shriek, like the enraged, pain-filled cry of some newborn creature.

As Celestia hauled the root across the clearing towards them, Cade saw it deflate, like a bladderball with a puncture. Celestia gave a final tug, and the shriekroot came to rest at their feet. Fascinated, Cade bent down to inspect it. Close up, the mass of soft, hairless protuberances were like the appendages of something half-formed, with a misshapen head, a distended stomach and numerous weird, mutant limbs.

'The sound,' he murmured, examining the snapped tendril, from which a wisp of water vapour was rising. 'It seems to be caused by air escaping.'

But Celestia was paying him no attention. Instead, she was staring back into the clearing, her brow furrowed.

'I don't understand it,' she said. 'The tarry-vine should have reacted to the shriek of the root, lashing down from the branches to grab it. I've lost several that way,' she added as she untied the rope and placed the shriekroot in her backpack. 'But it didn't even seem to notice—'

Her words were abruptly drowned out by an agonized scream.

The next moment Cade saw the tarry-vine for the first time, and gasped. It was a broad, green, muscular-looking plant which was indeed rooted somewhere in the darkness at the top of the trunk, and hung down from the branches to the forest floor. As Cade scanned the length of the vine, he could see that it had been lying across the clearing behind the tree the whole time, still and dormant, concealed from their sight by the bloodoak's trunk. Now, as it flexed and bucked, Cade saw that the other end of the vine disappeared into the forest beyond the clearing.

As Cade watched, the bloodoak became more and more animated. Viscous red liquid oozed from the nubs on its pulsating trunk and a strange click-clacking sound came from the top of the tree where its branches met. The sound rose to a crescendo as, in a flash of green, the tip of the tarry-vine snaked into the clearing.

Cade trembled. The vine was coiled tightly around a terrified hammerhead goblin. A *wild* hammerhead goblin, judging by the black tattooed bands and spirals on his torso and the gleaming metal rings through his ears and around his neck. He looked no older than Cade himself.

Cade shrank back, his stomach churning as the goblin let out another agonized scream. It made the sounds from high up in the tree grow even louder.

The bloodoak was hungry and the tarry-vine was about to feed it.

· CHAPTER TWENTY-EIGHT ·

Celestia was running. Cade saw the glint of the knife gripped in her hand. And he too was running, swinging his phraxmusket from his shoulder and pointing it at the vine as the hapless goblin was dragged over the bone-strewn ground towards the flesh-eating tree.

But it was no good. He couldn't fire – not without the risk of hitting the hammerhead. *And* Celestia, who had leaped down onto the vine just beyond the goblin, wrestled it flat to the ground, and was hacking at it savagely with her knife. Cade dropped the phraxmusket and drew his own knife.

The vine was writhing. A thick foul-smelling liquid oozed from the lacerations that Celestia had inflicted with her blade.

Cade dropped down onto the vine, his back to the hammerhead, facing Celestia. The tarry-vine bucked, but Cade held on tight. Behind him, the vine must have tightened around the hammerhead's neck because Cade heard him gurgle and splutter, and when he glanced behind him he saw the goblin's face turning from red to purple, his eyes bulging and his swollen tongue gagging.

Celestia was still desperately hacking at the vine. There was thick slimy juice up her arms, splattered on her leather jerkin, her face, her hair. A long jagged rip in the green skin gaped, but the tough sinews beneath seemed resistant to the knife blows. Writhing and pulsating with a horrible energy, the tarry-vine pulled all three of them towards the bloodoak, which was clacking and slurping and spitting out gobs of bloodflecked saliva.

They were being dragged over the bone mound at the base of the tree now. With immense strength, the tarry-vine reared up into the air.

Cade's feet left the ground. He clung onto the vine with one hand while stabbing down with the other. Celestia lost her grip and was thrown clear, tumbling back and slamming down on the bone mound. The rank smell of decay intensified and, looking down, Cade saw that he and the hammerhead were being pulled towards the bloodoak's gaping mouth.

Gleaming ridges of woody gum flexed and gurned. Like the iris of a monstrous eye, the mouth slammed shut then opened up again to reveal row upon circular row of triangular yellow teeth that glinted and clacked and slavered. And below the mandibles, deep inside the trunk itself, a dark, convulsing tunnel opened that led down into the bowels of the bloodoak.

Cade gagged emptily as the stench billowing from that black pit wrapped itself around him. He turned away. Below, Celestia had her phraxpistols in her hands. She aimed and fired.

The leadwood bullets sliced through the vine's tendons and bloodsap-vessels, which exploded in red spray, and with a wet, splintering crack the vine finally snapped, sending Cade and the hammerhead tumbling back down to the ground.

'Quick!' Celestia cried urgently. 'We've got to get him out of here!'

Cade frowned. The vine was severed. Surely there was time to catch their breath . . .

But Celestia, already tugging fiercely at the truncated length of vine that encircled the hammerhead's motion-less body, was insistent.

'Come *on!*' she shouted.

Cade joined her and between them they managed to loosen the hold of the tarry-vine and pull the hammer-head free. The heavy coils slumped to one side. The young hammerhead was pale now, his black tattoos stark against the waxen skin. Pale and still. Cade couldn't tell if he was even breathing – and Celestia was in too much of a hurry to check.

Instead, she took hold of him under the arms, shouting at Cade to take him by the legs. Together they carried him back across the clearing, away from the bloodoak. They were halfway to the lufwood tree when Cade became aware of something moving behind him.

There was a slithering noise. There were soft, slurpy popping sounds, coming one after the other . . .

Cade turned.

From the oozing end of the severed vine, five new vines had burst out, emerald green and whip-thin. They rose up, swaying, lurching, and growing thicker with every passing second. Their bright green tips quivered. There was another *pop*, then another, and two more vines burst out from the congealed stump; then two more . . .

Suddenly the new vines hurtled towards them, flailing like a cat o' nine tails.

Cade let go of the hammerhead's legs, picked up the phraxmusket he'd dropped earlier and cocked the trigger. Closing his eyes, he blasted the writhing mass of vines. Foul-smelling sap flew in all directions, covering him in warm, fetid wetness. Opening his eyes, he saw the shattered vines twitching at his feet. In a few moments, he realized now, they would regenerate into dozens of new shoots.

He turned and, together with Celestia, picked the hammerhead up and fled full pelt into the depths of the forest.

· CHAPTER TWENTY-NINE ·

Celestia and Cade plunged deeper into the trees, supporting the hammerhead goblin between them. Weaving in and out of the gnarled trunks, skirting thickets and undergrowth and ducking beneath low branches, they half ran, half stumbled through the Western Woods and away from the bloodoak glade.

Finally they stopped, and as Cade fought to catch his breath, Celestia looked up at the treetops and whistled. In answer, moments later, the prowlgrins came bounding down through the branches and landed, one after the other, on the forest floor before them.

Calix and Burrlix observed the hammerhead goblin, their flared nostrils twitching suspiciously, but Rumblix was less restrained. With a high-pitched yelp, he launched himself at the goblin who, still weak and dazed, lost his balance and landed heavily on his back. Rumblix dropped down onto his chest. His mouth opened and, for a terrible moment, Cade could only stand and stare as the prowlgrin bared his teeth.

But instead of savaging the goblin, Rumblix stuck out his long prehensile tongue and began licking at the hammerhead. At his shoulders and neck; his exposed chest. Under his arms. The goblin squirmed helplessly, convulsing with laughter as the little prowlgrin tickled him.

'Stop! Stop!' he spluttered.

Grinning himself, Cade pulled Rumblix off and held his halter while the hammerhead goblin climbed unsteadily to his feet. He looked down and wiped the slobber from his skin, then looked up at Cade. His face, with its broad brow, wide-set eyes and sweeping ears, grew more serious.

'You saved Teeg,' he said formally, touching one fist to his chest. 'From the strangle-vine. Teeg is grateful.' He crouched down before the prowlgrin pup, who was straining in Cade's grip. 'Teeg tastes good?' he asked, his eyes sparkling with amusement. He returned his gaze to Cade. 'Hammelhorn grease,' he said, tracing his fingers over his gleaming skin. 'Keeps cold out.' He smiled a broad, chisel-toothed grin. 'Your branch-leaper likes the taste.'

'Are you all right?' Cade asked.

'Teeg is unhurt,' the goblin said with a nod. 'Teeg was scouting ahead for the tribe. The Shadow Clan of the High Valley Nation . . . Teeg was careless.'

The hammerhead youth was taller than him, his build more muscular, and up close Cade could make out the markings on the goblin's face and arms. There were ironwood pines, curved cloud shapes and thin spidery black lines that curled over his brow ridge and round his upper arms.

Hammerhead goblins had always intrigued Cade. Back in Great Glade, hammerheads were used as muscle. Fierce, loyal and formidable fighters, they often became guards or soldiers – or skymarshals on board the skytaverns, Cade recalled, his stomach churning at the memory of how close he'd come to being skyfired by the hammerhead skymarshal on the *Xanth Filatine*.

This savage young hammerhead wore a leather jerkin and breeches, and his broad muscular feet were bare. On his brow, over each wide-spaced eye, he wore a ring, and several

more banded his neck. And when Cade breathed in, his nose was filled with the odour of the hammelhorn grease smeared over the hammerhead's face and arms. It smelled of stale meat and woodsmoke, and something else – something savage and untamed. Something far removed from the world of Great Glade with its stilthouse factories, academies and skytaverns. Cade's world. It smelled of the Deepwoods.

'Father,' said Teeg. He was looking past Cade and Celestia. 'These two heavy-foots saved Teeg from the strangle-vine.'

Cade turned and followed Teeg's gaze.

Before them stood the imposing figure of an adult hammerhead goblin. He was tall and heavily muscled, tattooed, ringed and coated with gleaming grease. He had a large backpack strapped to his broad shoulders and held a vicious-looking blackwood spear in one massive hand. He had approached them so silently that neither Cade nor Celestia had heard him, and the hammelhorn grease had masked his smell from the prowlgrins.

'Heavy-foots,' said the hammerhead, his broad-spaced eyes turning to Cade and Celestia. 'So far from the great water?'

As he spoke, Cade became aware that they were now surrounded by hammerheads, a dozen or so in number. They stood in a circle where, seconds before, there had been no one. Some, like Teeg's father, carried blackwood spears. Others bore bone-handled knives, or studded cudgels, or carved copperwood bows, the drawstrings loaded with stone-tipped arrows and pulled back taut. All of them carried heavily laden backpacks on their shoulders.

'We were foraging,' Celestia said, 'when we saw your son snared by the tarry . . . the strangle-vine—'

'Chert know you,' the hammerhead interrupted her. 'You are daughter of the heavy-foot from the cabin in the air.'

'Yes,' said Celestia, 'but how? I've never seen you before.'

'You don't see the clan, but the clan see you. Many times,' he added. 'On your branch-leaper in the forest.'

The hammerhead stepped forward and held out his huge hand. 'Chert of the Shadow Clan thanks you. Both of you.'

Celestia and Cade shook his hand in turn.

'Now,' he went on, 'you must make camp with the Shadow Clan.'

'We'd love to,' Celestia said, 'wouldn't we, Cade?'

Cade nodded.

The hammerheads had lowered their weapons, but their brutal, elongated faces showed no emotion. Chert and Teeg turned away and started walking, and Cade and Celestia followed, leading their prowlgrins by the reins.

Around them, the other hammerhead goblins spread out and kept pace, but so silently that Cade had to keep looking right and left to make sure they were still there. What was more, the tattoos on their heads and arms, together with the muted colours of their clothes and backpacks, meant that they blended into the dappled woods perfectly – so perfectly, in fact, that it was only when they stopped walking about half an hour later that Cade realized the twelve hammerheads had been noiselessly joined by many more.

Forty or so of them, Cade guessed as they gathered silently around Chert and his warriors on the edge of a small glade. Males and females. Young and old. All of them tattooed and ringed, and all of them carrying curious rolled-up bundles on their backs.

A hammerhead youth, similar in age to Teeg, was waiting for them in the centre of the clearing. His hands were cupped to his mouth and he was imitating the low, hollow cough of a fromp. It was this call, Cade realized, that the clan had been following. With their remarkable hearing, they had picked out the call of their scout from amid the clamour of screeching, whistling and howling of the forest creatures and made their way to him.

The glade they found themselves in was pale green and grey, and shot with shadows cast by the slender willoak saplings that grew there. It was sheltered from the wind by a stand of massive ironwood pines on the far side, and smelled of the nibblick and woodthyme which grew in dense clumps at the centre.

Chert strode over to the scout and laid a hand on his shoulder, nodding appreciatively before turning to the rest of the clan and giving a three-fingered signal.

In response, the tribe silently split into three groups and set to work. And as Cade and Celestia watched, the females and young'uns unrolled the bundles they had been carrying, which revealed themselves to be lengths of woven wicker matting.

The older males and the youths pulled the large packs from their shoulders and began methodically taking out their contents: machetes, scythes, jag-blade knives, as well as small cooking pots and various utensils for cutting, chopping, grating and skewering. Then, as the females tied the wicker matting together with strips of tilder leather, the males cut down a number of the willoak saplings and began constructing a large frame.

The third group, the hammerhead warriors – including Chert and his son, Teeg – laid down their backpacks and slipped away into the forest.

Meanwhile, in the clearing, in a matter of minutes, the older males had tied the saplings together to form a vast cone onto which the females attached the woven matting. Then, coming together, they all raised the wickerwork cone upright and hammered in copperwood staves around its base to anchor it.

Cade stepped back, wide-eyed with astonishment. From seemingly nowhere, and in almost total silence, a mighty hive tower had just risen in the centre of the clearing. The hammerheads then spread out. The females gathered kindling and firewood from around the fringes of the clearing, as well as bunches of the nibblick and woodthyme. The young'uns climbed up into the iron-wood pines, leather water-gourds on their backs. Up high, they selected those great hanging pine cones that had

collected rainwater in their upturned seedpods the night before, tipped them up and carefully poured the water into their gourds.

Weighed down by the various things they had gathered, the hammerheads began filing into the hive tower, brushing past the tilder hide that served as a door – and leaving Cade, Celestia and the prowlgrins standing alone outside. Evening was falling, with the shadows lengthening across the glade. Above their heads, wisps of smoke emerged from the triangular openings at the top of the hive tower.

'It's incredible,' said Celestia. 'I've seen evidence of hammerhead camps before. Cut saplings strewn about; circles of blackened stones from the campfires they set.' She shook her head. 'But to see an actual hive tower being built . . .'

Just then, Cade became aware of movement at the edge of the clearing, and turned to see the returning hammerhead warriors step out of the shadowy depths of the forest. Hanging upside down on a pole carried between them was a heavy-set creature, the size of a large bull hammelhorn and almost as shaggy. A single arrow had pierced its chest.

'It's a giant quarm,' said Celestia. 'I've never eaten quarm meat before.' She frowned. 'No idea what it'll taste like.'

'Looks like we're about to find out,' said Cade as the hammerheads placed the creature on the ground and began to skin it expertly with razor-sharp knives.

Rumblix, Burrlix and Calix bounded over to the hammerhead warriors, their tongues lolling eagerly from their mouths as they watched the goblins butcher the quarm. Meanwhile, Chert and Teeg had crossed the glade and greeted Celestia and Cade.

'Thank you for your patience,' Chert was saying. 'The hive tower is now prepared.' He led Cade and Celestia towards the entrance and pulled the tilder-hide curtain aside.

Although Cade had watched everything that had taken place, he still found it difficult to take in the scene before him as he stepped inside. His own modest little cabin had taken weeks to complete. In contrast, the hive tower had been constructed in minutes. It was, however, magnificent.

Dozens of tilder hides had been spread out upon the floor, at the centre of which a great fire blazed. A score of small pots nestled among its burning logs. Some of them were filled with water which was already coming to the boil, others contained hammelhorn grease that hissed and spat in readiness for the meat of the giant quarm being butchered outside, while others bubbled and plopped as a gruel of ground gladebarley and wood-thyme slowly heated.

The flames from the fire flickered on the inside of the woven matting walls, on the burnished pots, and in the eyes of each and every hammerhead goblin who, stopping whatever they were doing, turned to look at Cade and Celestia as they entered.

'Sit,' said Chert, gesturing towards two hides laid out close to the fire.

They took their places, and Chert sat down next to them. The other hammerheads returned to their chores: cooking the meat as it was carried into the tower, sharpening their weapons, mending their backpacks . . .

'Soon, the clan shall eat,' Chert told them. 'But first Teeg must gain his mark.'

Cade and Celestia turned to see the young hammer-head kneeling on a tilder hide on the other side of the fire, the firelight gleaming on his sweat-covered brow. Sitting cross-legged on the floor beside him was an older hammerhead, his brow creased with concentration. He held a needle-thin splinter of ironwood in his hand, which, as Cade and Celestia watched, he dipped into one of the two bowls which lay by his side. It contained a thick black liquid. When the pointed end of the splinter was covered, he reached up and punctured Teeg's skin with it, at the top of his right arm. Again and again, he repeated the action – until at last, sitting back, he observed his handiwork through narrowed eyes.

'The mark is done,' he announced.

Setting the splinter aside, he plunged his fingers into the second bowl, then smeared hammelhorn grease over Teeg's arm.

Teeg peered down, his eyes glinting with excitement, then climbed to his feet. He walked round the side of the fire and proudly showed Cade and Celestia his new tattoo – a circle of sharp-looking triangles, intersected by a wavy line. Cade recognized it at once as a representation of the bloodoak and tarry-vine.

'Every mark has its meaning,' Chert said as he observed the fascination in Cade and Celestia's eyes. He looked down at his own arms and touched a row of five ironwood pines, most with ten branches, one with only two. 'These trees are the number of years Chert has lived. These stars, the place of Chert's birth. These clouds, the ancestors . . .' He pulled open the front of his jerkin and tapped the inked spearheads and arrows that decorated his chest. 'These are battles,' he explained. 'The Shadow Clan has fought many.'

Cade nodded, the blood draining from his face. These Deepwoods hammerheads were warriors. Fierce and warlike. And the evidence was written on their bodies.

Chert reached up and indicated the tattoo of the bloodoak symbol on his son's arm. On either side of it were two stick figures. 'These marks are Cade and Celestia,' he said. 'Teeg came face to face with the tree of blood. And survived.' He tilted his angular head to one side, returning his gaze to Cade and Celestia. 'Teeg will not forget.' He turned to his son. 'Teeg?'

The young hammerhead goblin bowed his head, then looked at the two of them. He clenched his fist and pressed it to his chest.

'Teeg will not forget,' he said.

Then he turned and went over to the fire, returning moments later with a wooden platter heaped high with pieces of sizzling meat, which he served to Celestia. After that, he served Cade, then Chert. And the fourth time he returned, he sat down with a platter for himself.

Cade bit into a piece of roasted quarm and began to chew. The flavour was pungent and bitter, with an intense cloying texture that reminded Cade of brindled curds.

'The meat of the mighty tree-hugger is good?' asked Teeg, looking at Cade, then Celestia, and back again. Cade chewed and chewed, then with some difficulty swallowed. Beside him, Celestia smiled valiantly as she did the same.

'Delicious,' she lied.

'Meat tough,' nodded Teeg solemnly. 'Good for jaw muscles.'

Cade took another piece out of politeness, then passed his platter to a group of young'uns on the tilder hide beside him, and was relieved when they tucked into the meat hungrily.

'Celestia's father goes into the caverns of the great waters,' said Chert, leaning forward and staring intently at Celestia. 'Chert has seen.' He nodded gravely. 'The white trogs will be angry . . .'

Cade and Celestia exchanged glances. The white trogs. The fearsome tribe rumoured to live deep underground. Gart Ironside had mentioned them, and so had Celestia's father.

'White trogs,' said Celestia, putting back a piece of quarm and pushing away the platter. 'Have you seen them?'

Chert shook his head slowly, his brow-rings glinting in the firelight as he did so.

The low chatter of voices had suddenly stilled.

'No,' Chert said. 'The clans of the hammerhead nations – the High Valley, the Low Valley, the Western Peaks . . .' He paused. 'No clans venture into the caverns.'

'Why not?' asked Celestia, and Cade could hear a tremor in her voice.

Chert reached out a hand and beckoned to an old hammerhead who sat listening on the other side of the fire. The hammerhead climbed to his feet and approached them. He was stooped with age, but still muscular and powerful-looking. His face and arms were covered in tattoos. As he reached them, the old

hammerhead pulled open his leather tunic to reveal an image of a creature, fanged and clawed, devouring a stick-like figure. At its feet were several more figures, twisted and dismembered.

'Brack was just a young'un,' the old hammerhead said, 'when the white trogs caught Brack's family in the caverns.' His wide-spaced eyes widened as he tapped the tattoo with a wizened finger. 'Brack ran. Brack did not look back.'

· CHAPTER THIRTY ·

Celestia was the first to wake the following morning, a cold wind plucking at her clothes and ruffling her hair. She opened her eyes . . .

'Cade!' she exclaimed.

Cade started to wakefulness. He looked about him, bleary-eyed, unable at first to make sense of his surroundings. The pair of them were lying on their blankets on the soft grass in the centre of the deserted forest glade. Around them lay willoak saplings strewn haphazardly beside the dark-singed circle where the fire had been.

'They've gone,' Celestia was saying. 'The Shadow Clan. Upped and moved on . . .' She shook her head in wonder. 'Like shadows.'

Apart from the saplings and the scorched circle, everything had gone from the clearing. The woven matting walls. The animal hides. The pots and pans . . .

Cade climbed to his feet. He yawned, stretched. Rubbed his eyes. And it was then that his gaze fell on something glinting in the grass at his feet.

It was a bronze ring.

It had been attached to a leather thong and placed close to where his head had been. There was a second ring beside Celestia's backpack, which she'd used as a pillow. Celestia picked up the ring and put it round her neck, and Cade did the same with his.

She smiled. 'We're honorary hammerheads now,' she said.

Just then there was a yelping bark, followed by a snort, as the three prowlgrins came bounding across the clearing towards them.

'Rumblix!' said Cade as the pup leaped up into his arms. 'Whoa! You seem to be getting heavier by the day!'

'Looks like our "branch-leapers" had a feast of their own last night,' Celestia observed, patting Burrlix and Calix and adjusting their bridles and saddles. 'Fresh quarm offal, I'd say.'

Cade shuddered as he remembered the bitter taste of the quarm meat. Gathering up his phraxmusket, canteen and bedroll, Cade climbed into Burrlix's saddle. They leaped up to the treetops and set off across the forest canopy until the glittering waters of the Farrow Lake came into view.

'Breakfast at my house?' Cade called to Celestia.

'I'll race you,' she called back, and twitched Calix's reins.

With the riders on their backs, the prowlgrins sped through the forest, soaring effortlessly from branch to branch, then galloped along the lakeside so fast that Cade had to hold on for all he was worth, with Rumblix bounding along at his side.

As they rounded a bend where a spur of rock jutted out into the lake, Cade saw the roof of his cabin far ahead, glinting in the early morning sunshine. Exhilarated by the speed he was going, he pressed his heels into Burrlix's flanks – and the prowlgrin galloped even faster.

'Not bad, city boy!' Celestia called across as she drew alongside him. Then she flicked the reins and sped past. 'But not quite good enough!' her voice floated back.

Moments later, the pair of them arrived at the jetty,

Celestia first, but Cade close behind. He reached down and patted Burrlix, who was snorting and huffing, and wondered if he'd ever be able to ride as well as this beautiful green-eyed girl.

Steam was rising up from the prowlgrins' wet fur; white plumes of breath billowed out from their gaping mouths. Celestia slipped down from the saddle and let go of Calix's bridle, and the prowlgrin trotted down to the water's edge and began lapping up the cool lake water. Rumblix joined him. And when Cade had dismounted, so did Burrlix. Then all three of them plunged deep into the lake. Calix and Burrlix took in water through their mouths and expelled it from the nostrils at the tops of their heads. Rumblix copied them eagerly, sending two jets of water shooting high up into the air and making Cade and Celestia laugh.

Leaving the three prowlgrins to play, Celestia and Cade headed up the jetty towards the cabin. They climbed the stairs, and Cade was just pushing open the cabin door when a sound from below the wooden veranda stopped him in his tracks.

It was a soft groan. Celestia looked around.

'Did you hear that?' said Cade.

The noise came again, low, breathy, filled with pain. Celestia cocked her head to one side, and when it happened a third time, she stared at the boards beneath her feet.

'It's coming from below the cabin,' she said, grabbing the tallow lamp from the table.

The pair of them hurried down the steps, Cade pulling his phraxmusket from his shoulders as he went. Stooping down, they peered into the shadows underneath the veranda.

'There's something there,' Celestia whispered.

Cade squinted. She was right. Black against the gloom was something large and slumped over on its side. Cade's heart gave a lurch as he realized that he knew what it was. He gripped the phraxmusket tightly, his finger on the trigger.

'It's injured, whatever it is,' said Celestia. She pulled a couple of fire-flints from her pocket, lit the lamp and held it up.

The creature was curled up, its long arms wrapped around its chest. The large misshapen head, with its crooked jaw and thick skull ridge, was twisted round at an awkward angle, and when the light fell upon it, the tiny deep-set eyes opened and stared back at Cade and Celestia, pain-filled and pleading.

'Oh, you poor, poor thing,' Celestia whispered softly, reaching out and stroking the side of the creature's great lumpen face. 'Whatever's happened to you?'

She raised the lamp and leaned forward.

'Earth and sky!' she exclaimed.

The creature's right leg was swollen and discoloured. Down near the ankle, there was a thin, suppurating wound, inflamed and raw-looking. Celestia crouched down lower, holding the lamp above her head and inspected the wound more closely. The light glinted on

a twist of wire that was poking out from the side of the leg, and when she placed the lamp down on the ground, a short length of wood, and a piece of ragged-ended rope could be seen, half embedded in the infected wound.

'A snare,' said Celestia, straightening up as far as the low ceiling of the overhead veranda allowed. She shook her head. 'Judging by the infection, this happened some time ago.'

Cade swallowed. 'Six weeks,' he breathed.

Celestia turned to him. 'You know about this?' she said.

'It . . . it's my snare,' he said.

'Your snare?' Celestia sounded shocked.

'I set it when I first arrived here,' he explained, his voice low and emotionless. 'I . . . I was hoping to catch something to eat. A weezit maybe. Or one of those plump lakefowl. I heard the trap being sprung, but when I got there, it had gone. The tether rope had been torn apart . . .' He frowned, rubbed his jaw thoughtfully. 'Now it all makes sense . . . Something ransacked my camp soon afterwards. And then, on the night I fell ill, I saw a hideous creature standing on the edge of the forest. I thought – hoped – it was just the fever making me see things . . .' He looked up into Celestia's piercing green eyes. 'But now I realize that it was real and just needed help.' He hesitated. 'I had no idea.'

For a moment, Celestia simply stared back at him. Then her expression softened. 'You weren't to know,' she said. 'But setting snares isn't my way. I believe in seeing what I hunt and ensuring it doesn't suffer.'

Cade's face reddened and he put down the phrax-musket. 'Can you help it, Celestia?' he asked.

'The infection's serious,' she said, turning back to the creature. 'But I'll do my best.' She took off her backpack and opened it. 'I'm going to need a bowl and a pair of pliers,' she said.

Cade ran up the steps and into the cabin. He grabbed a bowl from the shelf, then disappeared into the store-room to look for the pair of pliers. Moments later, he was back beneath the veranda, the bowl in one hand and the pliers – which, like all the other tools, had been given to him by Gart Ironside – in the other. He held them up.

'These are what I used to make the snare in the first place,' he said.

'Good, good,' said Celestia briskly. She took the bowl from him and put into it a spoonful of salve, some chopped herbs and crushed berries, and several drops of a green liquid from a vial, then stirred the mixture vigorously. 'I'm making a poultice,' she explained.

Pungent smells filled the air: hyleberry, lakebane, deadwort, woodcamphor . . .

When she was happy that the ingredients were well enough mixed, she began applying the poultice. Cade watched as she dipped her hand in the bowl and scooped out a dollop of the pale green salve. She let it drop down onto the inflamed leg. The creature squirmed and let out a weak cry. But moments later, as the numbing tinctures and herbs started to work, it fell still. Celestia waited a moment longer, then reached out and began smoothing the poultice over the infected area of the leg.

Cade was impressed.

'Easy now,' she said softly. 'This should take the pain away . . .'

A thick coating of the poultice slowly built up over the lower leg as Celestia kept rubbing more in. Gently. Evenly. The creature seemed to relax, its breathing coming ever deeper and easier.

'That's the way,' she kept saying. 'That's the way.' Then she turned to Cade. 'I'll keep going,' she said. 'You cut the snare wire.'

Cade nodded. He gripped the pliers, realizing that his hand was shaking. He moved forward on his knees and took hold of the twist of wire that stuck out from the swollen flesh. The creature jerked violently, but Celestia kept stroking and whispering, and it fell still once more. Cade inserted the ends of the pliers between the wire and the skin, which was burning hot against the back of his fingers. He squeezed the handles of the pliers.

There was a click.

'That's the way,' said Celestia. She took the last of the poultice from the bowl and rubbed it in with the rest, still whispering softly, mesmerically.

Cade tugged at the broken wire. At first nothing happened. He placed the pliers aside, then pulled a little harder, using both hands. With a squelching sound and a gush of oozing pus that made him feel sick, the wire came free. Cade moved his hand round the leg until he felt the rope and the wooden stake, then slowly, gently, pulled them free as well.

'Well done, Cade,' Celestia told him. 'Now, you keep rubbing the poultice in while I prepare the shriekroot.'

'The shriekroot?' said Cade.

'The poultice is taking away the pain,' said Celestia, removing the monstrous-looking root from her backpack, 'but with an infection this bad, only shriekroot can save its life.'

Celestia drew her knife from her belt, cut off one of the larger nodules of shriekroot, and carefully peeled its skin to reveal the fibrous pulp inside. Then, having removed the glass from the lantern, she took the pliers from Cade and used them to pick up the piece of glistening shriekroot, which she held over the naked flame.

The root pulp began to sizzle, then glow a deep, pulsating red. It gave off wisps of rich aromatic smoke. Celestia reached out and stroked the underside of creature's chin. The creature opened its mouth. Huge angular fangs glinted as Celestia placed the red smoking ember of shriekroot on the creature's tongue and closed its mouth again.

'That's the way,' she said, and kept stroking under its chin until it swallowed.

Cade watched, fascinated, as the veins beneath the creature's skin began to glow red, standing out in a spreading tracery against the grey pallor of its skin. The red lines coursed throughout the creature's body until they reached the infected ankle, which glowed, first dark purple, then red, then a yellow tinged with white before fading. Beneath his fingers, Cade felt the heat leave the wound.

The creature turned its monstrous head towards Cade, and he found himself looking into its small dark eyes. Its lips parted into a twisted grimace that seemed to pass for a smile, and a sound, grumbling and raw, emerged from the back of its throat.

'Master.'

· CHAPTER THIRTY-ONE ·

The creature slept for the rest of the day. Its soft snoring blended in with the gentle lapping of the lake water against the stone jetty.

Before she'd left that morning, Celestia had helped Cade cut bundles of meadowgrass for the creature's bedding, which they had laid down beneath the veranda, together with a bucket of lake water and a pot of glade-barley porridge. Until they could work out what sort of creature this was, she had thought it best to offer it only the simplest of food.

Celestia had set off just before midday. Cade had waved her off, with Rumblix yelping and chittering mournfully from his perch on the veranda rail as he watched Burrlix and Calix gallop away. Then Cade had spent the afternoon scything weeds and digging up stones in the meadowland behind the cabin, in an attempt to clear a plot to begin planting a vegetable garden.

Every so often, as he strained to move stubborn boulders embedded in the rich earth, he would glance back at the cabin. Beside him, Rumblix, his nostrils twitching, did the same. In the shadow beneath the veranda, nothing stirred.

At last, having made painfully slow progress, Cade abandoned his stone-clearing efforts for the day and walked back to the cabin. The sun had set and a thin mist hung over the still lake. Now and again, at various points, Cade saw the lake dimple as the lakefish rose to feed. It was as though a pin had pricked the water, and circles spread out – circles that intersected with other circles before flattening out and disappearing.

Cade propped up his tools – spade, pickaxe, rock-hammer and scythe – against one of the ironwood pillars of the veranda, then walked to the end of the rock jetty. It was quiet; that brief, peaceful moment before dusk when the creatures of the day had retired and the creatures of the night were yet to stir. Cade could hear the soft snoring of the creature behind him, and far in the distance, a yodelling cry that echoed from the forest ridges somewhere beyond the Five Falls. He sat down wearily on the edge of the jetty and closed his eyes.

The call was melodious and resonant, and filled with a deep longing that, as he listened, made Cade feel inexplicably sad inside. It was the yodelling cry of a lonely banderbear calling out across the Deepwoods, though, it seemed to Cade, with little hope of a reply.

He opened his eyes and gazed at the beautiful Five

251

Falls in the distance, their waters glistening in the evening light. Then he climbed to his feet and turned back to the cabin, only to stop in his tracks.

The creature had awoken and emerged from beneath the veranda. It was sitting on its haunches with its back to Cade. The bucket was empty and lying on its side next to an ironwood pillar, but the pot of porridge hadn't been touched. Instead, the creature was hunched over a great bundle of meadowgrass, which it seemed to be munching its way through.

At that moment, from overhead, Cade heard a soft, chugging sound and, looking up, he saw a familiar-looking vessel approaching through the evening sky. Steam billowing from its funnel, the small phraxlighter drew to a halt and hovered above Cade. Then Gart Ironside's head appeared over the side, followed closely by the barrel of a phraxpistol, which was aimed over Cade's shoulder at the veranda.

'Need some help, neighbour?' Gart Ironside called down to Cade.

'No, no,' said Cade hastily, keeping his voice down so as not to alarm the creature. 'It's all right, Gart. Everything's fine . . .' He glanced back at the creature, which was so intent on its banquet of meadowgrass that it hadn't noticed the phraxlighter.

'Well, if you're sure,' Gart replied.

The phraxlighter hissed and hummed as Gart steered the vessel over the jetty and brought it down to hover above the veranda. Gart stepped down onto the boards,

gripping the end of a tolley rope, which he tied to the veranda's wooden rails.

Cade walked back along the jetty and approached the steps of the veranda. The creature looked up and, as Cade passed, it flinched as though expecting a blow. Despite the fading light, up close, Cade could clearly see an array of welts and raised ridges on the creature's back.

'That's an interesting guest you have there, Cade, my lad,' said Gart Ironside, greeting him at the top of the veranda. 'And it's been many years since I've seen anything like it.'

From behind Cade, Rumblix jumped up onto the veranda in one leap and landed on the balustrade, his tongue lolling out of the side of his mouth. Gart ruffled the prowlgrin pup's fur with one hand, and Cade saw that he still held the phraxpistol in the other.

Gart smiled apologetically. 'Forgive me, Cade. But I always carry a loaded pistol in my hand when I'm down here, away from my platform – which, I don't need to tell you, isn't very often—'

'You know what this creature is?' interrupted Cade. 'Celestia and I didn't. She was going to ask her father.'

Gart laughed. 'So you've made friends with the old explorer's daughter, have you?' he said. 'And built yourself a cabin, I see.'

'Thorne Lammergyre helped me,' Cade said.

'The fisher goblin from the hive hut on the west shore,' said Gart approvingly. 'Well, you've certainly settled down nicely. I needn't have worried about you, Cade, lad. And in answer to your question, yes, I do know what that creature is.'

Gart looked down at the creature, which had turned back to the meadowgrass and was grazing contentedly.

'It is a creature from the Nightwoods.'

Cade frowned. He had heard of the Nightwoods. They lay far to the west, between the Deepwoods and the waif city of Riverrise. It was an area where the forests were in perpetual darkness and were roamed by telepathic waifs, red and black dwarves and strange, half-formed giants that had yet to be named.

'That is a . . . a nameless one?' said Cade, wide-eyed.

Gart nodded. 'Not very old, judging by its size,' he

said. 'But it'll grow bigger. How big is anyone's guess. And as to what it'll end up looking like, who knows?' The pilot shrugged. 'What you've got to understand, Cade, is that all life in the Edge comes from the Riverrise spring, but the life seeded by the spring in the Nightwoods is different to that which was seeded in the Deepwoods. Without light, those seeds grew in strange ways. Waifs. Dwarves. And giants like this nameless one – they live and die in the Nightwoods, and no Deepwoods scholars or librarians have ever categorized them. It was only when trade routes were opened up to Riverrise that they were even discovered.'

Cade looked back down at the creature with its slumped shoulders, scarred back and mouth full of meadowgrass. Somehow, it seemed less monstrous to him now.

'You've heard of the Forest of Thorns, and the tunnel that leads through it to the city of Riverrise, I suppose,' Gart continued.

'Yes. Thorn Harbour,' said Cade. 'It's where the sky-taverns dock, isn't it?'

Gart nodded. 'But did you know that Thorn Harbour and the tunnel were built by the red and black dwarves, small, vicious, beak-mouthed goblins?' He paused. 'Or rather, by the nameless ones they enslaved.'

Cade drew a sharp intake of breath and shook his head. 'It spoke,' he said quietly. 'It called me "master".'

'The slavery of nameless ones was abolished when Riverrise became a free city,' Gart went on. 'But in parts of the Nightwoods, it still flourishes. I'm guessing that

this one must have escaped from its captors and somehow found its way here . . .'

'To me,' said Cade.

The nameless one finished the meadowgrass, then
turned and retreated back into the shadows beneath the
veranda. Cade smiled as the sound of soft snoring rose
up through the boards beneath their feet.

He had been lucky, he realized. Gart Ironside had
lent him tools. Thorne Lammergyre had fed him lakefish
and helped him build a cabin. And Celestia . . . She had
tended to him when he'd fallen sick, and then befriended
him and shown him the wonders of the Western Woods.
His friends had helped, tended and looked out for
him. Now Cade had the chance to do the same for this
nameless one.

'Thank you, Gart,' said Cade, turning to the pilot.

'What for?' said Gart.

'Everything you've done for me,' Cade said warmly.
'And now you've come for your tools and your musket
. . . I've had them too long, but they've been so useful.'
He smiled. 'I'm sure Celestia and Thorne can help me
find more . . .'

'No, no,' laughed Gart, holstering his phraxpistol at
last, and shaking Cade by the hand. 'I haven't come for
those. In fact, keep them, Cade, and with my best wishes.
No, I've come to say goodbye.'

'Goodbye?' said Cade. 'But why? Where are you going?'

'Let's just say I've chanced upon a bit of good fortune up there in the ridges above the falls.' Gart grinned

delightedly. 'And I'm off to Great Glade to sell it to the highest bidder, pay off my debts . . . No more sky platform in the middle of nowhere for me. It's back to the big steam. The phraxlighter's packed and ready to go.' His blue eyes gleamed. 'Wish me luck, Cade.'

'Of course,' said Cade. 'Good luck, Gart. But what is it? What have you found?'

Gart looked around as if afraid they might be overheard and Cade saw his hand stray to the phraxpistol holstered at his belt. Then he smiled again.

'Call me a cautious old fool, but until I get to Great Glade and shake a rich merchant by the hand, I'll just call my discovery' – he strolled over to the phraxlighter and climbed aboard – 'the nameless *thing*.'

· CHAPTER THIRTY-TWO ·

Cade awoke shortly after sunrise. He sat up and looked out of the window. The sky was cloudless and the sun shone down on the Farrow Lake, making its choppy waters glisten and glitter. In the distance the Five Falls stood out against the grey cliff face of the Farrow Ridge, stark white columns of water thundering down into the dark depths of the lake beneath.

Cade stretched lazily. His shoulders and arms felt stiff from his exertions of the day before, shifting rocks from the plot in the meadowlands behind the cabin. Despite all his hard work, he realized, getting out of bed, the ground looked barely touched.

But today was a new day, Cade told himself, and he would do better.

Rumblix stirred as Cade washed and dressed, and watched him sleepily through one eye as he fried a couple of gladefowl eggs in a skillet over the fire, and ate them with a slice of barleybread he'd baked in his simple oven, cut out of the cliff-face wall beside the fireplace.

Cade collected his tools from the storeroom – the spade, pickaxe and rockhammer – crossed the cabin and opened the door.

'Coming, boy?' he asked, pausing in the doorway.

From his perch at the end of the hammock, Rumblix sighed, closed his eye and went back to sleep.

Cade shrugged, smiled and stepped out of the cabin, leaving the door ajar, then descended the stairs to the rock jetty. At the bottom, he paused to glance underneath the veranda. The nameless one was awake and eating the last of its meadowgrass bedding. It looked up, and their eyes met.

'Enjoying your breakfast, I see,' said Cade.

The nameless one lowered its gaze. It balled up another wad of grass and flowers and pushed it into its mouth. Cade pointed towards the meadowlands.

'There's plenty more where that came from just over there,' he said.

Around the rectangle of land he'd marked out by scything down the grass, thick lush meadow pasture shimmered in the breeze. If he could just get rid of the rocks that littered the rich dark earth, he could dig the soil and sow neat rows of vegetables. Blue cabbages and polderbeets. Ochre-beans and glimmer-onions . . .

Taking the pickaxe in his hands, Cade strode across the meadowlands to his vegetable garden and started digging. He drove the sharp head of the pick into the ground next to a rock, levered it out, then tossed it to one side. He moved on, and did the same with another rock. Then another. He straightened up, leaned against the pickaxe and looked around. He had barely scratched the surface.

With a sigh, Cade took up the pickaxe again. He removed a couple more rocks. The sun rose higher and he took off his jacket, then his shirt, and continued working.

The next rock he came to looked manageable enough to start with, just a small nub of stone sticking up above the ground. But when he tried to lever it out of the earth, he discovered that it was much bigger, and went far deeper, than he'd thought. He dug down, gradually exposing more and more of the boulder. Sweat beaded his forehead; it coursed down his chest, his spine. He crouched and wrapped his arms around the rock.

'Tug,' he groaned. 'Tug.'

He strained and grunted. He cursed.

All at once, a shadow fell across him, and Cade looked round to see the nameless one standing over him. Without making a sound, it stepped forward and

261

gripped the boulder. Cade stepped back as, with its short but powerful legs braced, the nameless one pulled itself upright.

'Tug,' it grunted.

Like a tooth being pulled from a gum, the rock creaked, then abruptly came free from the ground in a shower of earth.

'Tug!' the nameless one growled.

Hugging the boulder to its chest, it crossed to the side of the plot, swaying as it went, then dropped the boulder on the ground. It turned and lumbered back to Cade.

'Well done!' Cade exclaimed. He reached out and patted the creature on the shoulder.

The nameless one flinched and lowered its head. It stared down at the ground, its nostrils twitching, and Cade noticed the white scars that crisscrossed the skin around its nose and ears.

'I'm sorry,' said Cade, his voice soft. 'I didn't mean to startle you.'

The nameless one looked up. 'Master,' it said in its low rumble of a voice.

Cade gestured to another boulder. 'Tug?' he said, tapping it with his rock hammer.

With a throaty grunt, the great creature strode across to the rock. It was smaller than the other one and the nameless one pulled it out of the ground with its bare hands, muttering 'Tug' under its breath. It pulled up the rock next to it, and the one next to that. Then, squatting down, it picked up all three rocks, strode back across the plot and laid them down carefully next to the first boulder.

'Good!' said Cade. 'Good! Lots more to tug!' He tapped rocks and boulders to his left and his right.

'Master,' growled the nameless one, and set to work.

For the rest of the morning the great lumbering creature worked tirelessly, removing the rocks and boulders from the earth and adding them to a growing line along the north, then the east and west sides of the plot of meadowland. It didn't need Cade's tools, but simply used its huge hands, scraping away the earth with its yellowed nails and yanking the boulders free with powerful spatula-like fingers.

'Tug,' it grunted as it worked. 'Tug . . . Tug . . . Tug . . .'

Cade laughed. 'Tug,' he said delightedly.

He patted the great creature on his shoulders and this time it didn't flinch, but regarded him with its deep-set eyes that seemed to sense Cade's approval.

'You're a nameless one no longer,' Cade told him. 'Your name will be Tug. Tug!' he repeated, tapping the creature in the middle of its barrel chest.

The nameless one's heavy brow knitted together in

a frown, then raised to reveal his twinkling eyes. He tapped himself on the chest in imitation of Cade.

'Tug,' he growled. 'Tug! Tug!'

'That's right,' said Cade, then pointed to himself.

'Master,' the creature growled.

'No, Cade. Cade,' he said, jabbing a finger into his own chest.

The nameless one that was now Tug spread his lips in what Cade could only describe as a crooked smile.

'Cade,' he growled.

Just then, there was a yelping cry of excitement and Cade turned to see Rumblix, who must have woken up at last, come bounding across the meadow towards them. Looking up, Tug let out a cry of alarm as the prowlgrin pup bounced up to them. Tug reared up, teeth bared and small eyes rolling, and backed away.

Cade stepped forward and gathered Rumblix up in his arms. 'Don't be frightened,' he told Tug. 'Rumblix is just trying to say hello.'

Cade put Rumblix down and got him to sit, then took hold of one of the nameless one's massive hands and brought it close to the prowlgrin's head. Tug flinched and pulled back, but Cade tightened his grip.

'Stroke him just above his nostrils,' he told Tug. 'Rumblix likes that, don't you, boy?'

At the feel of the prowlgrin's fur, the nameless one let out a grunt.

'That's it,' Cade reassured him. 'Now tickle him with your fingertips,' he said.

Rumblix began purring as Tug's great fingers gently ruffled his grey fur. Tug cocked his head to one side. The purring grew louder, and Rumblix rolled over onto his side. Tug crouched down, and kept tickling him, up and down his haunches, on his belly, under his chin . . .

Finally Rumblix could stand it no more. Jumping up, he leaped onto Tug's forearm and clung on tightly. Tug stared down at him for a moment, then slowly inclined his head. Rumblix rewarded him by licking his face, and Cade heard the most extra-ordinary sound bubble up from the back of the huge creature's throat. Part growl, part purr, part soft wheezing sigh, it was the sound of a nameless one from the Nightwoods laughing.

Just then, from far in the distance, there came a mournful yodelling call. Tug paused, cocked his head to one side and stared off into the forest, a puzzled look in his eyes.

'That's the call of a banderbear, Tug,' said Cade, patting his arm reassuringly. 'I'm pretty sure there aren't any of those in the Nightwoods where you come from.'

For the rest of the afternoon, as Rumblix bounded about the meadowlands, Cade and Tug worked together as a team. The sun was sinking by the time they had completely cleared the vegetable plot of rocks, which had been piled, one on top of the other, to form a rough drystone wall that enclosed the garden. Tired but elated, Cade returned to the cabin, followed by Tug and Rumblix.

He fetched some offal from the storeroom and set it down on the veranda for Rumblix to eat, while Tug sat beside him with a pile of fresh-cut meadowgrass which he chewed contentedly. When they had finished, the pair of them ambled slowly down to the lakeside and, lowering their heads, lapped at the cool lakewater side by side.

Cade pulled up a chair on the veranda and was just about to sit back and admire the fiery sunset over the Farrow Ridge when he spotted something out on the glittering lake. It was Thorne Lammergyre in his coracle, far out in the middle, a paddle in his hands. Seated behind him was Celestia, the pair of them paddling towards the rock jetty.

Cade raced down to the end of the jetty to meet them.

'Thorne! Celestia!' he shouted as they drew closer, then stopped as he saw the expressions on their faces. Thorne was frowning and Celestia looked white-faced and red-eyed, as if she'd been crying. 'What's wrong?' he called as the coracle approached.

Thorne raised a hand. He brought the coracle close to the jetty, but didn't moor it. Celestia rested her paddle across her legs and looked up. Cade stared back at her.

'It's my father, Cade,' Celestia called out. 'When I got back yesterday, he was just setting off for the caverns.

Said he'd return by nightfall, but he's still not back. It's just not like him. And I'm worried.' Her voice faltered.

Thorne reached back and placed a hand on her arm, then turned to Cade, his square jaw set.

'We're going into the caverns behind the Five Falls to look for him,' he said grimly. 'And we could use another pair of hands . . .'

Cade saw the old phraxmusket strapped to the fisher goblin's back, the telescopic sight glinting in the sunlight – *and* the two pistols at Celestia's belt.

He nodded. 'Give me a moment to get my phraxmusket,' he said.

He turned on his heels and raced up to the cabin. Caught up in the excitement, Rumblix scampered after him, Tug following on behind.

At the cabin, Cade hurried inside. He grabbed the phraxmusket and his backpack, then took two lakefowl from the store. He ran down the steps, two at a time. Rumblix and Tug were waiting at the bottom. He tossed the lakefowl to Rumblix.

'That should keep you going for a while, boy,' he said, before turning to Tug. 'Look after him, Tug,' he said, and Tug nodded his head – and as if in response, the prowlgrin pup jumped up onto the creature's forearm, one of the lakefowl dangling from his mouth.

Cade walked to the end of the jetty and stepped down into the coracle, which rocked from side to side. He sat on the bench next to Celestia.

'Let's go,' said Thorne.

He pushed the coracle away from the end of the stone jetty with his paddle, and brought it about till the rounded prow was facing the distant falls. Then, with Thorne at the front of the coracle, paddling first on one side, then on the other, and Cade and Celestia behind him, paddling in unison, port and starboard, they set off toward the glistening cascades of water.

It was Cade's first time out on the lake, and in the evening light, it looked even more beautiful than from the shore. Following Celestia, Cade got into a smooth and easy rhythm as he plunged the paddle deep into the water, pulled back; then withdrew and plunged it down again. He was soon sweating from the exertion. Behind him, when he glanced round, he saw a V-shaped wake, shot with late afternoon gold, spreading out over the surface of the lake.

The sound of the waterfalls grew louder as they approached the Five Falls, rising little by little to a deafening roar. Spray flew into their faces, fine and drizzle-like at first, but quickly growing heavier. As they drew closer to the falls, the water grew violently turbulent and Thorne's coracle was tossed about like a piece of flotsam. It was all the goblin could do to stop it being dashed against the rocks.

'Which way?' he called back to Celestia.

Celestia looked up, hand raised, shielding her face from the spray from the waterfalls. 'My father said the third of the five caverns led down into the crystal caverns.' She struggled to make herself heard over the roar of the falls. 'And then the drowning pools . . .'

'The drowning pools?' said Cade, gripping tightly to his paddle as the coracle bucked and swayed in the current.

'That's right, Cade,' said Celestia, leaning close to him and talking into his ear. 'I'd understand if you felt you couldn't follow us down there.'

Cade turned and looked deep into Celestia's green eyes. His face coloured up. She had saved his life; had become his friend. He'd hoped she knew just how he felt about her.

'You can count on me, Celestia,' he told her fiercely. 'I'd follow you anywhere.'

· CHAPTER THIRTY-THREE ·

'There's a mooring rock behind the waterfall,' shouted Thorne. 'If we can get to it without capsizing . . .'

Celestia pushed back her dripping wet hair and nodded. 'Get as close to the falls as you can,' she said, pulling a length of rope from her backpack. 'I'll do the rest.' She tied one end of the rope to the bow of the coracle and fashioned a noose at the other end.

Cade looked up at the Farrow Ridge, a sheer flat cliff face of glistening grey rock. The third cavern of the Five Falls was directly above them, water gushing down from its black mouth in a steady, unceasing torrent. Behind the falls, Cade could make out a definite ascent, a natural cutting in the rock that zigzagged its way up to the cavern entrance.

Thorne tapped him on the shoulder. 'Paddle, lad!' he bellowed. 'Paddle as if your life depended on it!'

Cade crouched forward and, shoulders hunched,

began to paddle. Thorne did the same. The pair of them drove the coracle through the swirling, bubbling water at the foot of the falls. The noise of the crashing water made their ears ring. Celestia stood at the front of the coracle, legs apart to steady herself, and tossed the rope.

The noose seemed to waver for a moment in the air, then dropped down over the spur of rock jutting out from the cliff face behind the waterfall. Thorne and Cade stopped paddling. The rope went taut. The wickerwork at the front of the coracle creaked under the strain.

Thorne reached forward, seized the rope and pulled. The coracle, buffeted by the boiling currents, inched forward. He pulled again, gaining enough slack in the rope for Cade to grab onto. The two of them pulled together, then Celestia joined in. Rocking and shuddering, the little vessel shot though the waterfall to the other side.

It was eerily quiet at the base of the cliff behind the falls, the roar of the torrent muffled by the wall of grey rock directly in front of them. Thorne stepped out of the coracle onto a thin apron of gravel-strewn rock. Celestia climbed out next, followed by Cade, and, soaked to the skin, the three of them looked up at the cliff face towering above them. Close up, it looked even more daunting than it had from the other side of the waterfall, the rock-ledge steps that rose up the cliff far more haphazard and precarious than they had appeared at first glance.

Thorne stepped up onto the first ledge, then paused. He pointed to a mark which had been scratched into the rock – a curved line bisecting a triangle.

'See this? It's a sky-shipwright's mark,' he explained. 'Blatch uses it to signpost trails when he's exploring. Leastways he did back when we were mapping the lake fringes of the Western Woods.'

Cade saw the look of relief that passed across Celestia's face as she shot a glance at the mark on the rock. Her father might still be in trouble, but at least they were going the right way.

Thorne started to climb the zigzagging steps, placing his boots down square on each rock ledge in turn and securing a firm handhold before stepping up to the next one, maintaining contact with the rock at all times. Loose-limbed and strong, Thorne made it look easy – as did Celestia, who followed close behind him.

But when Cade started to climb, he discovered that the spray from the waterfall had left a fine layer of water on the rock ledges. It made them slippery and cold to the touch.

He tried to copy Thorne – raising his arms and feeling round until he found a handhold to pull himself up. He took a step. Then another. And another . . .

He glanced over his shoulder. At his back, the waterfall was like a vast curtain, glittering and opaque. The chill generated by the water rushing past him made his teeth chatter. Drops of water splashed over the back of his collar and coursed down his back. His arms and legs ached and he gasped in lungfuls of air as he forced himself on. Looking up, Cade saw that Celestia and Thorne had reached the jutting lip of rock at the cavern entrance, and he gritted his teeth.

'You can do it, Cade,' Celestia called down to him as, hand over hand, foot after foot, Cade scrambled up the last half-dozen strides.

Reaching down, Thorne grasped him by the shoulders and pulled him up onto the ledge. Cade slumped to his knees, fighting to catch his breath. Directly beside him, the torrent of water gushed out of the inky blackness of the cavern and cascaded down to the lake far below.

Cade looked up.

Before him in the dappled sunlight, the Farrow Lake and its shoreline stretched out in a magnificent panorama. Far to his left lay the Levels, the flat marshy lowlands that bordered the forest to the west. To his right, Gart Ironside's sky platform rose up from the surrounding forest to the east. While in front of him, in the far distance, Cade was able to make out a thin ribbon of emerald green along the east shore.

The meadowlands . . .

Cade squinted, trying to make out his cabin. But it was impossible. Even the vegetable patch he'd cleared was not visible from this far away. He thought of Rumblix and Tug patiently waiting for him to return, and felt a lump rise in his throat.

'My father mentioned the crystal caverns,' Celestia was saying. 'And discovering the place he called the drowning pools. That's where he found the arrowheads,' she added, and turned to him, her green eyes narrowed. 'You remember the arrowheads, don't you, Cade?'

Cade nodded. 'Yes,' he said, climbing to his feet. 'He was examining them in his study.'

'Load your weapons, both of you,' Thorne broke in. 'Keep close behind me and look out for more marks.' He slipped his old phraxmusket from his shoulder and cocked the trigger, then unhooked the lamp that dangled from his belt. He took a wax-sealed box from his jacket and removed two fire-flints. He lit the lamp and raised it, then turned and headed into the forbidding blackness of the cavern. Celestia went with him. Cade followed, gripping his phraxmusket tightly.

After the sunset dazzle outside, Cade was struck blind by the dark of the cavern, despite the lamp. He paused and pressed his hand against the smooth cold rock

wall to steady himself as he waited for his eyes to grow accustomed to the darkness.

When they did, he gasped in astonishment.

The cavern they had entered was vast: a great domed chamber through which the water gushed in a deep channel on its way to the entrance. The light from Thorne's lamp illuminated the ridged walls of the cavern that stretched up high above their heads, and in the soft glow, Cade could see thousands of tiny, translucent creatures shimmering on shifting currents of air.

With translucent, bulbous bodies and heads set with bunches of pearl-like eyes and long thin feelers, the tiny creatures seemed to sense their presence and started drifting down towards them, their long tendrils trailing behind them. Cade was transfixed. They clustered around his face and hands, and his skin tingled as though from countless gentle pinpricks.

He swallowed. 'What *are* they?'

'Air shrimps!' Celestia exclaimed. 'They live throughout the caverns – my father showed me drawings of them in his notebook last week.'

Brushing aside the clouds of shrimps that hovered around them, they made their way through the vast cavern. It echoed with the roar of rushing water, which drowned out the sound of their footsteps on the loose gravel beneath their boots.

'Over there!'

Thorne pointed to one of Blatch Helmstoft's marks on the far wall of the cavern. It was beside a low-ceilinged tunnel, the smallest of three leading out of the cavern. Water spurted from cracks and fissures in the cavern wall in great jets, which they had to duck under to reach the tunnel.

Cade shivered as he followed the others. His wet clothes clung to his body, chilling him to the bone, and he wondered what could have possessed Celestia's father to enter this dark, inhospitable world, and not just once, but time and time again. The tattoo on the chest of the old hammerhead goblin came into his thoughts, and Cade flinched.

White trogs . . .

Just then, something slithered over Cade's boot, and he gave out a shrieking yelp that made the others turn, their weapons raised in their hands. Thorne held out the lantern and Cade looked down at his boot. It was coated in a trail of a silver-white mucus-like sub-stance. Slowly making its way up the tunnel wall was a giant colour-less snail.

'Did your father ever draw that?' said Cade as the snail continued slowly on its way.

'Oh, yes,' said Celestia. 'That's a slime snail. A small one by the looks of it.'

She reached out and lightly touched the glistening trail. When she pulled her finger away, a long thin strand clung to the tip. It was transparent and smelled of spiced honey.

'My father collected a jarful of this stuff on his last trip,' she said. 'It's good for gluing broken pots back together, but not much else.' She smiled at Cade. 'You look cold.'

'Oh, I . . . I . . . I'm all right,' said Cade, trying to stop his teeth chattering.

'Here, take a sip of this,' said Thorne, pulling a flask from his back pocket and handing it to Cade.

Cade took a sip, and the warm, fiery glow of wood-grog filled his mouth and throat, and then his belly. 'Thanks,' he said.

They continued down the small tunnel, which twisted and turned and seemed to double back on itself, the floor sloping downwards all the while as they descended ever deeper. The air grew warmer the further they went, and Cade felt his clothes begin to dry out. Finally, turning a sharp corner, the air filled with a soft, mournful sound that reminded Cade of the sonorous windchimes that hung from the rooftops of the academies in the Cloud Quarter of Great Glade. Up ahead, the light from Thorne's lamp seemed to explode into great shafts of brilliant light as the tunnel opened out into a larger space.

The next moment, Cade emerged from the tunnel. He straightened up and looked around him. 'These must be . . .'

'. . . the crystal caverns,' said Celestia, finishing his sentence, her voice hushed with awe.

Thousands upon thousands of crystals filled the cavernous space in front of them. Hexagonal. Octagonal. They lay at angles to one another, crisscrossed and intersecting, like branches of trees. They towered above Cade's head. Thin and thick. Long and longer still. Some were bifurcated, some were branched; some came to angled points, while others split into dozens of smaller crystals that splayed out like spiky seedheads. It was a forest of crystals stretching off into the distance, and as Thorne held up his lamp, the light bounced from facet to facet, intensifying as it did so. The whole cave was illuminated. It glowed through the flat, polished faces of the crystals; it glinted at the angled edges. It flashed

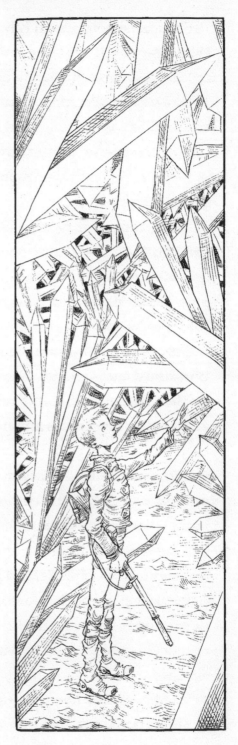

and shimmered while an echoing, bell-like chiming filled their ears.

Cade touched the hard surface of the nearest crystal. It was gently vibrating, and the eerie sound it emitted rose and fell as he trailed his fingers over it.

'They seem to be sensitive to the smallest disturbance in the air currents,' said Celestia, looking around, fascinated.

They stepped forward and as they picked their way through the forest, the crystals chimed and sang all around them.

'If Blatch is down here, he'll certainly hear us coming,' said Thorne, and in the sparkling light Cade could see the fisher goblin's finger tighten on the trigger of his phraxmusket.

They made their way through a succession of caves, each filled with crystals and the haunting, vibrating music they produced. Finally Thorne found what they were looking for: Blatch Helmstoft's mark. It was scratched into the rock above the entrance to a downward-sloping tunnel that led out of the last of the crystal caverns.

'This way,' said Thorne, entering the tunnel.

Celestia ducked down and followed him. Cade stepped past a large, round boulder at the tunnel entrance, and hurried after them. As he did so, he felt something brush against his ankle, and looking down saw that he had snagged a strand of what looked like a cobweb. At the same moment, he heard a low creak behind him.

He glanced back . . .

The other end of the sticky strand was attached to a small wedge-shaped rock that held the big boulder in place. As Cade watched in horror, the cobweb plucked the wedge from beneath the boulder, sending it rolling forward.

'Run!' Cade shouted to the others as it rumbled down the tunnel towards them.

The boulder gathered speed, its surface grazing the pitted sides of the tunnel as it rolled. Just ahead, Cade, Celestia and Thorne dashed headlong down the increasingly steep incline in a desperate bid to outrun the oncoming boulder.

Before them, the end of the tunnel was in sight. With his lamp swinging violently from side to side, casting wild shadows across the walls, Thorne threw himself through the narrow opening, followed closely by the others. As they fell sprawling to the floor there was a crash behind them as the boulder slammed into the opening, sealing it shut.

The three of them picked themselves up. Thorne raised the lamp and they looked about them.

They were in a small cavern. Clusters of pearly stalactites hung down from the low ceiling; stalagmites rose from the floor. And set between them at various points were a dozen bowl-shaped depressions with holes at their centre.

Celestia turned and stared at the boulder blocking the end of the tunnel. It was wedged tight like a stopper in a bottle.

'We're trapped,' she said, and Cade could hear the panic in her voice.

Thorne knelt down at the edge of one of the depressions in the cave floor and examined the small grooves on the surface of the rock. When he looked up, his brow was furrowed.

'These aren't natural formations,' he said. 'They've been created – cut into the floor with rock chisels . . .'

Just then, with a deep echoing gurgle and a sudden roar, water gushed up from the holes at the centre of the depressions, one after the other, until twelve mighty geysers of water were pouring into the cavern. They hammered against the ceiling, coursed down the walls and swirled around their feet . . .

'The drowning pools,' Celestia breathed.

· CHAPTER THIRTY-FOUR ·

The gushing water flooded the cave. Strong, swirling currents seized Cade's legs and threatened to spin him round. His boot went over on a lump of rock. He stumbled, lost his balance, fell forward and landed with a splash. The stock of his phraxmusket swung round and struck him on the side of his head.

Sprawling and splashing, he managed to grab a stalactite and pull himself back onto his feet; then, legs braced, to push himself upright.

'Are you all right, Cade?' Celestia shouted above the roar of rushing water. She was clinging to a stalactite over by the cave's entrance and was waist deep in the surging water. Thorne stood beside her, furiously swinging the butt of his phraxmusket against the boulder that blocked the tunnel.

Cade moved towards him. The water was up around his chest now, currents beneath the surface threatening to pull him under with each step. As he reached Celestia and Thorne, the fisher goblin took another swing at the boulder, only for the copperwood butt of the phraxmusket to shatter. Thorne threw the old musket aside in disgust.

'Stand back,' said Celestia. 'I've got an idea.' She pulled her phraxpistols from their holsters and aimed at the side of the boulder, where it formed a watertight seal with the cave wall. 'Cade, you take the other side . . .'

Cade pulled his phraxmusket from his shoulder and took aim.

'Fire!' Celestia shouted.

With a blinding flash and a deafening crack, the phraxweapons discharged. The bullets struck the rock, sending splintering fragments off in all directions. They reloaded. Fired again. More rock crumbled.

But the seal between the boulder and the cave wall remained watertight.

Cade reloaded again. 'Move, curse you!' he roared. '*Move!*'

He fired again, and again. And again . . .

The water was now up around their necks, submerging the blocked entrance and threatening to drag them under.

'It's no good,' Thorne told Cade. 'We need to get up as high as we can.'

Stalactites hung down from the roof of the cave in needle-like clusters, and as the level rose, the three of them trod water and rose with it. Thorne held the lamp above his head. It cast an eerie, shadowy light on the hanging rock formations. Below their feet, the dark water bubbled as the jets continued to surge up from the cave floor.

Reaching up, Thorne grasped one of the ridged stalactites and, with the handle of the lamp clamped between his teeth, hauled himself up out of the water. Celestia grabbed another stalactite and did the same, and Cade followed, the three of them scrambling up towards the roof of the cave.

Shivering, Cade gasped in lungfuls of air. It tasted stale and dank in his mouth. He looked up. A little way off, Celestia clung to the top of a stalactite, her face drained of colour. Their eyes met.

She winced. 'I'm so sorry I got you into this,' she said, and glanced across at Thorne. 'Both of you.'

'Your father is my friend,' Thorne said simply.

'And you and Thorne are *my* friends,' added Cade.

Celestia nodded, and in the light of the lamp Cade could see that her eyes were brimming with tears.

'So what do we do now?' she said, voicing what they were all thinking.

Thorne flinched and held up the lamp, illuminating the turbulent depths below. The water was rising towards them, already lapping at their boots.

Cade looked up, searching the ceiling for any sign of a crack or fissure that might offer a way out. But there was none he could see. The space between the rising water and the rock ceiling would close up. And they would drown . . .

Cade swallowed.

'There must be a way out,' Thorne muttered. 'When your father mentioned the crystal caverns and the drowning pools, Celestia, did he say anything else?'

Celestia frowned. 'You know what he can be like, Thorne,' she said. 'Vague, distracted, lost in his thoughts . . .'

'Think, Celestia!' urged Thorne. 'Anything he said. Anything at all . . .'

The water had spilled over the tops of their boots and Cade could feel its icy touch moving up from his ankles to his knees. He shuddered and closed his eyes, pressing his cheek against the smooth, cold surface of the stalactite he was clinging to.

'He took his pack, his lamp . . .' Celestia recounted. 'I gave him salve and some hyleberry-soaked bandages in case he needed them . . .' She let out a sob, then collected herself. 'And . . . and he said that on his last trip, he'd explored some "very interesting" caves beyond the third of the falls . . . He mentioned the crystal caverns, where he found the arrowheads. And the drowning pools . . .'

The water was now at chest height, and Cade jerked his head back, fighting the rising panic surging up from within him. He opened his eyes. To his right, its surface illuminated by the lamplight, was a small stalactite, its grey-green colour different to the pearly white stalactites around it.

'He said the drowning pools were "fascinating". That was how he described them. "Fascinating" . . .'

Celestia's voice was beginning to crack, and she was

speaking very fast as she fought against the same panic that Cade was feeling. It wouldn't be long now before the water was at neck level and Thorne's lamp would begin to gutter and then go out, pitching them into darkness . . .

'His last words to me were that he was going to explore beyond the drowning pools, "as silently as a slime snail" . . . Oh, Thorne, Cade, I'm so sorry . . .'

Cade stared at the stalactite. There, carved into its surface was a skyshipwright's mark – scratched hastily, the lines wobbly and uneven, but unmistakable. A line bisecting a triangle.

'He was here!' Cade shouted out. 'Your father was right here! Where we are now!'

Just then, with the water in their faces and the ceiling grazing the tops of their

heads, Thorne's light went out. In the pitch blackness, Cade blindly reached out for the stalactite and grasped it with both hands.

The stalactite abruptly lurched forward.

As it did so, there was a loud grinding sound from somewhere within the walls of the cavern followed by stone scraping against stone. Around them, the water seemed to tremble. The next moment, a broad shaft of light appeared below in the cave floor and the water was sucked rapidly away, taking them with it.

Twisted and spinning, his hands raised protectively to his head, Cade closed his eyes as the powerful current dragged him down, down, down. His lungs were burning. His temples throbbed.

Suddenly he was falling through the air in the cascade of water. His arms flailed. He snatched a breath. Then, with a great splash, he struck more water and plunged deep into a seemingly bottomless pool.

He kicked his legs. He drove upwards with his arms. And he broke the surface, gasping and spluttering.

'So, you followed me,' came a thin, reedy voice. 'I was afraid you might . . .'

· CHAPTER THIRTY-FIVE ·

Cade was treading water in a deep dark pool at the centre of a vast domed cavern, its steep, faintly luminescent walls lined with gouged-out alcoves. Waves caused by the cascade of water slapped at the sides of the pool, and the sound echoed around the cavern.

Close by him, Celestia broke the surface and gasped for breath, followed, moments later, by Thorne.

'Celestia!' It was the same thin voice that Cade had heard before. 'Thorne!'

Cade looked across to where the words had come from, and there, hunched down low in one of the shadowy alcoves carved out of the wall, was Celestia's father.

'I'd come and help you out of the water, but . . .' He nodded down at the glistening rope that crisscrossed his body like the laces of a shoe. 'The white trogs have bound me up in this slime-rope of theirs!'

Blatch was wearing a scuffed leather jacket with a high

collar and studded patches reinforcing the shoulders. Attached to the front, on cords looped around buttons, were various brass instruments with glass panels and dials, together with a notebook and leadwood pencil. He was half sitting, half crouching in the alcove, his hands bound tightly to his sides by the slime-rope. His feet were bare and blistered, and there was an angry-looking welt on the side of his cheek.

'Oh, Father,' Celestia said, swimming over to the side of the pool below the alcove. 'What have they done to you . . . ?'

Just then, the cavern filled with a deep, sonorous sound and, looking up, Cade saw a huge white spider emerge from a crevice high up in the roof. On its back was a figure sitting astride a curved saddle. The spider scuttled across to the stone trap door in the vaulted ceiling through which Cade and the others had fallen.

The rider paused beside the opening, looking up into the cavern and then down at the swimmers in the pool below. He took a shell from his belt and blew into it, once, twice, three times, then reached out for a stalactite beside the opening. The rider pulled the stalactite back and, with a grinding sound, a stone slab slid back across the opening, sealing it once more. Then, turning, he urged his spider down the cave wall towards the pool, where Cade, Celestia and Thorne were treading water.

As the spider approached, Cade noticed the figure on its back was clutching a length of glistening rope in one hand and a jagged shard of crystal in the other.

As if in response to the first rider's call, two more spiders emerged and scuttled down the walls, their riders arching back in their saddles as they hurled strands of glistening rope down at the surface of the pool.

Cade felt a sudden stinging sensation, as if from a slap, and looking down saw that a coil of rope had struck his chest and stuck fast. The next moment, he was yanked up out of the water and the cavern walls blurred as he felt himself being spun bodily round and round, then dropped. He landed heavily, the wind knocked out of him and his head spinning. When it cleared and he got his breath back, Cade looked up and saw that he was lying in a shallow alcove, his chest tightly laced with slime-rope that bound his arms to his sides, just like Celestia's father.

From the alcoves on either side of him came gasps and grunts that told him that Celestia and Thorne had also been captured. Above the alcoves, sitting back in their saddles as their spiders clung motionless to the cavern wall, the white trogs eyed their prisoners silently.

Cade stared back at them, his mouth dry.

The white trogs were tall and brawny. They had cowl-shaped ears that flexed and quivered; they had broad flat noses and sunken eyes, and bumpy bone-ridges that crossed their scalps from the top of their brows to the nape of their necks. In the stirrups of their saddles, their three-toed feet were bare, and they wore bleached-out snailskin capes over white robes that shimmered and glowed in the dim light. The barbed crystal spears they carried were pointing down at the alcoves.

One of them reached inside his cloak. He looked older than the others and more powerfully built, and Cade assumed he must be the leader. He drew back his hand and Cade saw that he was holding the shell of a slime snail, which he raised to his lips and blew into. The cavern filled with the deep, sonorous sound once more – but this time Cade heard a similar sound answering it from somewhere in the distance.

The trogs twisted in their saddles and dug their heels into the sides of their spiders, which turned and scuttled back up the walls of the cavern before disappearing into the shadowy crevices in the ceiling.

Cade shuffled forward on his knees, and heard the others do the same. They leaned out from the alcoves. Below them, the dark surface of the pool was mirror-still, reflecting their faces back to them. Cade trembled. Bound tight by the slime-rope as they were, one slip and they would tumble from their alcoves, and drown. In the reflection of the pool, Cade saw Blatch Helmstoft's face, his dark beady eyes glinting from behind his wire-rimmed spectacles.

'You followed my marks, I take it,' he said sadly, looking at each of their reflected faces in turn. 'My loyal friend, my brave daughter and her new young friend . . . I wish you hadn't. The marks were for me to find my way back, not a trail for you to follow.' He hesitated. 'I'm so sorry I've led you into this misadventure of mine. I'm only grateful that you didn't all perish in the drowning pools.' He shook his head. 'Oh, when I heard the water come rushing in—'

'I saw your mark,' Cade broke in. 'On that stalactite.'

'Thank Earth and Sky for that much at least,' Blatch said with a sigh. 'Though this, I fear, is where the journey ends. The trogs have been holding me captive here and, despite my best efforts, have yet to communicate their intentions – or, indeed, utter a single word in my presence . . .' Blatch frowned and pointed to his left and right. 'Though these alcoves do the white trog's talking for them,' he added grimly.

Cade heard Celestia gasp and, looking down into the pool, he saw the reflection of the alcoves on either side of them. Hanging from slime-rope slings in the shadowy recesses were various victims of the drowning pools. The corpses of half a dozen tilder calves. Several plump lemkins. And a bedraggled-looking weezit . . .

They were clearly in some sort of larder where the trogs kept their fresh meat. Was this to be their fate? Cade

wondered. He remembered the gruesome tattoo on the hammerhead's chest and shuddered.

'You see,' Blatch was saying, 'the crystal caverns warn the white trogs of any intruders into their realm. The lightest touch, the brush of a fingertip, the tremble of footfall, and the crystals start vibrating, producing that eerie sound – and alerting the trogs to prepare their defences . . .'

'The drowning pools,' said Celestia.

'Precisely,' said Blatch. 'Though I didn't know that at the time.' He frowned. 'I'm afraid it took the misfortune of another creature to unlock that cave's terrible secret.

'It was on my fourth trip, and I was taking my usual meticulous care not to touch or disturb anything – and thank Earth and Sky I did! – when I discovered the pools. I realized instantly that they were not a natural feature, though their purpose was a mystery to me. The cave seemed to be a dead end, so I withdrew. It was only when I was back in the crystal caverns that I realized I was not the only one there. Somehow, a weezit had made its way into the caves.' He shrugged. 'I've seen them on the cliff-sides behind the falls, grazing on crevice-moss. This one must have got lost . . . Anyway, it blundered past me, and the next thing I knew it had run down the tunnel and into the cave I'd just left, tripping the spiderweb trap as it went. The great boulder rolled down into the tunnel and wedged itself tight at the far end . . .'

In the pond's reflection, Cade and Celestia exchanged glances.

'I went back down and pressed my ear against the boulder and listened,' Blatch went on, 'which is when I heard the sound of water flooding the cave, and the sound of the weezit crying out in alarm . . .' He paused. 'When it fell silent, I heard the rush of the water draining out again. Then the boulder shuddered, as if something was pushing it from the other side. I retreated back to the crystal caverns and waited. And that's when I caught my first sight of the white trogs . . .'

Blatch's eyes twinkled with excitement as he remembered the moment.

'As the rock boulder moved, I realized that two spiders were pushing it. The white trogs were riding them. When the spiders had shoved the boulder back up to the top of the tunnel, the trogs reset their ingenious trap. Then they returned to the cave, and I silently followed.

'One of the riders climbed the wall to the ceiling, pulled back a stalactite lever and released the trap-stone in the floor of the cave, then they all disappeared through the hole beneath it. The stone closed again and, after marking the stalactite, I returned home, my head swimming with thoughts of the white trogs and their hidden world deep in the caverns.'

He turned to his daughter, a smile on his face.

'I'd already shown you my drawings of slime snails and air shrimps, Celestia. But now I dreamed of the new wonders I'd discover beyond the crystal caverns and the drowning pools; wonders that I would return and delight you with . . .'

Blatch paused and shook his head sadly. 'But it was not to be. Despite the care I took on my return, making my way through the crystal caverns without a sound, and avoiding the cobweb snare, the white trogs must have sensed my presence somehow. For no sooner had I entered the cave than the boulder rolled into place and the drowning pools erupted . . .'

Just then, the surface of the pool rippled, breaking up their reflections as the sonorous sound of the slime-snail shell filled the cavern once more.

· CHAPTER THIRTY-SIX ·

As the sound of the snail-shell horn faded, four huge grey spiders emerged from a crevice in the cave ceiling. They scuttled down the wall, and as they descended the white trogs on their backs sent glistening coils of rope shooting down towards the alcoves.

Cade ducked his head. The end of a slime-rope landed on his shoulder with a gloopy squelch. The next moment there was a sharp tug and his stomach gave a lurch as he found himself being hoisted upwards. Beside him, the same was happening to Thorne, Celestia and her father.

For a moment, Cade dangled upside down far above the inky black water, before a powerful hand reached out and grasped him by the shoulders. Cade felt queasy and dizzy as the white trog turned him the right way up, then, tearing the end of the rope from Cade's shoulder, stuck him unceremoniously to the curved pommel at the front of his saddle, the slime-rope that crisscrossed Cade's chest holding him fast.

The spider lurched into movement, momentarily winding Cade as it climbed back up the cave wall, its knee joints click-clicking. He felt hot fetid breath on the back of his neck, and heard the rattle of a crystal-shard necklace and the rasp of a snailskin cloak as the trog shifted in the saddle behind him.

The spider entered the crevice in the cave ceiling, and everything went black. Cade heard the click-clicking of knees echoing in the darkness behind him as the other spiders followed.

A rush of cool air blew into Cade's face as the spider speeded up, and he was pushed back against the pommel of the saddle. Far ahead, he saw a thin sliver of light in the darkness. It grew brighter as they got closer, and the air filled with sounds.

Flowing water. The clatter of tools. The grinding of rock against rock . . .

All at once, they were out in the open again, descending the walls of an immense glowing cavern, the biggest Cade had yet seen. The scale of the place was awe-inspiring. It was as big as the Farrow Lake, if not bigger, the floor a patchwork of canals, rock bridges and immense trenches that were filled with forests of luminescent fungi. Above them, the span of the cavern was crisscrossed with glistening cables of slime-rope, to which boulders had been attached to create a vast network of stepping-stone pathways through the air. Extending

far into the distance were stands of jagged stalagmites, as tall as ironwood pines and covered in billowing white clouds of glowing cobwebs, through which Cade could see spiders moving to and fro.

The white trog grunted, his foul breath hot on Cade's neck as he urged the spider down the cavern wall and onto one of the suspended paths. The landscape beneath sped past.

Cade glimpsed dwellings below him which had been carved out of the vertical cavern wall, dozens and dozens of them, their arched entrances shuttered with hanging snailskin. Suspended by cabled slime-ropes below each dwelling were slabs of flat rock, each one crowned with verdant lawns of moss and lichen, where herds of slime snails were quietly grazing.

And amid all this, Cade could see white trogs. Everywhere. Hundreds of them.

They were harvesting the fungi in the rock trenches; they were tending to the slime snails and herding the cave-spiders. Still more were in work parties, a hundred strong, constructing rock weights and waterwheels to channel water through the canals in the cavern floor and up to the dwellings set into the walls.

As the spider sped past, the white trogs looked up from their work. Cade flinched. Their jaws were set and their eyes blazed. Some of them shook their fists; others raised crystal-shard spears menacingly above their heads.

Behind him in the saddle, the white trog blew into his

snail-shell horn. The long booming call was answered by another in the far distance.

The stepping-stone pathway descended towards the cavern floor and, looking down, Cade saw that they were approaching a large lake, its waters as black and forbidding as the pool beneath the alcoves. The spider's clicking gait slowed and it came to a halt at the lake's edge.

The trog behind Cade reached forward and wrenched him roughly from the pommel of the saddle. He then grasped one end of the strand of slime-rope that crisscrossed Cade's body and tugged it violently. With a tearing sound, the adhesive rope came away, leaving a ghostly white mark on Cade's jacket. The trog coiled the rope around in his fist, which, Cade saw, glistened with a thin film of grease, then threw Cade to the ground.

He landed heavily on his hands and knees, which were tingling with pins and needles. Next to him, he heard thuds and grunts as Celestia, Thorne and Blatch were thrown to the ground in turn. Thorne rose to his feet, rubbing his arms to get the blood flowing once more, while Celestia helped her father up. Blatch looked dishevelled and confused, and Cade saw that his notebook and several instruments had been torn from his jacket when the slime-rope had been removed.

In the eerie silence, none of them spoke.

Before them, a thin aerial bridge formed of stepping-stones stretched out towards a flat island of rock situated at the centre of the dark lake. The island was fringed with a barricade of spiked rocks. At the top of each one, crystal spears gripped in their hands, were trog females. They were larger than their male counterparts, with more prominent ridge crests and dark pigment smeared around their eyes.

Cade felt the spear tip of a spider-rider nudge him in the back and he stepped onto the bridge, which dipped and swayed under his weight. With every step he took, the bridge threatened to tip him into the black water below. And when the others followed, the lurching of the line of suspended rock slabs grew more violent. Cade struggled to keep his balance. Behind him he heard Thorne curse with annoyance as his boot-heel skidded, and Blatch Helmstoft calling out to his daughter to take hold of his arm.

At the far side of the bridge at last, they stepped through a gap in the rock-spike barricade and onto the island. It was flat and circular and studded with upturned snail shells that were filled with burning slime-snail oil, the bluish flames flickering on the impassive faces of the trog females who stared down from the barricade. At the centre of the island was a high-backed throne of dark rock, its polished surface intricately carved with representations of snails and spiders: spirals and coils and circular eight-spoked waterwheels. A fan-shaped spray of gleaming crystals stuck out from the back of the throne like the rays of the rising sun.

'Incredible,' Blatch muttered, reaching for a notebook that was no longer there. 'The whole cavern . . . a marvel . . . I had no idea that the white trogs were so . . . so advanced . . .'

Cade glanced round at Celestia. He saw the mixture of fear and defiance in his friend's clear green eyes.

'What do you think they're going to do with us?' she whispered.

Cade shrugged. He'd been wondering the same thing himself.

Just then, the sound of a snail-shell horn boomed across the water from an entrance in the cavern wall on the far side of the lake, which was connected to the island by a second stepping-stone bridge.

'I have a feeling we're about to find out,' said Thorne darkly.

The next moment, the snailskin at the tunnel entrance was swept aside and a tall figure dressed in voluminous white robes that shimmered brightly stepped out onto the swaying bridge. Cade stared as the figure came closer, passing effortlessly over the stepping-stones and striding onto the island.

This white trog female was taller than any of the white trogs Cade had seen so far. She had a broad, curving ridge-crest and deep-set eyes, the lids picked out in vivid red. She wore a long cloak of bleached snailskin festooned at the shoulders with clusters of snail shells, drilled with holes that emitted hollow, haunting tones as the wind blew through them. At her throat was a necklace; on her heavy brow a crown, the pair of them made from shards of crystal, needle sharp, which caught the light and sparkled in the glow of her spidersilk robes.

In one massive hand, she held a ceremonial dagger of solid crystal. On the other was perched a hairless, white-skinned cave-bat, which flapped its papery dry wings as, with her back straight and her head held high, the white trog queen moved towards the throne. Not only was she tall, Cade saw, but her movements were sinuous and graceful as she swept up her shimmering train of lustrous spidersilk and took her place on the throne.

She turned her head and surveyed the female trogs looking down from the rock-spikes. Her mouth opened and she emitted a series of loud clicks and clacks with her tongue. In her massive hand, the tiny cave-bat flapped with agitation.

She looked down at it, petting it, tickling it beneath the chin. It quietened down, its huge eyes pulsing and snout trembling.

She click-clacked a second time.

Behind him, Cade heard the female trogs emit click-clacking calls in reply.

The white trog queen nodded, the light flashing on her crown and necklace of crystal shards, dazzling Cade and forcing him to look away momentarily. When he looked back, she had turned her head and was staring down at the four of them. The expression on her face was impassive.

'You do not belong here,' she said. Her voice was clear and level, and set the fan of crystals on the throne-back behind her resonating. 'You have dared to enter our realm.'

Next to him, Blatch cleared his throat and was about to speak, but she continued without waiting for any response.

'We do not trespass into your world,' she said, her tone cold. 'The lands-of-the-sky are of no interest to us . . .'

Again Blatch tried to speak. But he was silenced by the white trog queen, who pointed at him with the dagger, her eyes blazing.

'We saw you creep through the crystal caverns . . . Release yourself from the flooding cave . . . Force your way into our underground domain . . . In doing so you have angered the ancient ones.'

She glanced down at the small cave-bat in her grasp, its papery wings fluttering uneasily at the sound of her raised voice. She stroked and lulled it for a moment, and the creature's eyes widened with delight. Then she looked up again, her deep-set eyes glittering with an icy fury.

Cade swallowed and he felt Celestia's hand reach out and find his own. He squeezed it tightly.

'You have violated our world and caused the spirits of our ancestors to desert us . . .'

She inhaled deeply, her breath shaky with emotion.

'Their spirit-blood no longer bathes the walls of the High Cavern.'

The white trog queen's voice rose to an eerie scream that set the crystals at her neck, crown and throne humming.

'So instead,' she pronounced, 'we shall bathe the High Cavern in *your* blood.' She turned to her attendants. 'Take them away.'

· CHAPTER THIRTY-SEVEN ·

Cade's legs shook as he crossed the stepping-stone bridge from the island to the entrance in the cavern wall. The bridge climbed steeply and the gaps between the suspended boulders grew increasingly wide. Cade had to leap from one swaying rock to the next, praying to Earth and Sky each time that he wouldn't lose his footing and fall.

Looking down, he caught sight of his reflection in the deep dark water below. He looked scared.

'We shall bathe the High Cavern in your *blood . . .'*

The words of the white trog queen rang in his ears, and Cade's sense of dread mounted. It was the dread he'd felt when, as a small child, his mother was suddenly and inexplicably no longer there for him; the dread that had overwhelmed him when his father had come to his bedchamber to warn him of the danger they were both in from Quove Lentis, the High Professor of Flight.

In your *blood . . . In* your *blood . . .*

A trog female jabbed him impatiently in the back with the point of her spear, the crystal shard piercing the leather of Cade's jacket and pricking the skin beneath. With a yelp of pain, Cade jumped hastily across several stepping-stones and down onto the ledge in front of the curtained entrance.

Behind him, he heard Celestia encouraging her father, whose breath was coming in short, wheezing gasps. And behind them, Thorne, who was cursing under his breath and grunting with effort.

The trog female escorting him reached past Cade and swept the snailskin curtain aside, before urging him on with the tip of her spear. Cade stepped through the entrance from which, earlier, the white trog queen had emerged, and found himself in a narrow passageway. The walls showed signs of having been worked on with picks and chisels. It was cool and dark, the passageway twisting up in a spiral that, after several turns, began to make Cade feel dizzy. Behind him, he could hear Blatch muttering to himself. Without his notebook and lead-wood pencil, the explorer seemed to be attempting to commit his observations to memory.

'Spiral tunnel. Cut through vertical seam of seemingly soft, dark rock towards what trog queen referred to as "the High Cavern".'

'We shall bathe the High Cavern in your *blood . . .'*

At the top of the winding spiral, the tunnel came to an arched opening. The trog females jostled and pushed

Cade through into a cave that was far smaller than the main cavern, but immeasurably taller, almost like a great chimney, a hundred strides or more high, with hairless cave-bats fluttering in the shadows above their heads. The dark walls glistened with patches of luminescence, while the floor seemed to be coated in something shiny and hard, like varnish.

Thorne looked up. 'Air,' he said. '*Fresh* air.'

He was right, Cade realized. Gentle currents of air were touching their faces, cold and crisp and pure. Cade closed his eyes. The air tasted wonderful, and he realized just how stale the atmosphere of the other caverns had been.

Four rough-hewn blocks of rock stood in a row in the centre of the cavern. They looked newly made, their sides chipped and chiselled with tools. In front of the blocks was an immense carved stone bowl that, judging by the track marks on the floor, had been dragged into place. And propped up against the bowl, its curved blade of crystal glinting in the half-light, was a long-handled axe.

The white trog females escorting them pushed Cade and the others towards the stone blocks. Cade looked up to see one of them, tall and powerfully built, looming over him, her cold, hard face bathed in the faint glow of the cave. Her sunken eyes betrayed no emotion as she shoved him in the chest and forced him to sit.

All at once, from the far side of the cavern, there came a curious *squelch-squelch* sound. Cade glanced across at the entrance to the cavern and saw an enormous slime snail emerging from the darkness. Like the ones Cade had seen grazing outside the trog dwellings, the creature had an opalescent curled shell and a forest of long rubbery feelers snaking out from its head. Those snails, however, were small in comparison to this monster, which was easily the size of a bull hammelhorn.

As it slithered into the cave, Cade saw that there were two trog males behind it. The taller trog was holding one of the snail's rubbery feelers in his hand, and had a stone bowl wedged under his arm. As he walked, he pulled on the feeler, sending a spurting jet of oily liquid into the bowl. The other trog had a long-handled broom which he dunked into the bowl time and again, before sloshing the grease over the glistening trail of sticky slime left by the snail. As he did so, the slime trail dulled, so that when the two trogs walked over it, their feet did not stick . . .

'Fascinating!' Blatch exclaimed. 'They're neutralizing the effects of the slime with a secretion from the snail itself. The very substance that prevents the snail gluing itself to the ground . . . The same grease they put on their hands to handle the slime-ropes,' Blatch muttered. 'Ingenious . . .'

The snail paused for a moment next to Cade. Its feelers probed his legs, then it continued. Behind it, the two trog attendants stood back and watched.

Slowly, steadily, slurping and sloshing as it went, the giant snail slid over Cade's feet, secreting a thick slime. Cade shuddered. The slime flowed over the tops of his boots, ran down his legs and pooled between his toes. It was warm, and the sickly sweet honey-like smell made his stomach churn.

The snail slid slowly over Celestia's feet, then Blatch's, then Thorne's, before continuing across the cavern and climbing up the cavern wall, disappearing into the shadows above. The two trog attendants stepped forward and resumed coating the slime trail with the grease in the bowl. At the cavern wall, they stopped and put down the bowl and broom, then walked back to the entrance. Without uttering a sound, the trog females followed them down the spiral passageway that would take them back to the bridge.

Cade glanced round at

Celestia again; she was slumped forward on the rock seat next to his. She was staring down at her feet.

'They're stuck fast,' she said.

'Mine too,' said Thorne.

'Quite remarkable,' Blatch muttered beside him. 'The amount of slime that a snail of such immense size must generate . . . And to think I underestimated the extra-ordinary properties of these snails' secretions . . .'

'Yes, old friend, remarkable it may well be,' said Thorne, standing up and going red in the face as he strained to break the grip of the snail slime. 'But unless one of us can reach that grease over there, we're trapped here.' The grey goblin nodded towards the stone bowl and axe in front of them. 'And we all heard what that queen of theirs said . . .'

'*We shall bathe the High Cavern in* your *blood*,' said Cade miserably. He couldn't even feel his toes, let alone move his feet.

'Cade.' It was Celestia. Her voice was urgent and excited. She reached out and gripped Cade's hand. 'Cade, look!'

Cade tore his eyes away from the long-handled axe with its curved blade of crystal. 'What?'

She was looking up, her eyes narrowed and brow creased. He followed her gaze, puzzled at first. And then he saw it, a small patch of light high up in the darkness above. A small patch of light that was framed like a port-hole by the jagged rock of the cavern ceiling. A small patch of light that hadn't been there before . . .

'The sky,' he breathed.

'That's what *I* thought,' said Celestia.

'By all that is sacred, Celestia, I believe you're right!' Blatch Helmstoft exclaimed. 'It must be where all this fresh air is coming from!'

'A way out,' said Thorne bitterly, attempting to free his feet, then slumping back on his rock seat. 'If only we could reach it.'

Slowly the dark blue turned to silver, until the patch of sky looked like a coin at the bottom of a black pool, and a ray of light pierced the misty gloom of the cavern's vaulted ceiling.

Suddenly, through the light, a dark shape appeared . . .

· CHAPTER THIRTY-EIGHT ·

Just then, from far below, there was the sound of a snail-shell horn being blown, low, booming and sonorous. It was answered by another one, then another, and another . . .

'They're coming back,' Cade breathed.

Thorne slumped forward and Celestia groaned softly.

A voice rang out. 'Stay there! I'm coming to get you!'

It was coming from the patch of sky in the cavern ceiling. The next moment, a rope ladder tumbled down, unrolling as it came until it was hanging in the air, the bottom almost touching the floor of the cave. It flexed and danced, and as Cade peered up, he saw a figure emerging from the shaft of light and climbing rapidly down the ladder towards them.

'Gart?' Cade shouted. 'Gart, is that you?'

Stepping down onto the cave floor, Gart Ironside pushed his goggles up onto his head and nodded grimly.

'I saw you heading into the caverns yesterday,' he said. 'I should have warned you. You see, Cade, this is all my fault . . .'

'*Your* fault?' said Cade. 'But how?'

The sound of the horns reverberated through the cave.

'Never mind that now,' Thorne interrupted brusquely. 'The bowl over there,' he said, pointing to the base of the wall. 'We need it to get unstuck. And quick.'

Cade saw the confusion in Gart's eyes, but he didn't question Thorne's words. Instead, leaving the rope ladder dangling behind him, he hurried across to the bowl and brought it back to Thorne, who tipped it up and poured some of its thick oily contents over and inside his boots. Instantly the slime

started to dissolve, and when Thorne braced his leg his boot came away from the ground with a plashy squelch. He passed the bowl to Blatch, and worked away at freeing his other foot.

The sound of the snail-shell horns rang through the caverns once again. They were louder than before, and there seemed to be more of them, summoning white trogs from all parts of the vast cavern below, Cade guessed, to witness the coming execution.

'I've got the phraxlighter's flight levers on hover,' said Gart. 'But the wind's getting up, so we need to hurry.' He turned and started the long ascent of the swaying rope ladder. 'Climb up after me,' he shouted back.

Free now, Thorne got to his feet. He took hold of Blatch's arm and pulled him up out of the sticky slime that was slipping down his legs and gathering at his ankles. Celestia took the bowl from her father and poured the grease into and over her boots, then passed it to Cade.

Thorne held the ladder steady for Blatch as the explorer began to climb, then held out a hand and helped Celestia to her feet. Long silvery strands of gluey slime stretched from the soles of her boots to the rock floor, then snapped as she stepped free.

From the entrance to the tunnel came the ominous sound of shuffling feet and the *clink-clink* of crystal shards.

Cade tipped the heavy stone bowl and sloshed the oily liquid down into his boots, then over the toe-caps and heels. The grease felt warm and fiery on his skin, making his feet tingle. He felt the slime melt away as he wiggled his toes.

The snail-shell horns echoed around the High Cavern again, a dozen of them, one after the other in quick succession. And Cade heard the click-clack of the white trogs' strange language coming from the entrance to the spiral tunnel.

Celestia turned to him. 'Are you all right?' she said.

'I'm fine,' said Cade. One foot was free now and, with his hands gripped around his knee, he was struggling to release the other. 'You and Thorne go. I'll be right behind you.'

'Hurry, lad,' said Thorne, climbing the ladder, followed by Celestia.

Cade wrenched at the boot and, with a sudden squelching *crack*, it came free. He leaped to his feet and ran to the bottom of the rope. Celestia had already climbed half a dozen rungs or so.

Hands shaking and heart thudding, Cade began to climb as fast as he could – but the rope rungs sagged under his weight, making the going hard. Hand over hand, foot after foot, he climbed higher.

The gap between Celestia and himself was growing. She was silhouetted, dark against the shaft of light shining down from the opening in the ceiling. It illuminated a large white stalactite that hung down from the centre of the cavern roof. Beyond her, Cade caught sight of Thorne, who was climbing up through the opening towards the hovering phraxlighter.

The cave was echoing now with the rising click and clack of the white trogs. It sounded like a night-chorus of woodcrickets.

Cade glanced down. Hundreds of the trogs were spilling from the tunnel entrance and spreading out across the cave floor, their faces raised as they stared up at him. In their midst, standing on one of the blocks of stone, was their queen. The expression on her face was one of cold fury. As Cade watched, she twisted round, and the crystal dagger in her hand glinted as she drew back her arm . . .

Cade turned away, reached up and hauled himself higher into the shaft of light. All at once, he felt a heavy thud at his shoulder. Then pain. A white searing pain that shot down his spine, along his arm, up his neck and across his back.

His head swam as he dragged himself up another rung of the ladder. Then another. His body felt as though it was loaded down with leadwood. His legs trembled. His temples throbbed.

His shoulder was burning . . .

He looked up. Celestia was being helped up through the hole in the roof. The shaft of light from the opening in the roof of the cavern filled his head with pain, and he screwed his eyes shut. He hugged the rope ladder. He tried to climb further, but couldn't.

He could not move.

'Cade . . . Cade . . .'

Cade opened his eyes. Gart was descending, coming

down towards him.
Below Cade, the rope
ladder juddered rhyth-
mically. White trogs
must be climbing up
towards him. Cade kept
his eyes on Gart, will-
ing himself not to look
down.

A few rungs above
him now, Gart stopped,
then reached into the
depths of his jacket
and drew out his hand.
Grasped in his fingers
was a magnificent
blood-red jewel.

Cade felt the last
of his strength ebb-
ing away, the pain
spreading out from his
shoulder to every part
of his body, so intense
that he could hardly
breathe.

Must hold on, Cade
told himself as the lad-
der juddered below
him. Must hold on . . .

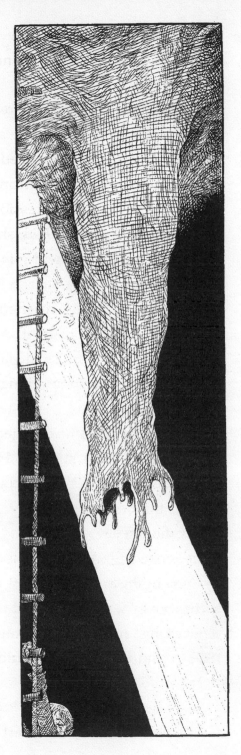

Gart reached out across the void towards the white stalactite. Cade stared up at him, unable to move. Any moment now, a slime-rope, a crystal-shard spear, a white trog fist would land on him, pull him back down, away from the light . . .

As Cade watched, Gart pushed the red jewel into the hollow at the tip of the stalactite. Its limestone tendrils gripped it like fingers.

All at once, the shaft of light hit the tip of the stalactite. It passed through the jewel and became defused, and bathed the cave below in a deep red glow.

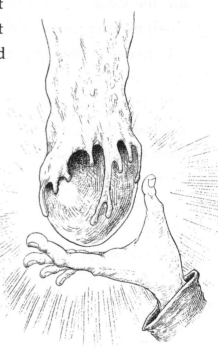

'The spirits have been restored!' the white trog queen's voice rang out. 'Their spirit-blood bathes the walls of the High Cavern once more . . .'

Cade's fingers peeled off the rung of the rope ladder, his head fell back and his legs buckled – only for Gart's arm to fold itself round him and catch him before he had a chance to fall.

'Lammergyre! Push forward on the flight levers!' Gart's voice sounded close in Cade's ear. 'Take us up!'

The next moment, the rope ladder gave a lurch and they started to rise. The luminescent cave walls slid by in a blur. Suddenly the opening in the cavern ceiling enveloped them and they emerged into a dazzle of sunlight.

Above him, Cade saw the blurry outline of the hovering phraxlighter. The rope ladder was winched up. Hands reached down and grabbed him and pulled him into the small vessel, then laid him gently down. Cade closed his eyes, exhausted by the pain.

Celestia's voice rang in his head. 'Stay with us, Cade. Open your eyes . . .'

He felt fingers probing . . . hands cradling his head . . . his jacket being pulled away . . . the clatter of a crystal shard hitting the deck . . . a warm compress enveloping his shoulder . . .

He couldn't breathe. The searing pain grew even more intense.

'It's no good,' Celestia breathed. 'We're losing him.'

· CHAPTER THIRTY-NINE ·

The pain throbbed. The pain burned.

Cade writhed and twisted. His fingertips explored the bandage at his shoulder. He probed. He smoothed. He tried to ease away the throbbing, burning pain that raged beneath it.

'Easy, Cade . . .'

'Lie still . . .'

The words buzzed and echoed. They made no sense. He *had* to soothe away the pain.

'Shhhh . . .'

Hands took his arm, folded it down, put it to his chest, gently but firmly. He felt himself being rolled onto his side. He heard sounds. Hissing and humming. Everything seemed to be gently swaying. Beneath him was a blanket that was warm and soft and smelled of woodsmoke.

He raised his head, opened his eyes . . .

Celestia was staring down at him, her green eyes

filling with tears. Behind her were Thorne, Blatch and, turned half away, his face in profile, Gart Ironside. A thin plume of steam drifted over their heads.

Where was he? Cade wondered.

'You were hit by a dagger,' Celestia said softly. 'In your shoulder . . . I've removed it. And I've applied a poultice and bandaged the wound.' She reached out and placed a hand on Cade's forehead. Her touch felt cool and dry. 'You're burning up,' she said, and her face grew serious once more. 'We think the blade of the knife was coated with some kind of poison.'

'Venom,' her father broke in. 'Possibly from the venom sacs of the cave-spiders.'

Thorne snorted. 'Poison, venom . . .'

'There's a difference,' Blatch said. 'Poison is ingested. Venom is introduced into the blood, with fangs, with knives. It's harder to counter its effects,' he added, his voice hushed. 'Far, far harder . . .'

Cade closed his eyes. The words were beginning to congeal; booming one moment, fading to nothing the next.

'Stay with us . . .'

'Hold on . . .'

'Cade . . . Cade . . .'

He thought of something he wanted to say, but when he opened his mouth, the words caught in his throat. And when he tried again, he couldn't remember what they were.

He was cold. So cold. The blanket had been wrapped around him, but he couldn't stop shivering; couldn't stop his teeth from chattering. His head spun, his body felt heavy. Everything became dark . . . and muffled . . . and numb . . .

And Cade melted into the blackness.

He dreamed that he was falling down a deep, dark well – only to be caught.

Hands. Cade could feel them. Hands shoving themselves under one arm, under his legs. More hands at his back and head. He bounced and swayed. The pain in his shoulder intensified. It felt as though he was being branded.

He was hot. So hot. His skin was on fire and his blood was boiling.

The hands shifted position, turned him round. He was back resting on something soft. The hands withdrew. Suddenly there was water in his mouth . . .

At least, that was what he thought at first. 'Drink this, Cade.' Except it wasn't like water at all. It was thick and claggy and sour, and he spat it out.

Cade's eyes cracked open. He peered groggily out through the narrowed slits.

Faces swam before him, refusing to come into focus. Creased brows. Red eyes. He wanted to talk to them; wanted to speak. But his lips were swollen and blistered, and his throat was raw. No words would come.

He gave up. He closed his eyes.

His mother's face appeared before him. He could smell her sweet perfume. 'Cade,' she whispered, and he felt a coolness touch his forehead, soft fingers caress his temples. 'Hold on, my sweet, brave boy,' she breathed. 'Hold on . . .'

Cade felt scalding tears streaming down his cheeks.

'Cade? Can you hear me, Cade?' It was his father, his kindly eyes full of concern. 'You're strong enough to beat this, Cade, I know you are.' He tapped the roll of scrolls he held in his hand against Cade's chest. 'You kept these safe for me. I knew you would. I could always depend on you, my dear, dear son . . .'

A deep, dark sob rose up from Cade's chest, catching in his throat, round and smooth as a lake pebble, and impossible to swallow back down. The faces of his parents faded back into the pulsing darkness, and he was alone again. Alone with the pain that burned his skin and gnawed at his bones. His head hammered. He couldn't breathe . . .

All at once, there was wetness at his face. He winced. Wetness again, across his nose, on his cheeks . . .

He parted his eyelids once more and peered out

through narrow cracks. Blurred before him was a creature. Round, grey. Yellow eyes. Broad, slavering mouth. A slurping tongue . . .

He jerked his head away.

Another creature stood close by. Huge and hulking, with a massive misshapen head. It loomed closer. Thin lips parted. Teeth bared.

'Master . . . C . . . Cade . . .' it growled.

'No, no,' Cade cried out.

He thrashed his arms. He kicked out with his legs. He struggled to escape the terrifying creatures that stood before him, threatening to tear him limb from limb, to devour him . . .

He slumped back exhausted and closed his eyes, and gave in once more to the pain and the darkness. As if stirred by pumping bellows, the fire in his shoulder and in his head suddenly raged once more. He felt sick. He felt dizzy. He couldn't move. It was as though he was above a blazing fire, tied to a spit that was slowly turning round and round. Then blackness . . .

There was something at his lower lip. It was hard and smooth. A bottle . . .

He tried to turn away. But his head was held still. He opened his eyes. Before him, blurred, as though he was looking up through a pool of water, he saw a large face – brown fur flecked with white bristles, large tusks, and the deepest, kindest, wisest eyes he had ever seen . . .

A trickle of water flooded over his tongue. This time it was neither thick nor claggy nor sour, and he did not spit it out. Instead, he swallowed, once, twice, three times.

The water extinguished the blazing fire, and the excruciating pain dulled to a throb – then faded away completely. The pressure on his chest lifted, and he could breathe easily once more.

The face rippled and shimmered before him and, as Cade relaxed, his eyelids became impossibly heavy. They closed . . .

With a contented sigh, Cade drifted into a deep, deep, dreamless sleep.

· CHAPTER FORTY ·

Cade opened his eyes and stared up. The pain hadn't returned and his head felt clear. He stretched where he lay, flexing his legs, arching his back, revelling in the feeling of his muscles tensing and relaxing.

Rumblix hopped down from his perch at the end of the hammock and bounded up Cade's chest to lick his face. The creature's breath was warm and sweet.

'And good morning to you too, boy!' Cade said, reaching up and tousling the thick beard beneath the pup's chin.

He sat up. The cabin was cool and bathed in early morning sunlight that streamed in through the windows and set the dancing motes of dust sparkling in its blade-like rays.

The last thing he remembered was clinging to the rope ladder, too terrified to look down, too weak to climb up, the sound of vengeful white trogs ringing in his ears. Yet here he was in his cabin, in his hammock, with an unfamiliar brown and white checked blanket over him that smelled faintly of woodsmoke.

Lying here in his bed, Rumblix purring contentedly in the crook of his arm, it was as if the events of the last few days had all been some horrible nightmare. The drowning pools . . . The execution blocks . . . The huge crystal axe . . .

Cade sat up and looked out of the cabin window. It was open and a soft breeze, laced with grassy freshness, was coming in from the lake. The sun was glinting on the water, on the meadowland flowers fringing the shore, on the jagged treetops in the distance and the rocky outcrops beyond.

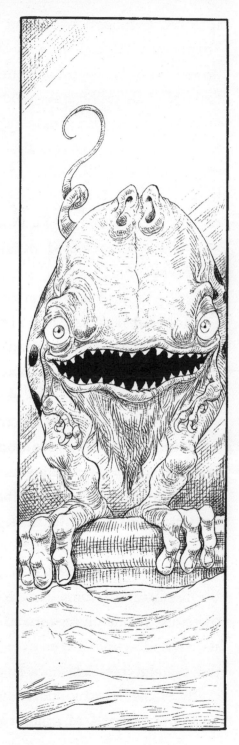

It looked as though everything had been freshly polished. There were hammelhorns on the west shore, their heads down and hoofs deep in swampy mud as they grazed on the seedheads of the spiky reeds. There were fowl coming in from the east, flapping low over the surface of the lake. From the distant ridges to the south came the chittering cries of gangs of weezits, and the booming cough of a rutting tilderbuck. Above, the sky was blue and clear, save for a line of fluffy white clouds that drifted slowly from east to west.

It was, Cade realized, a wonderful day. And he was glad to be alive . . .

At the far end of the Farrow Lake, the torrential Five Falls were cascading down into the waters below. Cade's gaze came to rest on the entrance to the cavern at the top of the central waterfall. It was the cavern that he, Celestia and Thorne had entered. He shivered at the thought of it . . .

Where were they now? he mused.

Thorne, most likely, was out in his coracle netting lakefish. And Celestia – well, maybe she had returned to the hanging-cabin with her father. He hoped that she'd be back soon . . .

Cade looked around the cabin. The table and chairs had been brought in from the veranda and were standing beside the hammock. His leather jacket hung over the back of one chair, torn at the shoulder and stained with blood, while draped over the other was a black scarf that belonged to Celestia.

The tabletop was strewn with Celestia's medicines. Unstoppered pots of creams and salves were clustered together with vials containing liquids of various colours: purple, green, yellow, clear. And a charred ash-fringed ember of something soft that lay on the blade of a knife.

Frowning, Cade reached out and took the knife by the handle. He brought it to his nose and sniffed.

'Shriekroot,' he murmured, remembering the bitter taste in his mouth.

He had been close to death and Celestia must have fought hard to save him.

He reached up and slipped his hand down the back of his shirt. His fingertips glided over smooth, unblemished skin, with trace of neither wound nor scar, and he frowned as he recalled the crystal dagger that had struck him there. The venom-coated dagger . . .

Celestia had thought he would die, he remembered. There had been tears in her eyes.

He looked down at the salves and potions. At the bloodstained jacket. And at the nub of shriekroot.

He shook his head. She had tended to him, looked after him, tried everything she could think of to bring him back from the brink of death; from the burning fever and racking pain.

From the blackness . . .

Cade swung his legs over the side of the hammock and pulled himself to his feet. But the nightmare was over. The fact was, he'd never felt so well as he did now. Fit and healthy and strong – and very, very hungry. He padded over to the fireplace, where a pot of barley broth was bubbling over a crackling fire.

His gaze fell upon the mantelpiece, with the spyglass at one end and the glass vial of perfume at the other, and pinned to the log wall above it the parchment scrolls his father had entrusted him with . . .

'Father . . . Mother . . .' Cade whispered, his eyes misting over.

Picking up a mug from the table, he peered down into the steaming pot. There wasn't much broth left, but enough. He ladled some of it into the mug, then took a sip.

The barley broth, he discovered, was seasoned with meat stock, nibblick and peppercorns, and tasted delicious. Cupping the mug with both hands and sipping at its thick, peppery contents, Cade sat down at the table and gazed out of the window.

Rumblix jumped from the hammock to the back of the chair next to Cade's, his dextrous hind paws gripping the wooden frame. He kept turning his large head and looking at Cade as if to check that he was still there, and every so often, he would stick out his long prehensile tongue and lick at Cade's forearm.

'Were you worried about me, boy?' Cade asked.

He smiled, absentmindedly stroking the loyal pup's thick grey fur. Rumblix purred contentedly and nuzzled up against Cade's side.

'It's all over now,' he said. 'And it's a bright new day.'

He drank the rest of the soup and, wiping his mouth on the back of his sleeve, crossed back to the fire to see whether he could scrape some more out of the pot. Rumblix followed Cade, leaping across the cabin from the chair to table, table to floor, where he squatted at Cade's feet looking up, his head cocked to one side.

The pot was all but empty, Cade discovered, and he noticed the stack of bowls and spoons in the wash-bowl suggesting that the others had also eaten. Cade smiled. His friends had saved his life. Thorne, Blatch and Gart, pulling him out of the cavern and into the phraxlighter; Celestia tending to his wounds, and then . . .

Cade paused in his thoughts as he remembered the bottle at his lips. The fur-faced creature with the kindly wise eyes; the life-giving water which had taken away the pain . . .

Just then, there came a knock on the door. Rumblix, who had been balanced on the back of one of the chairs, jumped down and raced across the floor, yelping and purring. Cade paused. Thorne's knock was usually louder. Celestia's, a familiar *rat-a-tat-tat*. This knock was soft, almost hesitant.

Rumblix was jumping up and down excitedly on the spot, until the door handle turned, when he sat down and looked up expectantly as the door slowly opened. Fingers appeared, gripping the edge of the door. Then a head; thick hair, goggles. Dark blue eyes scanned the room . . .

'Gart,' said Cade, leaping to his feet.

'Cade, lad,' said Gart, stepping inside the cabin and closing the door behind him. 'Good to see you back on your feet.'

'I've got to thank you,' Cade said. 'For rescuing me from the cave—'

'Cade,' Gart interrupted him. He reached up and twisted the points of his moustache, his expression troubled and grave. 'There's something I must tell you.'

· CHAPTER FORTY-ONE ·

Gart raked his oiled hair back across his head with his fingers, then looked up and held Cade's gaze.

'I'm not a bad person,' he said quietly.

'Of . . . of course you're not,' Cade began.

Gart cut him off with a raised hand. 'Hear me out, Cade,' he said, sitting down at the table. 'I came to say goodbye, remember?'

Cade nodded.

'Well, that morning, I had been hunting weezits over the upper ridges. It was dawn and the sun was rising, and as the first rays hit the High Farrow, I saw a red glow shining up from a cleft in the rock . . .'

Cade leaned forward. Gart had tried before to explain, he remembered, down on the floor of the cave. *This is all my fault*, he'd said.

'The jewel,' Cade breathed.

For a moment Gart did not move. Then he sat back

335

in his chair and nodded slowly. 'I laid eyes on it when I took the phraxlighter down for a closer look and saw that the cause of the glow was a shaft of light hitting the tip of a stalactite and being diffused by the magnificent jewel embedded there. I'd never seen a jewel so large, so flawless. So valuable . . .' He paused. 'And I knew in that instant that I had to have it. It was the answer to all my problems . . . So I set the phraxlighter to hover and climbed down to get it. And that's when I saw them . . .'

'The white trogs?' said Cade, the hairs on the back of his neck standing on end.

Gart nodded. 'Hundreds of them, bathed in the red light like . . .'

'Blood,' said Cade.

'They were on their knees, heads bowed and arms raised, making a kind of clicking noise . . .'

'That's their language,' Cade said. 'Only the queen used words, and then only to speak to us.'

Gart was looking out of the window at the distant view of the Five Falls.

'Then the sun shifted, the shaft of light was extinguished, and with it, the blood-red glow. I was frozen to the spot, clinging onto the rope ladder as the trogs all filed out of the cavern. Then I reached out and prised the jewel free with my knife. It was so easy, Cade. So simple . . .'

Cade watched Gart. He seemed to be avoiding his gaze.

'Eight years. Eight long years I've been up on that platform. Eight years to think about the merchants who

swindled me out of my business, sold me a phraxmine that was played out and useless. The great swindle,' he snorted. 'I lost my wife, my children, my home, my money, my reputation . . .' He shook his head. 'Eight years to think about the gambling debts I built up on the skytaverns trying to get my fortune back. Shuttle, rumblestakes, carrillon, splinters. I played them all, and won. At least, at first . . . But then I lost. And I kept losing . . .'

Gart's eyes narrowed as he stared out across the lake.

'Eight years paying off those debts,' he said quietly, 'working on that platform in total isolation, setting foot on solid ground only once in all that time – on the boards of your cabin that day I came to say goodbye . . .'

'But you didn't leave,' said Cade softly.

'I was going to,' said Gart. 'When I left you, I went back to the platform to pick up some tarpaulin in case of bad weather. Opened a bottle of woodgrog to toast my departure. And sat up there drinking alone far into the night. I fell asleep just as dawn was breaking . . . When I woke up, I realized I'd slept most of the day away, but I set off at once, despite a sore head.'

He suddenly turned and looked at Cade, and Cade saw the guilt in his face.

'And then I saw you climbing up the cliff face at the Five Falls,' he said. 'The three of you. Thorne, Celestia and you, Cade. I saw you enter the cavern. And at that moment it was clear to me: *I could not leave*. I flew down to the cavern entrance and shouted out warnings to you, into the darkness, but got no response, and I couldn't bring myself to step out of my phraxlighter and follow you.'

Gart looked down at the table. 'So I flew up to the High Farrow and hovered above the cleft in the rock, trying to summon up the courage to climb down and look for you. I failed. I had taken the jewel and what happened to you was all my fault, Cade.'

Cade stared back at Gart. He was right. It *was* his fault. He had caused everything that happened. Yet he had tried to put it right. And he had done so. After all, thought Cade, Gart could have simply left them to their fate and returned to Great Glade. No one would ever have known. And even after he had rescued them in the phraxlighter, he could still have kept the jewel. But he didn't. He had decided to return it to its rightful place.

No, thought Cade, you're not a bad person. You made a mistake, that's all.

'It's over,' he said simply. 'No hard feelings.'

Gart stared down at the salves and ointments and tinctures spread out on the table. 'We thought you were going to die,' he said, his voice little more than a whisper. 'I thought my greed had killed you.'

'But it didn't,' said Cade. 'I'm fine. We all are, thanks to you, Gart. You saved my life, not once, but twice. First up in that ironwood pine when I jumped from the skytavern. You gave me tools, provisions and a phraxmusket. I couldn't have survived without them . . . without you. And then you saved my life by coming back to the cavern when you didn't have to. I owe you everything.'

'But you saved *my* life, Cade,' said Gart quietly, look-ing down at the floor. 'You have shown me the value of friendship.'

When he looked up at Cade, his eyes were glistening, but he was smiling. He laid a hand on Cade's shoulder.

'They're wonderful friends you've made, Cade. Thorne and Celestia – and her father, Blatch. While you've been ill, I've been getting to know them, and it's made me real-ize just how isolated and lonely I was up on that accursed platform. The trouble was, I thought I could live without others; I *wanted* to live without others.' He frowned. 'Having been betrayed so badly in Great Glade, I never imagined I would trust anyone ever again. How wrong I was . . . I only hope that, after everything I've done, they might also accept *me* as their friend.' He looked almost bashful. 'Thorne has invited Blatch and me to supper at his hive hut.'

'And Celestia?' asked Cade.

Gart crossed to the door and opened it, his smile grow-ing wider. 'Celestia's been very patient, letting me speak to you, Cade,' he said. 'You'll find her waiting for you down at the end of the jetty. *She* wants to speak to you as well.'

· CHAPTER FORTY-TWO ·

Cade stepped out onto his veranda. There was a chill in the air and the billowing clouds had melted away, leaving the sky an unbroken canvas of blue. Celestia was standing at the end of the jetty looking out across the mirror-still water, her back to him. Her gleaming jet-black hair was over her shoulders.

As he went down the steps, Cade heard a soft snort behind him. He looked round to see Tug and Rumblix snuggled up on a nest of meadowgrass beneath the veranda. Tug looked up and his face twisted into a lopsided, thin-lipped smile.

'Master,' he said, his voice like rumbling thunder.

'Cade,' Cade told him, smiling back. '*Cade*.'

'Cade better?'

'That's right,' said Cade, and stooping down, he patted Tug on his shoulder. 'Much better.'

Tug bared his crooked brown teeth happily, and

Rumblix, who had been asleep in the crook of Tug's arm opened one eye, saw Cade, then opened the other and purred loudly.

'Earth and Sky, you seem to grow bigger every day,' Cade murmured. He ruffled the fur around the prowl-grin's neck. 'I remember the moment you hatched, popping up out of your egg – and out of that porthole.' He smiled. 'You fitted inside my hat back then. And now look at you . . .'

Rumblix's purring grew louder.

'Won't be long now before we can ride over the tree-tops together,' said Cade, crouching down and tickling the prowlgrin on his belly. 'Will it, boy?'

That first ride Cade had taken through the Western Woods on one of Celestia's prowlgrins was still fresh in his mind. Gripping onto the reins of the sleek black creature as it had leaped from branch to branch through the forest had been exhilarating, but how much more wonderful it would be to ride on Rumblix's back – his very own pedigree grey prowlgrin that he'd raised from a pup.

Cade patted Tug on the arm, ruffled Rumblix's fur, then backed out of the shadows beneath the veranda and turned. Celestia hadn't moved. She was still standing stock-still at the end of the jetty, gazing out across the gleaming lake.

He crept along the jetty towards her, picking his way over the rocks as silently as he could, a smile on his lips. He stopped behind her. He breathed in the sweet jasmine-hay smell of her hair. Then, raising his hands, he was about to reach forward and cover her eyes when Celestia suddenly spun round, seized one of his wrists, twisted him about and brought his arm up behind his back.

'Don't mess with me, city boy,' she laughed.

Back bent forward and arm throbbing, Cade half laughed, half groaned. 'How did you know I was behind you?'

'This isn't Great Glade,' Celestia said, letting him go.

Cade rubbed his wrist and smiled ruefully.

'You need to look after yourself in the Deepwoods. There are no tavern waifs or Freeglade Lancers here to do it for you,' Celestia added.

Cade found himself nodding. The quiet cloisters and dusty colleges of the Cloud Quarter hadn't exactly pre-pared him for a life out here in the wilderness.

'You have to watch how the creatures of the forest behave,' Celestia was saying, her green eyes staring into his. 'Always stealthy. Watchful. Ready to react . . .'

Cade nodded again, realizing just how in awe of Celestia he was. She was so capable, so independent. So at home in the Deepwoods.

'Anyway,' she said, and laughed, 'I saw your shadow.'

Taking his hand, Celestia led him to the very end of the jetty, where the rocks went down in a series of nat-ural steps. The pair of them sat down on a flat, jutting boulder and dangled their legs over the water. Celestia turned her head and looked out across the lake. A family of paddlefowl passed by the end of the jetty, their flat orange feet pedalling hard at the water. Small waves from their wake lapped at the rocks. Cade picked up a couple of flat pebbles and skimmed one of them out onto the water, sending it bouncing off across the surface of the lake.

Celestia watched the ripples fade. 'Last night, I thought we'd lost you,' she said quietly. 'You were dying.'

Cade put down the other pebble and looked at her. Celestia's profile was dark against the sky. A tear caught the light as it trickled down her cheek. Cade reached out and took hold of her hand.

'Celestia . . .' He paused. 'What *did* happen last night? I mean, I can remember some of it. Lots of it . . . The rope ladder being hauled out of the cave. The flight. You . . .'

'I tried everything I'd ever learned,' Celestia said. 'Firebane tonic. Feverfew lotion. Healwort and hyleberry salves . . . Keeping you hot to sweat out the fever. Chilling you down with ice-cold water . . . The shriek-root was the last resort, and even that didn't seem to be working . . .'

Cade frowned as the memory of the looming figure with white-flecked fur and kind, wise eyes came back to him once more. 'Perhaps I was dreaming, but last night it seemed as if there was someone else there,' he said. 'It . . . it looked like a banderbear.'

Celestia turned to Cade, her green eyes sparkling. 'That's what I wanted to talk to you about,' she said. 'You weren't dreaming, Cade. It *was* a banderbear – he told my father his name was Goom.'

'I've never met a banderbear before,' said Cade. 'They were few and far between in Great Glade.' He frowned. 'I didn't know they *could* talk. I mean, I heard a banderbear yodelling somewhere far off in the High Ridges the other day, but—'

'That was Goom!' said Celestia excitedly. 'He told my father everything. You see, banderbears use a language of signs, of movements. My father learned their language from an old banderbear years ago, back in his skyship-yard.' She smiled. 'The thing is, while Goom was making signs with his paws and ears and the angle of his head, all I could hear him saying was *wuh*.'

'*Wuh*,' Cade repeated.

'*Wuh. Wuh-wuh. Wuh-wuh-wuh-wuh*.' Celestia laughed. 'At least, that's what it sounded like to me. Though my father understood.'

'And what *did* he say, this Goom?' asked Cade.

Celestia's face grew serious. 'He told my father that he had come from the Garden of Life,' she told him, 'far up at the top of the rock spike that sticks up out of the darkness, high above Riverrise. The city of the waifs.' She hesitated. 'According to my father, he'd been there for more than five hundred years.'

'Five hundred . . . But that's not possible,' said Cade.

'With the life-giving waters of the Riverrise lake, it is,' said Celestia. 'Apparently Goom was the sole survivor of a skyship crew that'd ended up there way back in the First Age of Flight.' She frowned. 'When we first saw him emerging from the trees behind your cabin, he had a glass vial of Riverrise water round his neck. It was half full, and Goom said it was what had been keeping him alive since he'd left the Garden of Life.' She paused. 'And that's what he gave to you. All of it.' A smile spread across her features. 'It was like a miracle, Cade. The spasms in your body stopped. You got colour in your cheeks. Your temperature dropped. And that wound on your shoulder, it just closed up and healed itself, right in front of my eyes. In seconds!' She reached out and clasped both Cade's hands in hers. 'We'd got you back,' she said. 'I'd got you back.'

Cade stared into Celestia's eyes. He felt oddly uneasy.

'But why me?' he asked. 'Why did he give *me* the last of his precious water?'

'Because of the nameless one,' Celestia said.

'Tug?' said Cade.

Celestia nodded. 'Since the opening up of Riverrise, Goom said he'd devoted his life to fighting the enslavement of the nameless ones. Goom had tried to save Tug's mother from red dwarf slavers in the Nightwoods beyond the city, but she died of her wounds. Tug ran away in the fight and was lost in the woods, and Goom said he'd been tracking him ever since. When he finally found him, you, Cade, had taken him in and given him a home.' She smiled. 'This was Goom's way of thanking you.'

'But what happened to him?' Cade asked. 'Where is Goom now?'

Just then, as if in answer, the distant sound of yodelling cut through the afternoon stillness, and Cade turned

to see a lone figure – broad of shoulder, though slightly stooped – standing at the top of the Five Falls. Swallowing hard, he watched as the distant figure of the banderbear stood there on the jutting rock, silhouetted against the sky. Then, slowly, stiffly, the ancient banderbear turned and shambled off, up the High Farrow to the forested ridges beyond, and disappeared from sight.

Cade turned to Celestia. There was a heavy ache in the centre of his chest.

'He didn't even know me,' he said, 'yet he sacrificed his life for me—'

'And willingly,' Celestia broke in. 'He told my father that he had lived a long, long life, Cade. And that he was ready to join his ancestors in Open Sky. The Final Convocation, he called it . . .' She frowned. 'And there was something else.' She paused. 'After he had given you the Riverrise water, he just stood there beside your hammock, staring down at you. It was so strange. Then he reached out and ran his great paw gently down the side of your face, and he said something – something that wasn't just *wuh*.' She looked at Cade. 'It sounded like *Twig*.'

'Twig?'

She nodded. 'Goom told my father that you reminded him of the captain of the sky-pirate ship Goom had been a crew member on. The captain he'd waited for at Riverrise all that time . . .' She shook her head in wonder, then reached out and took Cade by the hand. 'But what's important now, Cade – for you and me, and Thorne and Gart – and my father; and Rumblix and Tug,' she laughed, and fixed Cade with her green-eyed gaze, 'is the future.'

Cade nodded. Celestia was right, though he would never forget the banderbear's gift. The gift of life. And every time he heard that yearning yodelling sound of a banderbear calling, he knew he would remember Goom's self-sacrifice. He, Cade, would do his best to be worthy of it.

'Come on,' Celestia said, pulling him to his feet. 'They're waiting for us at Thorne's for supper. Thorne's got something he wants to talk to us about.'

'What?' said Cade.

'I don't know,' Celestia told him. 'But it's something to do with those barkscrolls of your father's that he made all those notes about.' She took his hand and led him back down the jetty. 'Something that Thorne thinks could change the Farrow Ridges for ever . . .'

HAVE YOU READ
THE QUINT TRILOGY?

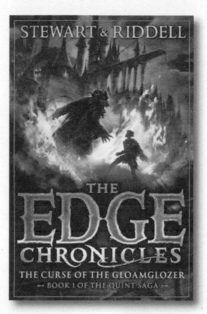

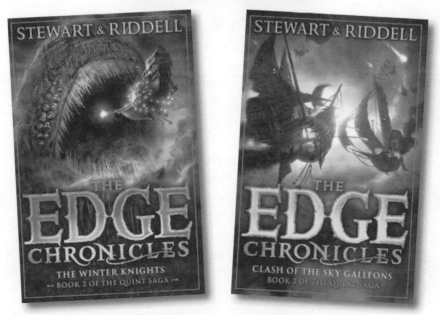

Available now in paperback, ebook
and audio download

THE EDGE CHRONICLES

Have you read them all?

THE QUINT SAGA

The Curse of the Gloamglozer
Deep inside Sanctaphrax, an ancient curse has
been invoked . . .

The Winter Knights
Quint struggles to survive the icy cold of a
never-ending winter.

Clash Of The Sky Galleons
Quint is caught up in a fight for revenge against
the man who killed his family.

THE TWIG SAGA

Beyond the Deepwoods
Abandoned at birth in the Deepwoods, Twig
does what he has always been warned not to do,
and strays from the path . . .

Stormchaser
Twig must risk all to collect valuable stormphrax
from the heart of a Great Storm.

Midnight Over Sanctaphrax
Far out in Open Sky, a ferocious storm is heading
towards the city of Sanctaphrax . . .

THE ROOK SAGA

Last of the Sky Pirates
Rook sets out on a dangerous journey in order to become a Librarian Knight.

Vox
Can Rook stop the Edgeworld falling into chaos from the evil schemes of Vox Verlix?

Freeglader
When Undertown is destroyed, Rook must travel to a new home in the Free Glades.

THE NATE SAGA

The Immortals
Nate is a lowly lamplighter, until treachery forces him to flee to the city of Great Glade.

THE EDGE CHRONICLES

Praise from critics:

'Stunningly original'
Guardian

'Beautifully illustrated'
The Times

'For children who've read the Harry Potter books
and want another world to explore'
Mail on Sunday

'Filled with delights . . . not least the extraordinary
world and its creatures captured in Chris Riddell's
endlessly beautiful, bizarre and marvellously
detailed line illustrations'
Independent on Sunday

'Each book in the series has grown swifter, tenser
and more tightly written'
New York Times

'Packed with action and adventure. There is a touch
of the Lewis Carrolls to its authors' enthusiastic and
uninhibited inventiveness and to the illustrations'
Starburst

'So exceptional . . . I'd bet good money on it still
being in print a century from now'
Interzone

'Stupendous . . . surely in years to come new
fantasy creations will be compared with Tolkien,
Pratchett and Stewart & Riddell'
The School Librarian

THE EDGE CHRONICLES

Praise from readers:

'The Edge Chronicles are the best books I have read so far in my life. My favourite book out of all the trilogies is *The Last of the Sky Pirates*'
Aranga, Macclesfield

'I really enjoy your books The Edge Chronicles – they are the best books that I have ever read, and trust me that's a lot. My favourite book is either *Stormchaser* or *The Last of the Sky Pirate*s. I think that you guys are a perfect team!'
Tommy Legge, website

'I think the simplest thing to say is that your books ROCK!!!'
Robbie, Dublin

'. . . your books are a real gift to literature. The illustrations are beautiful and the stories are exceptional. I love how the books fit together like a jigsaw and how everything falls into place. When I read them I feel happy, excited, sad and moved all at once. I was constantly amazed and surprised. Thank you for creating The Edge Chronicles. They have touched my heart and I'm sure they've done the same for many others'
Katie, Oxon

'I enjoy your vast imagination on the series Edge Chronicles. Your books grip me into turning each page with thrilling adventure and murderous betrayals.'
Jonathan, Vancouver

'I wanted you to know how much The Edge Chronicles have meant to my children – you have encouraged them to enjoy reading.'
Diana, Brighton

PAUL STEWART is a highly regarded author of books for young readers – everything from picture books to football stories, fantasy and horror. Together with Chris Riddell, he is co-creator of the *Far-Flung Adventures* series, which includes *Fergus Crane*, Gold Smarties Prize Winner, *Corby Flood* and *Hugo Pepper*, Silver Nestlé Prize Winners, and the *Barnaby Grimes* series. They are of course also co-creators of the bestselling *Edge Chronicles* series, which has sold over two million books and is now available in over thirty languages.

CHRIS RIDDELL is an accomplished graphic artist who has illustrated many acclaimed books for children, including *Pirate Diary* by Richard Platt, and *Gulliver*, which both won the Kate Greenaway Medal. His book *Ottoline and the Yellow Cat* was shortlisted for the Kate Greenaway Medal and won a Gold Nestlé Prize. Together with Paul Stewart, he is co-creator of the *Far-Flung Adventures* series, which includes *Fergus Crane*, Gold Smarties Prize Winner, *Corby Flood* and *Hugo Pepper*, Silver Nestlé Prize Winners, and the *Barnaby Grimes* series. They are of course also co-creators of the bestselling *Edge Chronicles* series, which has sold over two million books and is now available in over thirty languages.